# What the critics are saying about...

### *Ellora's Cavemen: Legendary Tails I*

**5.0!** "This anthology is one of the best I have ever read. All the novellas are quite diverse in settings, subject matter, and hero/heroine interactions... I highly recommend this anthology for quick, exciting stories that will put a spark in your day or keep you up all night." – *Callista Arman, Mon Boudoir*

**5 Cups!** "All of these stories were great for me and I couldn't pick just one. I thoroughly enjoyed the differences in them all and found all of them to be wickedly sensual and greatly appealing." – *Sheryl, Coffee Time Romance*

**5 Hearts!** "Ellora's Cavemen: Legendary Tails 1 is a fantastic collection of stories that I enjoyed reading from start to finish. Normally when I read collections like this there might be one or two stories that aren't as good as the rest, but this time every one of them shined..." – *Julia, The Romance Studio*

### *Ellora's Cavemen: Legendary Tails II*

**4.5 Roses!** "Ellora's Caveman: Legendary Tails 2 is an amazing anthology filled with so much heat and emotional turmoil in its stories that it almost self combusts... The stories are well written and filled with so much mystery and danger that the reader will not be able to stop reading once they start." – *Angel, A Romance Review*

**4.0!** "This is a collection of incredibly hot and steamy romantic, erotic stories. The authors all do a fantastic job of setting the scenario and having you fall in love and lust with their characters. An easy fun read that you will want to break out whenever you need a charge!" – *Thia McClain, The Romance Reader's Connection*

Legendary Tails II has something for every reading taste…This book brings together six new sizzling tales from some of Ellora's Cave very talent authors all in one book. An anthology is always a great buy for your money, and it's a wonderful way to sample an author's work…" – *Luisa, Cupid's Library Reviews*

# ELLORA'S CAVEMEN: LEGENDARY TAILS III

## The Last Bite
### By Melani Blazer

Once the hunter…

Laura hasn't seen her partner in six years—when an easy bounty capture went horribly wrong. She's back with a secret that threatens the man she once loved, who still sets her blood on fire with little more than a look.

Now the hunted…

Elliot has his sights on one vamp—his brother's killer. He's swayed from his mission only by the reappearance of his former partner. Their blistering passion makes him forget her cryptic warning, until he's forced to face it. Will Laura fare as well when *his* secret is revealed?

## Hard Lessons
### By Nikki Soarde

Kaley Carrone discovers that her wealthy husband has been cheating on her. She wants out of the marriage, but their prenuptial agreement will deny her the money— as well as the revenge—that she feels she is due.

So she enlists the help of an old lover and his friend to stage a kidnapping that will net them a tidy sum of money, as well as make her husband suffer. The plan is good! However, spending three days alone with two handsome, dangerous, multi-talented men, a video camera and an assortment of Chinese takeout food has some consequences that Kaley didn't foresee.

## Close Encounters of the Carnal Kind
### By Delilah Devlin

Cajun Etienne Lambert, ex-soldier fresh from the horrors of the war in Iraq, doesn't believe her when the alien woman on his doorstep says she's there to take him home. When he resists, she kidnaps him. He learns he is the last potent male of the ruling class of their planets and it's his duty to sire the next generation of rulers.

Mariska is a fightership commander who succeeded where all the mages and trackers have failed. She's found her race's last hope for salvation! When the future king demands he start work immediately on the primary mandate of his rule — to sire children — she can't refuse his command.

## Tight Places
### By Arianna Hart

Savannah Malone has wanted to meet Carrick for months — but not when she's soaking wet and trapped in an elevator. Now that she's close to him she can tell there's more to him than meets the eye. But she has no idea how much more is waiting to be discovered under his expensive suit. Little does she know his real secrets are buried deep under the clothes he's oh so willing to shed. Exploring tight places has never been so exciting before.

## Pleasure Port 27
*By Kate Douglas*

An alien construct designed for pleasure, Mira provides sexual services for the men who travel the galaxies. Her place of business is Pleasure Port 27, otherwise known as Earth. But someone is watching her, someone is keeping track of each act she performs, each man she fucks. It is imperative the voyeur die before he discovers what she is…but once she sees him, understands him, Mira realizes there is more to life than one sex customer after another. There is Evan—there is love, there is a chance to live as a real woman. If only she is willing to take the risk.

## License To Thrill
*By Sahara Kelly*

When a flu epidemic at her top-secret Agency office thrusts administrator Jane Bradford into the front-line world of the agents themselves, the last thing she expects is to get a major thrill from the sexy voice at the other end of her communications headset.

Even less does she expect the owner of that voice to be the man of her dreams. Of course, he's not perfect. He's older than Jane, for a start. By about a thousand years or so...

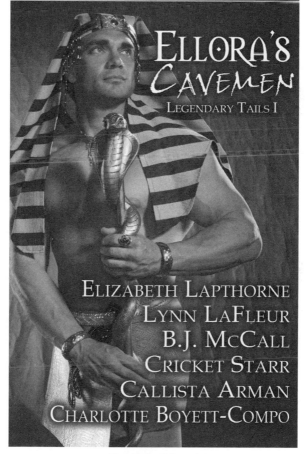

ELLORA'S CAVE PRESENTS

ELLORA'S
CAVEMEN
LEGENDARY TAILS I

ELIZABETH LAPTHORNE
LYNN LAFLEUR
B.J. MCCALL
CRICKET STARR
CALLISTA ARMAN
CHARLOTTE BOYETT-COMPO

On Sale Now!

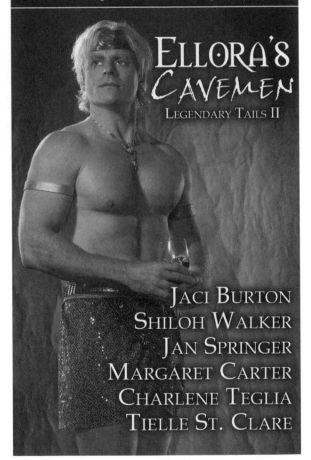

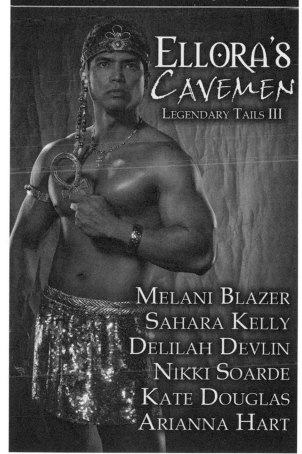

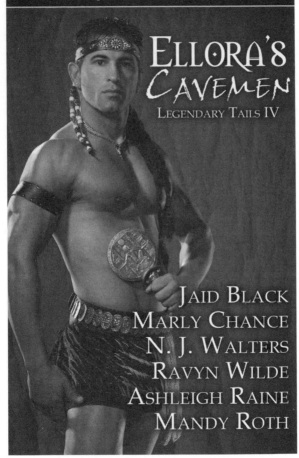

Available December 21, 2005

# ELLORA'S CAVEMEN

## LEGENDARY TAILS III

An Ellora's Cave Romantica Publication

www.ellorascave.com

ELLORA'S CAVEMEN: LEGENDARY TAILS III

ISBN # 1-41995-153-X

Edited by: Raelene Gorlinsky
Cover Design by: Darrell King
Photography by: Dennis Roliff

Electronic book Publication: September, 2005
Trade paperback Publication: September, 2005

# Warning:

The following material contains graphic sexual content meant for mature readers. *Ellora's Cavemen: Legendary Tails III* has been rated *E-rotic* by a minimum of three independent reviewers.

Ellora's Cave Publishing offers three levels of Romantica™ reading entertainment: S (S-ensuous), E (E-rotic), and X (X-treme).

S-*ensuous* love scenes are explicit and leave nothing to the imagination.

E-*rotic* love scenes are explicit, leave nothing to the imagination, and are high in volume per the overall word count. In addition, some E-rated titles might contain fantasy material that some readers find objectionable, such as bondage, submission, same sex encounters, forced seductions, etc. E-rated titles are the most graphic titles we carry; it is common, for instance, for an author to use words such as "fucking", "cock", "pussy", etc., within their work of literature.

X-*treme* titles differ from E-rated titles only in plot premise and storyline execution. Unlike E-rated titles, stories designated with the letter X tend to contain controversial subject matter not for the faint of heart.

# ELLORA'S CAVEMEN: LEGENDARY TAILS III

## The Last Bite
*By Melani Blazer*

## Hard Lessons
*By Nikki Soarde*

## Close Encounters of the Carnal Kind
*By Delilah Devlin*

## Tight Places
*By Arianna Hart*

## Pleasure Port 27
*By Kate Douglas*

## License to Thrill
*By Sahara Kelly*

# THE LAST BITE

Melani Blazer

# Chapter One

"I thought you'd be out of the business by now, Elliot." Laura Kline stood over him, arms crossed, legs spread. "Figured you'd had your fill of chasing vamps."

Elliot Simpson couldn't help but let his gaze linger on her toned thighs where they disappeared under the shadow of her short skirt. Damn. "Nice legs, hot stuff. Now quit pretending to be a badass and help me up."

"This smacks of déjà vu, doesn't it?" Laughing, she nudged him with her toe. A toe clad in a knee-high black leather boot. "I think when I saw you last, you were flat on your back trying to look up my skirt." She stepped sideways, closing those tantalizing legs and smirking down at him.

Why the hell did she have to remind him of that? Back then they'd been rival hunters—and explosive lovers. Independent contractors for a government department that officially didn't exist. Bounty hunters for criminals that weren't quite human. Until the night she'd walked away with his bounty—and his heart.

But instead of disappearing like she had six years ago, she reached for his wrist and easily hauled him to his feet.

Six years. A long damn time. She still looked hot as hell and his blood had started racing the moment he saw her. She'd left him—he'd have to remind her of that. But he had let her go. By the time he realized just what he'd lost, it was too late. The hunters were impossible to track if they were good at their job, and he and Laura were among the best. Sure, he made the rounds, used his years of seniority and tapped into the friends he knew in various other agencies to look for her. Nothing. Not even a hint that she was still out there.

He'd eventually come to the conclusion she didn't want to be found—that realization solidified by the fact she'd never make any effort to contact him. Until now.

"What's *her* crime?" Laura's eyes shifted sideways for only a moment. Her stance, her caution, her very attitude—made him wonder if she was still in the business—or one like it. If not, she hadn't lost any skill. She was on full alert.

He stared down at the lifeless eyes of the woman on the ground near his feet. "Sarah?" he asked, yanking his thoughts from the past. "She's a nobody—just the usual fucking vampire. Dealing, prostitution. Think she's drained a couple of those John Does sitting at the morgue. Caught me with a stun gun. The bitch."

There were no prisons for this kind of criminal— vamps who felt they were above the law. Harsh but true. Some vamps were decent folk, but when they went bad, there was only one punishment. Sarah found that out tonight.

Elliot was after one vampire in particular—the one who'd killed his brother nearly eight years before. After Laura left, that had kept him motivated. This surprise visit wasn't going to change that.

He holstered his gun and brushed off the street grime. His fingers slid over the ankle knife, the wooden stakes strapped to his thigh, and extra clips on his belt. Inventory intact minus one stake. The gun was to stun, the stakes to kill.

He didn't normally traipse down to the docks for a minimal bounty like Sarah. But hopefully her death would piss off her pimp, one of the main dealers on the street, and lure him out of hiding. Elliot was confident he could continue up the chain of command and get to the big kahuna, the one he desperately wanted to take down.

So what the hell was Laura was doing here?

"Can't say I've ever seen you out hunting in a dress. Pretty sexy. Is this some new sting operation or were you out sightseeing after a date?"

Laura's eyes widened. "Sting operation? Hardly. I don't waste my time with this business anymore. I've seen enough of vampires to last a lifetime."

He didn't believe her. No way was this meeting happenstance. He couldn't think of a single reason for her to be here in the middle of the night, on the docks, wearing little more than the hookers wore. Highly doubtful she'd missed him and wanted him back in her life. If that were the case, she'd have shown up at his house. He hadn't moved. Hell, she had a key. There was more to this. He might even be willing to take her to bed, just for old times' sake, but he wasn't sharing information on his cases. With *anyone*. That was long part of his past.

He lifted an eyebrow. "Working on the inside then, right? Sent to check on me? Part of some new secret department set up to make sure those of us in the trenches are doing this by the rules?" There's no way he'd believe she'd sunk to prostitution. There had to be a reasonable explanation. The jolt from the stun gun must have erased his ability to see the obvious.

When she simply shook her head, Elliot pushed a button on his cell phone, waited for the tone and then punched in the coordinates of the body. A recovery team would arrive in minutes to clean up the scene. He took a digital fingerprint—proof it was *his* catch.

The police were never involved. Most civilians didn't know they existed—the hunters *or* the creatures they hunted, vampires and werewolves.

Laura tilted her head and watched. The streetlight caught the highlights in her dark coppery hair. He'd never seen it loose about her shoulders except in the bedroom, where her hair hadn't been the only constraint she'd relaxed. The memories of her lack of inhibitions left his body damp with sweat.

But this wasn't the bedroom. This was where they— where *he*—worked. So *why* had she walked out of the mist with that same confident stride, but dressed in something so completely inappropriate? There wasn't a bulge on her formfitting outfit to indicate she was even armed. Yet, six years out of the business and she hadn't lost that composed take-no-bullshit stature that had his cock hardening.

"I'm not here on business," she said. But no explanation.

He'd work on learning more—he didn't give up easily. Right now he had some tension to work off and well, he'd rather missed her. "We need to talk."

He took a step closer and smiled.

Her lips parted, her chest rose and fell heavily. Hell, he could practically smell the spicy musk of her arousal. His mouth watered as he remembered how sweet her cream was when she came on his tongue.

"Well?" he asked, letting his breath fan over her cheek. An inch closer and he'd be able to taste her.

"Um. Yeah," she faltered.

As he was trained to do, he went in for the kill.

What was she thinking, coming here, determined to say what she had to and resist any of his advances? *Because the alternative was unthinkable.*

Laura's last coherent thought fell to the wayside as Elliot's mouth descended on hers. His warmth enveloped her, swirling inside her, all the way to the tips of her toes. He tasted of fine whiskey, the flavor as intoxicating as the man who shared it with her.

The cool breeze off the water played havoc with her feverish skin. She shivered. Six years hadn't changed him at all. Memories assaulted her with the same ferocity as his kiss. That strong, angled jaw that was always covered in sandpaper-like stubble. Eyes that were blue or gray, or even the palest hint of green. They sparkled with playfulness, deepened with anger and darkened with passion.

She leaned against his broad chest as he outlined her lips with his tongue before sinking inside with a moan. Hot. Wet. Just like she craved. Just like she remembered. Using her teeth, she lightly grazed his tongue before suckling. That had always driven him crazy.

Still did.

He rocked against her, holding her hips against his. His erection branded her lower stomach.

It had always been this way with them. Like a match, one strike and there was fire. The flames burned low in her belly. The air whirled around their legs, flitting up her skirt. The cold gusts against her wet panties heightened her senses.

She knew what she wanted.

Elliot. Any way she could get him.

"C'mon," he hissed, breaking away and pulling her toward the safety of the shadows.

She glanced behind her, seeing the glint of light off the windows of a truck and the silhouettes of three men erasing any sign that Elliot had been here.

Laura shook off the distraction. "And?" she asked, wondering if he'd changed his mind.

Her hand found the bulge of denim and rubbed. "Christ, Laura."

He pulled her hands above her head and kissed her senseless. She struggled against the restraint, but not enough to break free. He did maddening things to her body this way. Damn shame he couldn't reach to lift her skirt. What she wouldn't give to feel the cool air and his hot mouth caressing her pussy.

"We're supposed to be talking," he panted.

"Later." Right now her body hummed with need and never had Elliot turned her down. It'd been six years. And she felt each and every one of those empty minutes pounding through her racing bloodstream.

"Sure?"

She nodded. They clashed together in a tangle of searching fingers and probing tongues. Like two animals let loose, their minds on a single goal.

Carrying her this time, he returned to the shadow of a shed and pinned her between the hard wood and his hard body. She squirmed, hating the skirt that kept her from being able to wrap her legs around his waist and rub her aching mound against him.

Her mouth felt bruised from the onslaught of his kisses, but she liked it. Liked every bit of what he gave. Hard. Fast. Sometimes even rough. She took, demanded, and he let her.

Their hot, sweaty bodies fit together like pieces of a puzzle.

"Yes!" she cried as he dragged her skirt up over her hips. She shifted and locked her ankles behind his ass, propelling him closer.

It might not be the reason she'd sought him out, but right now it was the only thing that mattered. She tugged at his shirt, slipping her hands underneath to feel the hard muscles there. His skin jumped. The electricity of flesh on flesh coursed through her.

He kneaded her thighs, holding her up as he countered her actions, rubbing against her. The friction set her on fire.

He caught her moan in his mouth, plunging deep inside. Teasing as he tasted her.

"Get these off," she said, tugging at his waistband. "Or down." Reluctantly she uncrossed her ankles so he could release her.

As soon as he released the button of his jeans, she brushed his hands out of the way and pulled the zipper down herself. A rough moan, more like a growl, rumbled in Elliot's throat as she palmed his cock through the material.

Her mouth watered with the anticipation of feeling him pounding inside her.

His hands shook as they shoved denim and cotton out of the way. The rush of sensations continued to hit her like giant tidal waves. The power she still commanded over him — at least his body — awed her. And made her horny as hell for him.

"I want it like we were, hard up against the wall."

He knew how she meant. Despite the time away, they read each other so well. He slid his hands up her skirt and pushed down her panties. She wiggled until they fell and she kicked them away.

His hot fingers brushed against her thighs, smoothed over her ass. She could barely breathe for the need, yet she relished every moment of his skin against hers. Then he picked her up, his capable hands clutching her buttocks as he positioned her back against the wall.

His swollen cock twitched against her palm. She closed her fist around it and stroked it until a drop of pre-come appeared at the tip. She wiped it off, then licked her finger. If only she could see his features. But his groan was enough.

Using more of the fluid to lubricate his shaft, she squeezed as she thrust him through her fist, with each stroke remembering the way he filled her, the way her pussy stretched to accommodate his generous length. Her gasps mixed with his groan. His fingers tightened on the flesh of her ass. The rush of pleasing him made her body tremble with need.

"Give it to me," she commanded, leading him directly to the throbbing lips of her pussy. She rubbed his velvety tip against her clit, crying out as the heat seared through her entire being. His pre-come mixed with the cream of her arousal as she stroked his cock up and down the length of her slit, teasing both of them.

He shifted her weight almost without effort and grabbed her hand from between their bodies. Holding her gaze, he lifted it to his mouth and suckled.

She moaned, surrendering all inhibitions as she rocked her pussy against his engorged shaft.

"My turn," he whispered, then kissed her. She greedily licked his tongue, then his lips, feasting on the taste of their arousal.

He reached down and rubbed his cock against her pussy, burying just the tip into her tightness before removing it. No matter what she did — twist, buck, grind — she couldn't force him farther in for the sensation of being filled that her body craved.

He withdrew his cock and stroked it. In the half light, she could see the darkened head disappearing within his grasp and then reappearing, the pearl of more fluid glistening as he drew his grip all the way to the base.

She couldn't tear her eyes away from watching his cock. It was as if she felt each stroke inside her. The muscles along the walls of her pussy convulsed, needing to be filled.

He finally shifted his hold on her again, positioning her over his cock. Gravity would drive him into her. But he held her up, that slickened tip of his cock positioned right at the opening of her slit.

She squirmed, caught in a love-hate moment as he teased her a final time.

Then he thrust, bringing his hips up as he pulled her down onto him. She cried out, feeling his cock stretch her, fill her. He continued to drive into her, just like she'd asked for it. Never stopping, never slowing, just hard, almost animal-like movement until they were both covered in sweat and gasping for breath.

She came first, holding on as long as she could, but finding nothing left to grasp as rational thought spiraled away and exploded in a white light. Biting her lip to keep from screaming out, she shook with the continual earth-shattering orgasm.

He tensed, paused, then rammed her deeply. There was no pain, just the ultimate feeling of being both the conquest and the conqueror. Each thrust left her body shuddering with aftershocks. She held on tightly to sweat-slicked skin, reveling in the muscles that bunched beneath her grip.

She whimpered as he nipped at her shoulder. "Elliot, yes!"

Elliot drew a ragged breath, then roared out her name, his fingers squeezing her ass as he filled her with his hot come.

Dropping her head to his shoulder, she waited. He held her there, the cool breeze welcome on feverish skin.

That was good. Elliot was good. More than good. As she expected, he'd done more than satisfy her physically, he'd resumed his place in her life as if it'd been six hours, not six years. Of course, she had no idea if he felt the same way. He might have moved on.

"We, uh, should go," he said, finally backing up and lowering her to the ground.

While he righted his clothing, she found her panties, then looked at him.

Now what? Sex hadn't been in her plans. She hadn't intended on sticking around beyond sharing her news. But she had to tell him — soon.

"What's your next stop?" she asked, biting her lip. Despite the heat that still coursed through her body from one helluva orgasm, she felt cold.

"Coffee, of course," he said. "And yours?"

"Elliot," she blurted, unable to keep the secret that would destroy them. "I was sent here to kill you."

# Chapter Two

So that was it. Funny, the news didn't surprise Elliot at all. He just hadn't anticipated the chance to fuck her first.

"Really," he countered and stopped to face her. "Just which one of my enemies put the most attractive price on my head?"

He had to say, she had obviously underestimated him. He laughed at Laura's wide-eyed expression, her face all flushed, lips swollen from his kisses. Had she expected him to be shocked, even worried? "C'mon, tell me. I mean, it's not like you're going to be able to finish that mission, are you? Might as well humor me with the details."

"You think I couldn't kill you?" Her confident tone didn't match the trembling of her body. Or the glassy look of fear in her gaze.

"Honey, I wouldn't let you."

She reached up to slap him. He stopped her hand. Without a moment's hesitation, she countered with the opposite fist to his gut.

Elliot just smiled. *Good one.* "Now, let's get out of here."

To his surprise, she followed him off the dock and got into the passenger seat of his four-wheel drive. She didn't say a thing until he'd pulled into a motel lot and parked in front of the end room.

"Why are we here?"

"This is where I tie you to the bed and torture you until I get the answers I want."

He saw her eyes widen. She had to know he'd do it. Dealing with miscreants of all kinds had stolen any patience and sympathy he had. What she didn't understand was that he could never hurt her. Even if she *tried* to kill him.

"Well?" he prodded, killing the engine. This shanty of motel wasn't what he had in mind for a reunion with Laura, but these weren't the conditions he'd dreamed of either. He dug in his pocket and tossed a key at her. "Open it up."

"No."

God, he loved it when she stood up to him. But he'd never tell her that

"Fine." He got out, then yanked open the passenger door. "Last chance, sweetheart. Then my mercy ends."

"I am *not* going to—"

He grabbed her and tossed her over his shoulder.

She gasped and tried to reach her skirt, which of course had ridden up and exposed her bare ass.

"Now that's a sight." He caressed the back of her bare thigh.

"You bastard."

He laughed. Yeah, he was being a prick. After her little revelation, who could blame him?

"I don't recall it being my fault you lost your panties. Besides, there's no one here but dopeheads and transients. They're more interested in drugs and money than your ass. You're safe."

She kicked and pounded as he carried her into the room and dropped her on the bed. "Don't make it harder on yourself, Laura. You used to love it when I tied you to the headboard and had my way with you. Relax. You might enjoy this."

He nearly laughed when she turned away, but remained silent. He might just enjoy this himself.

"Sorry these aren't fur-lined, babe." With a wink, he yanked her wrist and snapped it in a police-issue handcuff that was already attached to the metal bed frame.

"Fuck you, Elliot Simpson. Fuck you and your goddamn games."

"Games?" *Oh here we go.* "That little up-against-the-wall routine just an impulse, or were you testing…just to see if you still had it?" Despite her attempts to fight him, it took very little effort to finish cuffing her spread-eagle on the full-size mattress.

Then, before his libido got the better of him and he envisioned the games they used to play in the same position, he turned off the light and left the room.

Back in his truck, he clicked open his cellular and called the one person whom he trusted.

"Dispatch."

"Gimme Mario. Stat."

Mario alone knew Elliot's secrets, even those he hadn't ever spoken out loud. "Yo."

"Who's hot on my heels this week? Got the latest hired gun cuffed to my bed at the Cabana."

He was rewarded with a laugh. "You need Disposal?"

"It's not one of them. I'll be taking care of this one myself."

"Elliot..." came the warning.

He hadn't called for a damn babysitter. He wanted answers. "Gimme forty-eight hours. I'm not taking another case before then. Buzz me as soon as you figure out who sent her."

The hierarchy of evil was going to crumble, and he was going to be the one to do it. He'd spent eight fucking years ripping at the foundation, one little brick at a time. But their numbers were multiplying. The street-level vamps were better prepared and anything but stupid. He needed to get to the powerful ones who drove lavish cars and never got their hands dirty. Drugs, alcohol, firearms, they were in on it all. They all had an insatiable thirst for money, power...and blood.

Elliot had a thirst for blood too—theirs.

\* \* \* \* \*

Laura didn't bother to scream or fight. She wasn't a fool. Elliott would have made sure her cries for help went unheeded. He was thorough like that. But that didn't mean she liked her current situation.

Damn him. Didn't he comprehend that he wasn't safe out there? She'd walked right up to him on the dock. Could have killed him. Could have picked up his gun and leveled it right at his forehead...

Lot of good "could have" did her now. How degrading did he have to be? Her skirt was still bunched at her waist, where it'd hiked as soon as he'd tossed her over his shoulder. She tested the cuffs one last time.

*Stupid.* He had them here for a reason. Likely she wasn't the first person to be tied up like this. Her mind wandered where it had no business going. Like wondering if Elliot had ever strapped another woman to the bed like this, for reasons other than torture. *That* thought got her blood boiling. She didn't want to imagine Elliot with another woman. Period. Though it was ridiculous to think he'd been celibate for six years.

She had. There hadn't been a choice. Unless of course, she wanted to fuck the underworld guards that had held her captive. She was probably lucky they hadn't raped her. She could thank their fear of Elliot for that.

Their last bounty had been a trap. They were getting too close to the top of the power triangle that controlled nearly all illegal movement around the Northeastern portion of the US.

The vamps had hunted them, using one of their own as bait. When Disposal arrived, they'd attacked. She'd seen one of the Disposal guys go down. Cold raced through her body as she remembered the panic she'd felt as Elliot turned back. She'd kept running.

Then things went blank.

And she'd woken up in a position similar to this one — only standing.

Spent way too much time that way, questioned and quizzed and degraded. Fed God only knows what for food. There'd been times she'd prayed for death, but had believed Elliot would come for her.

Days passed, then weeks. She heard his name on conversations that trickled through the ventilation and occasionally wondered if he'd tried, and failed.

"I'd forgotten you were still here, my love. I'd have expected you to expire waiting for your partner to rescue you from the bowels of hell. I see his mercy doesn't extend that far, eh?" She'd never met this man, but knew him the moment she saw him.

She'd been so exhausted and frozen with fear that she'd been unable to retort. The chains had made escape impossible.

"Would you like your freedom?"

She knew it was a trick, but she'd had to take him up on the proposal that he would spare her life if she'd end Elliot's. Of course she wouldn't, but prayed that if she could find Elliot, together they'd figure a way out.

Yet here she was, helpless and chained while Elliot was out there, unaware that fresh orders had been sent down from above to erase him. They'd come for her too, she didn't doubt that at all.

If only he had listened to her! What would it take to make him understand? Her muscles ached, but her heart ached more. "Elliot!" Her voice reverberated through the room.

Breathing out, she accepted the truth. Her fault. She should have figured he'd gotten harder and colder—just like her. What had she been thinking to just blurt out her mission?

Because she'd been scared for him. He'd been flat on his back when she'd walked up on him. Vulnerable. What if it hadn't been her lurking on that dock?

She had more to tell him. Through the years, she'd learned more than anyone had before about the hierarchy and relationship between these gang kings and "kingpins". The agency would love to know about vulnerable spots, connections to politics and businessmen that they'd never believe. But that information was for later. First they had to live through the night.

"Elliot!" she screamed one last time, jerking against the cuffs.

Where had he gone? Was he leaving her here? For what, Disposal to come get her? Disposal would take her in where she could get help. She'd be safe.

But Elliot wouldn't be. After all, she wasn't the only one looking for him. She'd just known where, and how, to find him. After all, she'd followed him for years, learning his tricks, admiring his talents. He knew the vamps, understood them, which was more than she ever could fathom. There had been times when she'd thought he was one of them. She nearly laughed remembering the one time when they'd first met, when she'd point-blank asked him if he was a bloodsucker.

That's when she'd fallen for him, seeing the emotions roll over his face like a midwestern storm over the plains, his eyes cloudy, sparks of lightning in the dark gray depths.

Despite the chilling memory, her body warmed, remembering how explosive Elliot had been in all aspects of his life back then. Still was, if this evening was any indication. Those memories had kept her alive. Memories of his anger and frustration and pain all building up. Hers too. They'd often joked that no one else could understand the emotional damage one suffered when driving a stake through another man's heart. Outwardly there was no difference between a man and a vampire except the teeth. It never got easier. Their lovemaking had often bordered on violent as they exorcised their demons with passion.

Her nipples tightened, sensitive nerve endings there brushing against her shirt. She shifted, but it only heightened the experience, the material pulling tight over the ripe buds that needed attention. And she couldn't even do it herself.

*Damn you, Elliot. Damn you.*

What would it be like, if he came in right now? Her pussy quivered in the cool air. Her juices flowed onto her thighs and dampened the bed beneath her — the mix of her current arousal and remnants of his come.

She wriggled, trying anything to alleviate the building pressure. But the idea of Elliot standing there watching her, knowing she was primed and needed release but unable to take it herself, sent sparks through the most sensitive parts of her anatomy.

A whimper escaped her as she willed the fantasy version of Elliot to climb onto the foot of the bed and position himself between her thighs. If she closed her eyes, she could almost feel his breath there, the very heat of it sending shockwaves to her womb.

She jolted, lifting off the bed as high as her bonds allowed as her fantasy took over. Memory and desire were enough to practically give life to the feeling of having Elliot's hot mouth on her pussy. At least before, when she'd conjure up these erotic thoughts, she could use her own hand to take herself to the brink. Trapped like this...she rolled her head from side to side and clenched her internal muscles, aching to find a way out.


Laura counted. Out loud at first, but then to herself. She closed her eyes. Tried to ignore the thudding of her pulse against the cool metal at her wrists and ankles. Failed completely at shutting out the way this position made her think sex. All sex. Nothing else.

She groaned. But kept counting. Fifty-two, fifty-three. Lord, where was he? She was past caring why—

Wait.

Was that a car door? She opened her eyes and struggled to look toward the entrance to the room, but couldn't lift her head far enough.

She was going to kick his ass for making her worry. After he made her come. Several times.

Waiting sucked. She hadn't been this impatient in prison. But she hadn't been turned on and helpless about it either. Nothing had come of the car door she'd heard. Probably another tenant. One free to get up and move around. Besides, she hadn't seen the glow of headlights hitting the window. Not that it mattered. He could roll in with them off or park farther down so that she couldn't see.

"Elliot!" she screamed one last time.

A figure burst through the door. Barely any light followed him in, just the briefest glint that meant his gun was drawn.

She dropped her head back to the pillow. "Thank God. Now get me out of here."

The door closed with a crash and Elliot's light chuckle filled the already cramped space. The deep sound vibrated across her skin, teasing like a light touch.

The whimper escaped before she could stop it.

"It's funny, Laura. No one at headquarters knows where you've been the last several years. They were surprised you were even alive."

She swallowed and followed his movements by the direction of his voice. "I—I know..."

"Get yourself a new boss? Go from bounty hunter to hit man? Interesting switch, considering I recall you feeling a bit burnt out on all the crime and death you had to deal with."

"It's not like that."

He stood beside the bed. She still couldn't see him, just sense him, feel the heat from his body.

"Not like that, eh? What am I supposed to think when you prance up after six years and announce you're here to kill me?"

No. No. *No.* "I told you I was *sent* to kill you. Didn't say I was going to. Damn should have, though. Now let me loose." She jerked, rattling the cuffs against the metal frame.

"Not just yet, sweetheart. Seems you're still withholding some vital information. Like *who* sent you."

She wouldn't tell him yet. Wouldn't send him to a certain death. And that's what it would be, despite his intense training and immeasurable luck that had kept him alive this long. She knew Elliot too well. Despite his nonchalance about being hunted, she knew he'd quickly shift gears and become the hunter. But this wasn't a normal job. They were expecting him. He'd be outnumbered and way out-armed. They were immortal— he was human.

Bad combination. She'd have to get him to trust her, then she'd explain and he could work with the agency on some sort of plan.

"We'll talk about that later, Elliot. It's not the who. It's the why, anyway." She winced at the little white lie. For him it'd be entirely about *who.* "You've cleaned up this town. Likely made yourself a rich man in the process. So why do *you* still do it?"

Laura sucked in a breath as Elliot traced his hand lightly up the inside of her leg, ankle to thigh. Her entire body trembled at the contact.

His silence spoke volumes.

Shit. She was in trouble now.

"Because, Laura dear, I'm good at it." His laugh did little to cool the fire he fanned with the light stroke of his fingers on her sensitive skin.

She moaned and lifted her hips, unable to disguise her need to be touched.

"Fiery little vixen, aren't you. Think I'll be dragged in by that warm…" He scraped his palm between her legs.

"…wet…"

Two fingers slid inside her, then back out. So quickly, such a tease.

"…pussy, and forget all about what brought you back to my bed?"

She couldn't breathe. The muscles in her stomach convulsed. The hot cream of her arousal soaked her legs and buttocks even more. How could he do this to her? How?

"I came—" She could cry for the torture he put upon her. God, how she wanted, no, needed him. Now.

"Yes. You came. I remember. And you'd like to come again, wouldn't you?"

*Whimper.*

"No, I, um, yes." She hated that he had so much control, yet mentally pleaded with him just to touch her one more time. Just a little more. A little faster. *Please!*

"Well?"

God, he knew well what he was doing. One finger drew circles on her thigh, getting so close…then spiraling away. Fighting the bonds was useless, yet she did it anyway.

"I wanted to…to warn you— Oh!" He brushed her clit, the shockwave vibrating her entire body. Yet when she lifted her hips, his hand was gone, only the cold air hitting the dampness of her pussy.

"Warn me, eh? That you were going to kill me? Is that how you've been trained to work now?"

He lifted his hand, not touching her at all. That had to be the worst of all.

"Warn you that they want you dead. Won't stop until you're down— they even talked about making you one of them."

"Honey, lots of people—wait, scratch that. Lots of vamps want me dead. C'mon, Laur, I kill them for a living. Not that they don't deserve it or anything, but yes, dealing with death threats and a price on my head is part of the job, or had you forgotten? I do recall hearing you were a wanted woman at one time, as well."

Everything he said was true. He wouldn't take this any more seriously than the next threat. And there wasn't much she could do to make him believe it—until he trusted her.

"I'm serious." Her voice trembled, her body strung so tight she thought her muscles and tendons would just snap from the pressure.

"Mmm." Elliot's voice faded as he walked.

The strike of the matchstick froze her pulse. The sudden yellow-white flare sent shadows dancing over the amused look on his face. He stood between her feet, his eyes fixed not on her face, but right at the juncture of her thighs. The muscles there convulsed in reaction to his stare.

Then just as quickly, the light went out.

"So tell me. What did you learn to bring you out of six years of hiding to hunt me down and tell me something I live with every day?"

There was no way to process what he said. Her nerves had all turned into one-way streets. She heard what he was saying, but only in reference to the driving need that thundered between her legs. Her voice refused to work. Formulating a sentence would have been impossible anyway.

"Ah, Laura, Laura…" Elliot leaned forward and placed his hands above her knees. She felt his weight there. Knew exactly the distance between his mouth and her aching clit. "You'd like me to help you out, wouldn't you?"

She whimpered. Couldn't help it.

"You'd like me to put my mouth right here," he whispered, a deep, gravelly sound that would have been enough — but he grazed the back of his knuckles over her pussy lips, a touch so light it hurt.

"Yes," she hissed through clenched teeth. At this moment she'd do about anything, yet she couldn't think of anything except the driving need. Never, *ever* had she felt this…intense.

"So sweet. God, Laura, I could eat you up."

*Please!*

"You won't kill me, will you? Given the chance, would you try?"

She shook her head violently on the pillow, willing to agree to anything to just release her from this tightly coiled knot of tension.

"Laura?"

His thumb brushed the sensitized nub, causing her to jerk against her bonds.

"You didn't answer me."

"Please," she whispered. "Won't hurt you. Promise."

He laughed as he slipped a finger into her pussy and drew it back out, lightly thrusting. "You wouldn't just say that to get me to fuck you, would you?"

He toyed with her, tracing his wet fingers over her pussy lips, pinching her clit and then dipping back into the slit that begged to be filled.

"No!" she practically screamed.

"No? You want me to stop?"

Maybe she *would* kill him. Later. "No. Please."

She held her breath, waiting for his next touch, praying he wouldn't leave her like this. His breaths were heavy, fast. He was just as aroused as she was. God. If she could only touch him. That's all it would take to convince him to bury his thick cock inside her and find that desperate rhythm that would push them both over the edge.

"Oh!" she screamed as his mouth descended on her mound. His hot breath and even hotter tongue seared her skin as he lapped up the cream that poured out of her. Then he turned his attention to her clit, finding the nub and laving it with his skilled tongue.

She died. That was the only way she could explain the sensation of flying higher than science allowed, yet still feel empty. She wanted him inside her.

"You taste so good. I've been hungry for you for a long time."

That, while said to arouse, shot straight to her heart. Just fleetingly, as he lowered his mouth and thrust his tongue into her. She pushed against him, every cell screaming for just another lick, another stroke. One step closer to oblivion.

Elliot couldn't believe what he was experiencing. Especially after earlier. Hell, he'd told Mario he'd have a woman more pissed off than a wet cat to deal with when he walked back into that motel room, not a wet pussy begging for some petting.

What had gotten her aroused? Whatever it was, having the woman he'd loved for so long, the only woman he'd found to be his equal in the sack, spread-eagle and dripping with want for him…well, he wasn't a fool.

Still, he used the moment to see what he could elicit from her.

Satisfied that it wasn't an act, he dove in.

Laura was hot. Remembering how sexually responsive she was back when they dated hadn't been enough to prepare him for the way she jerked and shuddered beneath him now.

Feeding on that juicy cunt wouldn't be enough for him. No way. He wanted to taste her orgasm, then climb on up and plunge into her hot depths until she squeezed every drop of come from his body.

Eventually he'd let her go. She might be turned on now, but that wouldn't last. After all, he knew—he'd be the same way were the tables turned.

Besides, they couldn't spend all their time fucking. There were criminals to catch—especially the bastard that had sent Laura here to kill him.

Something about that raged raw in him, hardened his hands on her thighs and made him even more determined to claim this woman as his. His. No one else manipulated her. Or touched her. Or asked her to do a job.

Not anymore. She probably wouldn't like what he had to say, but she'd get over it.

"How many times have you been bitten, love?"

She tensed beneath him, likely from the shock of him interrupting such an intimate moment with a serious question such as that. While he waited for her answer, he vibrated her clit until she cried out.

Knowing she was seconds from the edge, he quickly loosened his jeans and climbed up. He wanted this. Needed this. Inside her, possessing her, convincing himself this wasn't a dream. He pressed against her slick lips, barely letting the tip of his cock slide into her wetness. "Sweet—" he couldn't finish it. She rose up, practically pulling him inside her. He lowered himself, sheathing his cock inside her tight walls.

The cuffs rattled against the bed as she fought to be free. Her moan turned into a low wail. He caught it with his mouth, entwining his tongue with hers as his hips rocked hard and fast against hers. Laura sent him to the edge the moment her pussy squeezed and then quivered with the force of her orgasm. God, she was tight. Too many years away from this feeling had built up unchecked need.

Her body seemed to fill him, not the other way around. They were a perfect fit, her hot wetness latching onto him and drawing out the spiraling pleasure until he thought he'd explode from the force of it.

"Get me out of these goddamn cuffs," Laura whispered when he nuzzled her neck. He laughed into the hot skin there, feeling her racing pulse just under the surface.

"I like it like this. You're at my mercy."

She gasped as his tongue traced over her collarbone. Laura was as formidable in the bedroom as she was in a life or death battle, but there was something damn erotic about the times she let him dominate her like this.

"Do you really want me to let you free?" he whispered into the valley of her breasts, teasing the skin he knew was ultra-sensitive to his soft touch.

He could practically feel her heart thundering beneath the surface. He knew the answer before she even nodded her head. "I want to be able to touch you, Elliot. I want my hands on you, my legs wrapped around you as you fuck me."

"I'll think on it." He slid out of her body and smiled down on her. It was an age-old game, one that brought them both to the edge of reason. Then he'd release those cuffs and their lovemaking would be as frantic as it ever could be.

He kissed his way up the generous globe of flesh and circled his tongue over the areola, wishing he'd thought to remove her shirt before starting this torture. Her breathing tore ragged from her lungs. He couldn't help but smile around the nipple as he suckled it into his mouth and lightly bit down.

"Elliot!" she screamed. The cuffs rattled against the bed, her hips bucked off the mattress.

He wanted to pound out his orgasm—hard and fast. His cock ached at the slow friction. His balls were tight with need. The salty taste of her skin, the musky smell of her cream, the tiny mewls that were punctuated by gasps and moans—recipe for the most satisfying lovemaking of his life.

Eager to please her to the same pinnacle, he left one breast and traced his tongue to the peak of the other. There he lapped and suckled, alternating between light touches and lightly scraping his teeth over the nipple through the thin fabric.

She hid nothing of her reaction. She wanted more. Her hips bucked up, silently offering up the spoils of victory.

He pushed up her skirt until it bunched about her waist. "You know," he said, lowering his mouth to her stomach, "I always thought you'd look sexy as hell with one of those belly chains that hooked to a piercing here." He slipped his tongue into her navel, then kissed all the way around it. "Many nights I imagined you walking in to my room wearing nothing but delicate chain lying on those gorgeous hips."

He smoothed his hands over her gentle curves and gritted his teeth against the power of that memory. That image had never failed to send blood rushing to his cock and now, with his hands once again on the very flesh he'd dreamed about, he was ready to explode.

"If I buy you one, would you wear it?" he asked, knowing this conversation was quickly disintegrating. The sweet perfume of her pussy was infiltrating his nostrils. He had about as much control as a bull seeing red. Talking to her about some useless but sexy piece of jewelry was his only way to keep from draping himself over her and pounding out his release.

"They have jewelry you wear down here, too," he said, his mouth just above her clit. He was certain she could feel his breath there, heating up those moist lips and igniting more fires within her. "I've heard about little clips that don't require piercing. Damn, if I knew you were wearing something like that I'd lose control."

She murmured something he couldn't decipher and lifted her hips even higher. That ended that discussion. Like a starving man, he cupped her bottom and feasted on her scorching flesh.

Her voice tore from her in gasps and moans—nearly a howl as he grabbed her clit between his lips and suckled. He alternated between quickly flicking his tongue over the most sensitive areas to slowly laving her pussy lips, leisurely sliding his tongue into her pussy before making his way back up her luscious cunt to start again.

He sensed it building. Felt her muscles convulse, her breath catch. "Give it to me," he prompted, positioning his mouth tightly over her and sucking the sweet honey from her as she shuddered her orgasm.

The bed shook, the cuffs protested against the metal and her wail filled the room. Quickly he climbed up and thrust into her still-spasming walls. They clenched around his as he slowly withdrew.

Christ, she was heaven. He fed her more, nearly dying each time he pulled back. She was hot—burning him with her passion. But it was always this way—every time.

He closed his eyes and concentrated on anything other than the woman beneath him. Not knowing what would happen after he released those cuffs, he wanted to postpone ending this decadent bout of sex.

Her breath hitched. He knew he'd hit that magic spot that would send her higher and harder to the edge than the time before. Using his hips, he shifted back and forth to rub over that pleasure nub until she was gasping and panting again.

She pushed against him, begging for it with her actions—wanting it hard, deep and explosive. His balls slapped against her as he picked up the pace. He saw the emotions, the pleasure cross her features, reading the exact moment the earth crumbled around her. And he let go, burning up in the pleasure of her pussy convulsing around his cock, milking him until there was nothing left.

He wanted to whisper what he hadn't uttered in six years. What he swore he'd never tell another woman—even Laura, if she ever returned. Yet here he was, overwhelmed with the feeling of contentment, completeness and utter satisfaction. He loved her. Probably would never stop loving her.

But he couldn't tell her. Not until he knew she wouldn't walk away and shatter his heart again.

\* \* \* \* \*

Laura dozed. Elliot lay beside her, the thin blanket pulled up over their hips, their body heat more than enough to fight off the evening chill. There were so many questions. Not only the standard, *Where have you been and why did you leave?* But now, *What happened to you during that time? Did you think of me? Miss me?*

God, he sounded like a desperate soul. But how was he supposed to feel when the love of his life walked back into his life, announced her intention to kill him and then fucked him like they'd never been apart?

She looked like an angel while she slept. Her cheeks were rosy—he detected just a hint of color in the light that spilled from the small desk lamp, her lips pink and slightly parted. Dark eyelashes touched her cheeks. He wanted to be that close—always.

He leaned down to kiss her forehead.

"My arms are asleep," she whispered without opening her eyes.

"I told you I like you this way. You can't run."

"Promise I won't."

"If you try, I'll follow and drag you back—this time I'll find a cozy house in the wilderness where no one can find you, no one can save you and if you run, you'll never find your way out."

"Funny, Elliot. I came back, didn't I? Did you think it was just for sex, then see ya later?"

"No, you told me already," he said with a laugh as he touched the tip of her nose, then traced her lips with his thumb. "You came to kill me. How perfect would it be to announce it, seduce me, gain my trust and then stab me as I sleep blissfully beside you. Then, I think, you'd leave to go claim your bounty."

She pushed up against the bindings, clearly trying to separate the intimate way their bodies were tangled. There wasn't a chance in hell that was going to work.

"Goddammit, I told you already that I came to warn you that someone wanted me to kill you. You should know already that I couldn't kill you."

"Then answer some questions."

The angelic innocence was gone from her face. Lines marred that smooth forehead. Her lips were a tight, pale line. The miniscule dent in her chin was visible—a sign her temper was threatening to explode. "Ask then. And take these damn cuffs off." He didn't doubt for a moment that if she had her hands free she'd fold them over her chest and assume a defiant pose. One that was hot as hell to see.

Before he started thinking with his cock again, he needed to learn a few things. "You never did answer me earlier. How many times have you been bitten?" Three was the magic number. Three would turn a mortal into a vampire. He needed to know, needed to understand how vulnerable she was.

"Twice. Now get me out, Elliot. This isn't right."

There was an edge there he didn't want to cross. He didn't need her pissed at him. After grabbing his pants and fishing out the key, he held her wrist and felt for the lock mechanism. "Twice?" Not good. "When—"

"*That's* why I left," she shot at him, her voice little more than a hiss. "I'm not interested in that third one."

Icy fingers found their way to his heart and squeezed.

"And then? You just walked away, but where did you go?"

"Turn on the light and get these fucking cuffs off me and I'll tell you, dammit. I'll tell you everything."

His hands stopped. "Everything?"

She groaned. "Yeah, whether you want to hear it or not. And trust me, you won't want to hear it."

Laura squinted against the sudden brightness and rubbed her wrists and ankles.

"Well?"

She avoided his gaze as she stood up and righted her clothes. Her cheeks stained as she thought about how easily he'd shifted from passion to this distant, detached man who watched her with one eyebrow lifted.

After pacing the length of the room, she admitted, "I got scared, okay?" She sucked in a deep breath and leaned against the dresser. She avoided eye contact and prayed he bought her lame excuse for a reason. "I had that cushion, having only been bitten once, way back in the beginning. You remember that…"

Absently, she touched the pulse at her neck. Though the scars had long healed, she had spent nearly six years waiting for one of the guards to decide to thwart authority and feast on her fresh blood. She'd once vowed that if that happened, she would break out, find Elliot, and plead for a quick death.

"Things sure didn't end up the way we had planned, did they?" She realized she mused out loud only when she saw the look of surprise on Elliot's face.

"We still have a future, Laura. Now that you're back, we can readjust them and still turn them into reality."

She shook her head. He didn't understand. Sure, she could still retire from street work and work on the inside. She had enough skill with a computer to work in dispatch or even recruitment and training. Women were just as successful as men in those fields. She could be useful.

But Elliot wouldn't leave the streets. One day after a round of lovemaking, he'd said he would, but they both had known it was a lie meant to keep from spoiling the moment. They'd created hope that day—admitted their mutual affection and vowed to grasp the fragile relationship with both hands and make it work.

"Things haven't changed," she said with a sigh. "You're still chasing a phantom — and we both know you'll never let go."

He fell silent.

"So those dreams of the past aren't going to help us at all."

"You're dismissing the time we had together as nothing? You've known from the beginning that I…"

"What do you want me to say? I've never asked you not to search out your brother's killer. Never stopped you from following leads or questioning your bounties."

"I can't stop now, I'm too close."

"I didn't ask you to stop. But then what? Will you still be out in the trenches when you're forty? How about fifty? What if you haven't caught him by then? He's a fucking vampire, Elliot. He'll still be in his prime and untouched by age. Then what?"

"I'll get him before then. The force is growing. We've doubled the number of hunters in the last two years. Have nearly twice as many recovery teams. Dispatch now has two offices. We network with DC, Boston and Philly and are working with the other locales. We are making strides."

"When will you stop pretending this is a one-man war, then?"

"When I win."

\* \* \* \* \*

Laura shook her head and then locked herself in the bathroom. The cool water she splashed on her face did little to clear her head. What a mess! But so typical of life with Elliot.

He'd come to her rescue once, about six months after she'd started hunting—just a few raw weeks after his brother had died. Jack had been a hunter too. She'd never met him, or Elliot for that matter, but their reputation was well-known across the agency. Sometimes they worked together, sometimes alone. They always got their vamp. Hell, they were legends. Modern-day superheroes.

She was taking down what should have been an easy case—a prostitute whose taste for blood had spawned a killing spree. Laura had approached her and asked her secret for snaring johns. Two minutes later she'd been flat on her back with three hungry vamps eyeing her jugular.

She hadn't seen Elliot until two of the vamps crumpled to their knees. Her target was startled by the sudden demise of her bodyguards. Laura reacted and plunged a stake into the other woman's chest.

God, had she been sick that day. More scared than she'd ever been in her life. And then Elliot had grabbed her by the shoulders and hauled her to her feet. He never said a word, just picked her up, threw her in his car and drove back to agency headquarters.

She splashed more water on her face and then ran her damp fingers through her unruly hair. That day had changed her life in so many ways.

Elliot had been in her life every since. She rather thought they'd dumped her on him. Even so, he made it sound like his idea. He was going to watch her back and they could be more effective as a team.

They worked well together. Kicked some vampire ass. Now they were going to die together, because Elliot was so goddamn hardheaded that he wouldn't listen when she tried to explain it would be nothing short of a lynch mob coming after them.

She walked out of the bathroom and almost directly into Elliot's arms.

"I've got to know, Laura. You said you'd tell me everything."

If she blurted out the whole truth, he'd likely slap her back in the cuffs and take off to find the bastards and kill them all—and likely die in the process.

He stood before her, his legs brushing against her bare knees. The friction of denim against skin sent the butterflies in her stomach into frenzied flight. He reached up and touched her chin, whispering, "Tell me."

"They are... He is..." Her voice cracked as she looked up in his eyes and admitted it. "The bastard, the very one you've spent your career looking for, locked me up in their dungeon and used me as bait. Waiting for you to come save me so they could—"

His face turned to granite, white and hardened with his obvious anger. "Goddamn it, Laura. I didn't know. I didn't know!" He pulled her up and framed her face in his hands. The mere gesture stole her breath and twisted her gut. She'd given up the hope that he'd ever come for her. This was the reaction she'd waited for, spent hours and days and months imagining.

"I'm so sorry," he muttered against her chin, then neck. Her body quaked as nerve endings came alive.

"Wait," she said, getting her arms between them before he could make her forget all about the world outside their door. "I've got to finish."

"Talk." His voice vibrated against the flesh of her shoulder, the aftershocks spiraling straight to her feminine core.

She had never expected to find him again, much less rekindle the flame that burned so bright and hot that they often joked they would spontaneously combust one day. It was more than sex. They knew that, refused to talk about it. And that hadn't died either. At least on her part.

His fingers smoothed her hair, the backs of his fingers drifting down to stroke her face. God, how could she even speak?

"I—I—" she stuttered. "I need you to take off my shirt."

He threw his head back and laughed. "Okay." Immediately he started picking at the buttons of her blouse.

"Um, no. I mean, yes. Take it off."

His hands faltered. "Laura?"

She nearly laughed. Her mind and body were at war and dammit, her body was winning. "I need you to check, to see if they've tagged me in some way. Implanted a tracer. I can't imagine they let me go—with orders to find you—if they didn't have a way of finding me."

He stepped back then, the playful glint faded from his eyes. "You're serious."

"Dead serious. And that's what they want. I'm expendable here. They'll kill us both."

"Laura…"

She hated the almost...pang of sympathy she heard in his voice. She didn't come here to die. She came here to save his ass, the way he had hers. "You know you can go. Run. I'll tell them I couldn't find you."

"Son of a bitch," he roared as he pulled the shirt from her back. "They do this to you?"

Old-fashioned whippings. They just wanted information. She didn't comply then. Neither did she answer Elliot's emotional outburst. Just stood still while his fingers slid over her skin and prodded her hairline, the length of her spine and the dip of her back.

Elliot felt his blood pressure raise a few dangerous notches. The beautiful, flawless skin of Laura's back was now marred with angry pink scars. He bet she carried many more than that. He vowed to find the creatures that did this to her and double the agony before he finally killed them.

"I don't see anything. No signs. But you know that doesn't mean anything." She sucked in her breath as he traced the lines. "My God, Laura. I'm sorry." He should have gone after her.

But then he'd have to tell her the truth, tell her why he couldn't stop her when she'd claimed the kill and walked off. She hadn't been the only one bitten that day.

The noise outside caused them both to jerk. "How long have we been here?" she whispered. She couldn't believe she hadn't been more careful.

"About four hours total. I called in the last kill just after midnight. It's nearly four-thirty."

"Then they're still out there."

They had until daybreak. That's all the time he had, too. "Laura?" He nudged her chin upwards. Screw it all. His heart was going to break whether he said the words or not. "Whatever happens. I love you."

"Shut up, Elliot. Nothing's going to happen." But his words didn't go unnoticed. "What supplies do you have here? They'll come after me. If not tonight, then tomorrow."

"And in the meantime, shall we sit at the window and wait?"

She didn't have time to answer that. The glass behind her shattered with gunfire. Laura screamed and dived onto him, taking both of them to the floor.

"Where's your gun?" she gasped.

Elliot stretched and reached for the handgun he kept tucked in the small of his back. He thrust it into Laura's outstretched hand and crawled over to the dresser where he had a high-powered rifle propped up.

He flinched as someone—or some*thing*—rammed against the door of their motel room. Laura was right. There must be a tracer on her. Why hadn't he listened? Why couldn't he believe that somehow he'd given one of the major drug lords or arms dealers a potent hit in the revenue? But *six years*? Why hadn't they come before now?

"Stay down!" he commanded to Laura as he rolled away from the door and leveled his gun just above the door handle. The room shook with the force of their blows. It was no match for them. The wood of the doorframe was already splintering. He just hoped Laura was the crack shot she had once been.

The fatal mistake was looking back.

Laura used the bed as a shield, the gun nearly hidden in the wadded-up sheets.

He felt fear. A foreign, metallic bitch of a taste that took an edge off the adrenaline rush and need to get this done. She was vulnerable. If he didn't succeed, she would die today.

With one hand he supported his gun, the other closed around one of the wooden stakes he never let out of reach. He wouldn't fail. It wasn't an option.

The door gave.

Without hesitation he squeezed the trigger and dropped two of the vampires in the doorway. Hopefully they'd stay down long enough that he could finish them off.

Gunshots echoed around him. One of the two bedside lights shattered, deepening the shadows. Hopefully making Laura less visible.

An icy-hot flame shot though his thigh. He fell backward, firing at the silhouettes in the doorway as he did. Blood scalded his leg. "Bastards. Fucking hell." He gritted against the pain, knowing it'd soon fade. Wasn't going to help him get to his feet, however.

He needed a new plan.

Laura took careful aim before firing. She'd downed three of the monsters who'd pushed past the splintered wood of the door. Their eyes were black. Programmed hate. It turned her blood to ice, but gave her the ability to squeeze that trigger and then breathe when the shape fell. But they kept coming. She knew it would be this way. The vamps had no intention of losing this battle.

From the corner of her eye, she saw Elliot stumble backward with his fingers pressed to his thigh. Her stomach twisted, her heart lurched as she saw they were coated with blood.

That just made her all the more determined. She would die here if she had to. Under no condition would she go back to that dungeon. There would be no mercy for her this time. If she had to do it alone, she'd spend every damn bullet she had and use splinters from the doorjamb to slay these empty souls.

"Jack."

Elliot's voice forced her eyes away from the next silhouette in her sights up toward the doorway. There, framed by the blood-splattered frame, stood a man who could be Elliot's twin.

"Join me, Elliot. I'm tired of fighting you."

Laura swallowed, setting the sights right on the middle of Jack's chest. Her hands shook with the force of her anger. No way was this bastard leaving. But for all her anger, the mix of emotions she'd seen on Elliot's profile tore at her soul. She should have told him. Jack hadn't died that day at the hands of the vampire. They'd turned him into one of them. And he'd become a very powerful and angry leader. He blamed Elliot for everything.

"Jack? But I thought — "

She felt as Elliot must have. A deep, ragged knife turning and slicing right through the heart of her as she listened to Elliot's shock and disbelief. Eight years he'd spent, eating, sleeping and dreaming of the day he could avenge his brother's death. All for nothing. She blinked back tears but kept the gun aimed at where Jack's heart had been, a place now black with hate.

"You left me for dead. I wish you'd finished me off, rather than leaving me to this hell of a life."

"But why—why do you want to kill me?"

"Because you continue to take my life away from me. I finally had to accept who I was and realized there's only one choice for me. Regardless of what we try to do with our lives, all of you stereotype us into one category—bad. So if I was going to be bad, hell, I was gonna be the baddest there was. And I made it. Killed the bastard that did this to me and took over. But there's nothing about being a vampire that's glorious, no matter how much power you get. Then you started snooping around and made it worse—took even my prestige away from me. My business is failing, the gangs from Philadelphia and DC have moved in and taken over. And you're a worthless piece. I had your woman in my possession all that time and you never came for her. You don't deserve to live."

Laura gasped as Jack turned directly to her and grinned. "Feisty little thing, isn't she? I was tempted to keep her for myself, but at least I wasn't cruel enough to doom her to hell. What will you do, brother, when I put a bullet in her chest?"

Laura gasped and tried to scurry back, down, anywhere out of his line of view. Her fingers had gone numb, and her hands were shaking so badly that the bullets would be wasted. She did manage to squeeze off one round, the repercussion of the explosion knocking her backward.

The rest happened in slow motion. She saw streaks of white and black, like fireworks right in front of her eyes. Then there was a second explosion. She heard someone, Elliot she thought, scream "No!"

Then the white-hot pain lanced through her chest and shoulder. She tried to speak, to scream, but couldn't. The ache turned to ice and it spread slowly through her body. She could hear the mayhem—more shots fired, male voices yelling, sounds of furniture crashing—but it was so far away. And she didn't care. She was so tired. So tired…

Laura was down. Elliot felt as if he'd taken the shot himself. But he couldn't stop until the rest of the vamps were dead. Including the man who shot her.

His strength was nearly gone when he finished off those vampires they'd downed, using every available piece of wood to do it. He stood over the last vampire. This was his brother, a man he'd once considered his hero. He never, ever wanted to face this irony. Had never considered it. Eight years he'd hunted because of his love for this man.

"Do it if you're going to. I want out of this hell," Jack growled.

Elliot swallowed and looked back toward Laura's pale and limp form. How dare this fool curse her that way? How dare Jack empty *her* life on the ground to get his revenge? At least her shot had been accurate. Blood seeped from Jack's chest, a mere symbol of his life source emptying out.

Enraged, Elliot leapt forward, stake ready. That gunshot wouldn't kill him. He could.

He expected Jack to fight. Elliot paused when Jack said, "Do it. Give me peace, brother. Finally do something right. Give me *peace*."

"Why didn't you come to me? Why didn't you let me know? There were options. Still are."

"Not anymore. I gave Laura back to you. I didn't put her in the dungeon, Elliot, but I made sure she was never harmed. I waited for you. She waited for you. I've given up. There's no life left in me."

"Let me take you in. I'll find a way."

"I'm a wanted vamp. If you don't kill me, another hunter will. I'd rather die by your merciful hands. Give me peace. That's what I ask of you. Death."

Elliot choked back a sob. He understood too well. Not about Laura's part in this, but that didn't matter now. His brother said he'd killed the man Elliot had spent years hunting. He owed him this final request.

"Sleep well," he muttered, feeling the pain of the stake as he drove it through his brother's heart.

Jack smiled as the light in his eyes flickered and died.

Elliot felt numb. Empty. Never before had anything drained him, not since Laura had left and replaced his heart with a block of ice.

Jack. He'd been alive. How didn't he know? How didn't anyone know? It slowly dawned on him. Laura did. She tried to tell him, tried to warn him.

"Shit. Laura! Laura!"

He lifted her on the bed. So much blood. The bullet wound was too close to her heart. He didn't have much time.

She moaned and rolled her head. Her glassy eyes tried to focus, but fell closed again. Her breaths were shallow, her skin cold.

He couldn't—wouldn't lose her again. Not like this. "Laura, listen to me."

Nothing.

Shit. The tightness in his chest had nothing to do with physical wounds, but emotional ones. She had a piece of his heart he'd long thought had gone cold.

There was only one answer. Only one way...

Closing his eyes, he did something he'd sworn he'd never do to any human. He opened his mouth, unleashed the vampiric canines and pressed them to the faintest trace of pulse in her neck.

Tears poured from him as he understood the curse he'd give her. Was this too selfish? Would she hate him for being forced to live like this?

There was no time. As gently as he could, he let the razor-sharp edges break through her skin. The tang of her blood as it rolled from her flesh and onto his tongue revitalized him—strengthened him. Yet he felt incredibly weak. Helpless.

He prayed she'd told him the truth, that she'd already been bitten twice, or this was all in vain.

He pressed a kiss to her neck beneath those twin puncture wounds, the touch of her skin already warmer. It was working.

Instead of feeling better, he felt terrible. He should have died himself. He knew what it was like to live this life, to struggle to survive in a world that didn't accept his kind.

Elliot left her to sleep and limped out to his truck. There he radioed Mario and requested a recovery unit. At this point, he was nothing but a robot doing his job.

Then he dragged the vamps' bodies outside and waited.

\* \* \* \* \*

Laura slowly became aware of the ache in her chest and the coldness that surrounded her. It all had to be a dream. Everything was so...quiet. She must have imagined the last few hours. The shootout with Jack and his crew must have been a dream, a nightmare. But she'd imagined pulling that trigger and seeing Jack fall.

Then getting shot herself.

Her eyes flew open.

Pain and cold weren't indicative of the happy "died and gone to heaven" feeling she'd have expected. She was very much alive.

How?

"Stay quiet."

Elliot. She had to see for herself that he was all right. She struggled to sit up, fighting the nausea that swirled in her stomach.

"You'll want to stay down, too. The first few hours are the worst. Let your body get through all the changes."

*Changes?* She breathed out carefully, wincing at the tenderness on her left side. "I got shot."

"Yes, you did."

Why was he there, sitting cold and unmoving? She could barely make out his silhouette in the darkness. "Did you?"

"Yep."

"Oh God." That's right. She remembered now. Her head spun, images of the room blurred into a black-and-white landscape. She closed her eyes and let her head relax on the pillow. She would not succumb. Not until she had answers.

"I'll be okay, if that's your worry. So will you. As okay as you can be now."

There was a level of tension in his voice she didn't want to try to translate. "Tell me, Elliot. What happened here?"

"They're dead."

It was pain. He'd killed his brother. She ached for him, felt it tightening in her chest even as a tear slid down her cheek. "All of them." A statement, not a question. She had to know. Hated to make him say it, but she had to know the threat was gone.

"All of them. Outside, waiting for Disposal."

She sighed. "Then someone's coming for us, to take us to the hospital, right?"

Silence.

"Elliot?" She choked on her fear. There was something else wrong. Very wrong.

"No."

Squeezing her eyes closed, she felt for the wound. Her shirt was torn, but the flesh beneath it whole. Bruised. She'd taken a bullet to the shoulder and she felt bruised.

It could only mean one thing. "They got me, didn't they?" Knowing the answer, refusing to accept it, her heart rate picked up and her breath came in hysterical sobs. "Please. Please no. No…"

Everything was lost. Everything. A vampire. Now she understood the coldness in her body. The changes Elliot mentioned. The metamorphosis from a warm-blooded human to a blood-dependant creature of the night.

Everything she hated. Everything she sought to eliminate.

"Kill me, Elliot. You've got to. I can't..." She swallowed and continued in a stronger voice, "I won't."

"You have to. You don't have a choice."

She struggled for composure that just wasn't there. What room did society have for her now? "I have nothing. There's no reason to live. I can't live."

"I do it."

The iciness flowed over her like a tidal wave. She shivered and squeezed her eyes closed. When she could breathe again, she whispered, "What?"

"Hate me, Laura, for what happened. I did it. I couldn't let you die. And I won't kill you now."

The cold she felt was nothing compared to the ice that formed in her veins. *I did it,* he had said. Which meant — no. She choked back a sob and squeezed her eyes shut. She didn't want to look. Didn't want to see the truth. The man she loved, the man she'd made love to just *hours* before — was a *vampire.*

"Damn you, Elliot!" she screamed and jerked up from the bed. The dizziness kept her from getting to her feet, the stiffness in her back and shoulder paralyzing her arm. She pushed against her eyes to stop the stabbing pain there. "How *could* you?"

"Sit down. You'll make yourself sick. I need you to heal."

"Fuck healing." How could she cope with this? Six years in that prison was a piece of cake compared to this revelation. *Elliot was a vampire?*

She heard him get up, noting already that her senses were sharper. God, it really *was* happening. "Don't. Please. Don't."

Yet she couldn't fight it when he wrapped his arms around her and held her against his frame. His strong, warm body supported her as she cried. Sobbed for all that she lost. All the while hating this miserable weakness.

"I got bit the night you left," he whispered against her hair. "Number three. That's why I couldn't follow you. And then I wasn't sure I wanted to find you. Wasn't sure of anything for a long, long while."

"El—"

"Shhh. Let me talk. I tried to pretend nothing was wrong. Stayed in all day, worked at night. But Mario in Dispatch figured it out. Forced me to come in. Turns out I wasn't the only one on the team who'd been afflicted. They have a program. Research. Shots we can take to allow us to venture out in daylight, a feeding program that harms no one. They can't reverse it, Laura, but we aren't prisoners of what we are. We are stronger because of it."

She didn't want to hear this, didn't want logic to invade her pain and horror. *A vampire.* Elliot had turned her into a vampire. Yet she understood what he was saying. They would be more efficient. Immortal beings fighting immortal. No more would the criminals have the edge.

"Is this true? You've survived all this time as a vampire?"

"Survived." His laugh was riddled with sarcasm. "I haven't lived a day since you left."

Her breath hitched. He pulled her even closer and buried his face against her neck. She understood. Upon laying eyes on Elliot on the dock just hours ago, she knew that the past six years were nothing more than a blink of an eye. "Me either," she answered, daring to hope.

"I did this because I couldn't let you die. I don't want to lose you again. Not after what I know has happened, how we've lost six years. Don't ask me to kill you again."

Right now she couldn't imagine wishing anything else. "I've spent six years wondering if dying was a better alternative. I can't imagine ditching that thought anytime soon."

"Think about it, Laura," he said, stroking her hair gently. "Before we worried about dying, now we can concentrate on living. And I intend to. We can't let this be a curse. This is an opportunity to share forever. How many people can say that?"

She smiled bravely. It would take some getting used to before she accepted this new life, but with Elliot beside her, she was willing to give it a try.

"That said," Elliot dropped a kiss to her lips, "I need to call Mario and let him know what's going on. You get back in bed and heal. You're gonna need your strength. We've got all day to spend in bed, waiting for the sunlight to go away."

"And then?" she asked, knowing she was going to need a bit more time to adjust to this new state.

"And then we'll stay up all night getting to know one another again. I told Mario I needed forty-eight hours before I'd be ready to take another case."

"Tell him seventy-two and I'll go with you. I think."

"Hell, I'll take a week. I haven't had a vacation in over six years."

Laura grinned and let him guide her back to bed. She slid under the sheet and relaxed, for the first time in way too many years. His was a proposal worth living for.

# About the Author

Melani Blazer has a taste for the unusual. She loves books and movies that take her far from reality and test the edge of her beliefs. Which mirrors her writing. Instead of trying to curb her wacky imagination, she's been able to morph it into sexy stories of were-leopards and mortal angels and sinister ghost-cars. Ideas pop into her head in the weirdest places, but often choose to challenge her in the shower or in those waking hours just before dawn. If she can catch them, she builds them into worlds and stories.

She's been married nearly half her life (how can that be, when she's still 29?) to her high school sweetheart who supports her, challenges her, and provides all of the entertai—research needed to write emotionally charged tales of true love (and hot sex). They spend their time raising their caboodle of cats, their teenage daughter and one another's blood pressure. Oh, and they work on their own Hot Rod (a '71 Chevelle) together as well.

Melani welcomes mail from readers. You can write to her c/o Ellora's Cave Publishing at 1056 Home Ave., Akron, OH 44310.

## Also by Melani Blazer

Dante's Relic
Hot Rod Heaven
Legend of the Leopard

# HARD LESSONS

Nikki Soarde

# Chapter One

The camera panned across the room.

The office was spacious, well-appointed with antique brass fixtures, a polished oak desk and wide, bright windows that looked out over the town of Squamish, British Columbia, and the Pacific Ocean that glittered in the distance.

A man strode into view. Tall and lean, with chiseled features and thick black hair swept back off his face, he had an air of authority about him—a man who wore power as easily as he wielded it. He sat down in the high-back leather chair and drew up to the desk. He bent to read a file that lay there, but looked up at the sound of the door opening.

He frowned. "I thought I told you I wasn't to be disturbed."

The door clicked shut and a woman approached. She rounded the desk and stood beside his chair. Red hair was swept back off her face in a neat French twist. She wore small wire-framed glasses and a trim-fitting suit that showed off long legs and an enticing bit of cleavage.

She held out a clipboard. "You need to sign this, Mr. Carrone. It's important."

His eyes blazed. "So important it couldn't wait ten minutes until I finished with this?" His finger stabbed at the file on his desk.

She swallowed, took a half-step back. "Well..."

He stood suddenly, shrugged out of his suit jacket and let it drop onto the chair. He stepped closer, towering over her, expression thunderous. "How often do we have to go through this, Cyndi? How many times do I have to say it before it finally sinks in?"

She licked a pair of full, gold-tinted lips. "Uh…I'm sorry, but—"

"Sorry? Sorry's not good enough. You've said it a hundred times but obviously it means nothing to you. You have no idea how to follow instructions! I'm afraid you need to learn your lesson the hard way."

The two weren't even touching and yet the sexual tension rippled off the screen in almost-palpable waves.

"Wh-what does that mean?" asked Cyndi.

"Take off your jacket."

She blinked, but hesitated only a moment before setting down her clipboard and obliging. The jacket fell to the floor revealing a simple, if somewhat snug-fitting, white blouse. Her nipples strained at the fabric, stiff and provocative.

He slipped a hand inside the neckline and she started, reaching reflexively for his wrist. "Mr. Carrone, I—"

He slapped her hand away, reaching deeply inside her blouse and obviously fondling her breast beneath the bra. "Stop it. You have to learn how to take orders, Cyndi." He lifted his other hand and gripped the lapels of the blouse. He ripped them apart, sending buttons scattering onto the desk and floor. "And this is the best way for you to learn."

Her chest heaved, breasts spilling out of the scanty cups of her white lace bra. "But—"

The bra came apart as easily as tissue paper in his hands. He tweaked a nipple hard enough to make her cry out. "Quiet," he commanded. "I don't want to hear your whining."

He tweaked the other nipple and she endured it, making only the slightest of gasps.

"Better." He pulled a pin from her hair allowing the thick waves to tumble to her shoulders. "Much better." He removed her glasses, set them on the desk. "Now remove your skirt."

She hesitated, licked her lips as if considering what to say, but then seemed to change her mind. She unzipped the back of her skirt and allowed it to fall to the floor. Only a thin triangle of lace covered her pussy.

He ripped it away.

She stood there, naked and quivering before him.

"Touch yourself."

She stared at him. "Please. I don't—"

He grabbed her, whirled her around, wrapped an arm around her waist and pulled her back against him. He reached between her thighs, obviously thrusting a finger deeply inside her.

She arched her back and gasped.

"Fine," he growled, fingers working. "I'll take you as I like. It seems that's all you understand."

The camera zoomed in on her pussy, on his hand and the moisture that now coated his fingers and the insides of her thighs.

She groaned slightly, covered his hand with her own.

He abruptly withdrew and she whimpered in frustration. "No," he growled. "I have control here. That's what this is about." He presented his fingers to her mouth. "Suck me clean."

She closed her eyes and drew his fingers deeply into her mouth. "Do you want me to fuck you?" he asked as she licked and suckled.

She nodded.

"How? On this desk, with your legs wrapped around me as I shove my cock inside your pussy until you scream for more?"

His fingers were deep inside her mouth. "Mm hmm."

"I know you do." He withdrew his hand and pushed her forward until she was leaning over the desk, her breasts pressed against the wood, her ass exposed. "But this isn't about what *you* want, is it?"

She shook her head.

He kept one hand pressed against the small of her back as he undid his belt and fly with the other. "Right. It's about what I want, and how you can please me." His trousers and briefs fell to the floor revealing a thick and throbbing erection.

He opened a desk drawer and pulled out a tube of lubricant, coating his cock with it as he continued. "Do you know how you're going to do that, Cyndi?"

"No," she breathed. "Tell me."

He dropped the lubricant back in the drawer and slammed it shut. "You're going to grab your behind and spread those sweet little cheeks and let me fuck you in the ass." He bracketed his hands on her hips, holding her firm. "Right?"

She merely nodded and did as he had instructed, pulling her cheeks apart and closing her eyes as she waited.

He pressed his cock against her anus. "And you're going to enjoy it, right?"

"Yes!" She screamed the word as he rammed himself deeply inside her.

"Fuck," he groaned, his thrusts fierce and merciless. "Sweet God, you're tight."

Sweat broke out on his skin and trickled down his face. His grip on her hips tightened as his assault continued. At the key moment he reached between her thighs to push a finger inside her pussy and press his thumb against her clit.

They both came in a cacophony of grunts, screams and, finally, laughter.

"Damn," he said as he withdrew from her and reached for a tissue. "That was hot." He looked at the camera as Cyndi pushed herself off the desk and flopped back into his chair, legs splayed, chest heaving. He cast a glance at her over his shoulder. "You okay, babe?"

She just murmured, touching herself. "Mmm."

Chuckling, he looked at the camera. "Did you get it all, Vince?"

"Oh yeah, Mr. Carrone." The bodyguard's voice was thick. "It'll make a great addition to your collection."

"Do *you* want to fuck her? Now that would be interesting."

Cyndi's eyes flew open and she glared at him, her eyes shooting fire.

Rae Carrone laughed and grabbed her hand, tugging her to a standing position and pulling her in tight against him. "Don't worry, babe. I don't share." He sank his fingers into her hair and held her firm. "With anybody."

He thrust his tongue inside her mouth and the screen went blank.

\* \* \* \* \*

Kaley Carrone stood in front of the computer screen, the rage pulsing through her veins so hot she was surprised she didn't incinerate on the spot. Her fists were clenched so tightly that she had to make an effort to unfurl her fingers and was surprised to find that no blood had dripped onto the carpet of their three-hundred-square-foot bedroom.

Very slowly and deliberately she popped the disk out of the CD drive—the disk that she'd found slipped into the pocket of the suit her husband had asked her to have cleaned for him.

It was labeled "An Office Fuck" and the title had piqued her interest enough to investigate further. For just a moment she wished she'd ignored it, wished she could have gone on in blissful ignorance.

But only for a moment.

She snapped the disk in two, walked into the en suite bathroom and tossed the remnants into the garbage. She noticed a pair of scissors on the counter and on a whim, picked them up. She strode purposefully to his closet and glared at the rows of neatly pressed Armani suits and Gucci shoes.

She grasped a sleeve, held it up, poised the scissors — and stopped.

What would this get her? Sure she'd have the momentary satisfaction of seeing his face when he came home and found his precious designer clothes in shreds. She could take a sledge hammer to his car and that would feel good too. But for all that effort the satisfaction would be fleeting.

She could divorce him, but thanks to a carefully worded prenuptial agreement, she'd get barely a quarter of a million and Rae Carrone was worth twenty times that. It hadn't always been so.

They'd been married five years and his assets had quadrupled in that time, thanks in no small part to her efforts. The advertising campaign that had sent their sales through the roof had been her idea, her *baby*. She had conceived the idea, and with Ray's full approval, had supervised it every step of the way right through to completion.

Initially Ray had balked at the cash outlay required for the kind of media blitz she proposed, but she'd convinced him it would be worth it. And she had been right. Carrone Fitness Clubs and Health Products had become a household name, and the money had come rolling in.

She'd earned her position as head of Promotions and Marketing, and she had *not* earned it on her back. Sure, she'd been married to Ray when she got the promotion, but dammit, she'd deserved it. Just as she deserved a bigger chunk of the pie than a measly few hundred grand. She'd brought up the prenuptial agreement once or twice in the years since the business took off, but he'd always laughed it off, minimized its importance or said they'd change it *later*.

Maybe she should have pushed harder, but surely a judge would look at the facts, and their history together, and throw out the contract. Or would he? She would like to think so, but how could she be sure? It wouldn't help that she hadn't been a functioning member of the staff for more than six months. She'd taken an indefinite leave of absence on the advice of her doctor, and eventually on Ray's insistence.

He wanted a child, and the doctor suspected that the stress levels she experienced with the amount of time she put in at the office were not helping their chances for conception.

She could still remember the conversation as clearly as if she were watching a video tape in her mind...

*"This is ridiculous, Kaley," ranted Ray. I won't argue about it anymore. I don't see why you're having such a hard time with this. You get an indefinite holiday. You get to shop to your heart's content and have as many facials as you like. Most women would swoon at the thought."*

*She tamped down a rare spark of temper. "I enjoy my work, Ray. I'll be bored."*

*"Well, once you have a baby to look after you won't be."*

*"But what if it's not that simple?" Her temper got the better of her. "What if I'm not the problem? If you'd at least get tested then we could be sure."*

*She shouldn't have said it. The moment it was out of her mouth she regretted it, but there was no taking it back. They'd been over this ground before and she knew what his reaction would be. She wasn't disappointed.*

*His expression turned to ice. "So, you don't think I'm man enough for you, is that it? You think I'm incapable of fathering a child?"*

*"No, Ray. I'm sorry. I didn't mean – "*

*"I know exactly what you meant, and this discussion is over. If you don't want to be bothered with a baby, then tell me now, so I can find someone who* does!*"*

*He didn't mean it. She knew he said such things out of anger and an insecurity that few would have guessed he harbored, but still...it hurt. "Of course I want a baby. And I'll do whatever it takes."*

*"Good. Now let's not discuss this again until you can come back and tell me the rabbit died." He smiled as if he were making a joke, but she couldn't bring herself to smile. "And let's hope it's soon."*

*He pecked her on the cheek and walked out the door. "Yes," she whispered. "Let's hope it is."*

But it hadn't happened "soon", and lately Ray had seemed even more restless than usual. His temper had been thin and his good humor thinner. He hardly seemed to notice her anymore, and if she admitted it to herself, when they made love it didn't feel like making love anymore.

It felt like he was performing a duty. It felt like procreation.

And now she wondered if he really was thinking of *procreating* with someone else. Well, she wasn't going to be discarded so easily. She'd given him her mind and her body, she'd made him a home and made sacrifices for him, and still it wasn't enough. And still he felt the need to look elsewhere.

Well, Kaley didn't intend to take that lying down. And she didn't intend to make his life easy by taking that prenuptial agreement at face value and paving the way to a nice, tidy—cheap—divorce.

She wanted more, dammit. She deserved more.

She just had to figure out a way to get it.

# Chapter Two

Mason inserted the forged key into the lock and hoped. The dead bolt slid open, allowing the two men to slip inside without delay.

He closed the door behind them and sighed in relief as Dan, his friend and partner, crossed to the alarm panel and proceeded to work his techno-magic.

"I don't like this," muttered Dan as he fussed and fiddled, pushing buttons and making lights blink. "I don't like the whole thing."

The console light blinked green and Mason breathed a sigh of relief.

"Oh, for chrissake, Dan. Will you chill?" He pulled his ski-mask off to take a few deep breaths of unfiltered air. "You'll like it fine when we rake in all that cash."

Dan leaned in close and hissed, "Just so long as we don't have to spend it from a fucking *prison cell!*"

Mason raked his fingers through his mop of thick, blond hair and studied his friend.

Dan rubbed his temples. His short, chestnut hair stood out at a variety of angles and his eyes were shadowed with fear. Daniel was afraid of too many things and Mason had made it his life's work to cure his friend of his perpetual hesitation. From bungee jumping to sky-diving, Dan balked at everything, but always succumbed to Mason's unique persuasive abilities. All Mason had to do was challenge his friend to a bet or a contest and Dan's normally mild, subdued nature was transformed. He had a fierce sense of competition and once it was awakened there was no stopping him. Mason took advantage of that, and Dan had never once regretted it, always enjoying himself and eventually thanking Mason for pushing and challenging him.

Mason hoped he wasn't about to break a perfect record.

"Are you finished?" asked Mason, keeping his voice even. "Calm? Collected? Because if you're not tell me now. Both of us have to be in top form or this isn't going to work. Or else we *will* end up in a prison cell."

Dan looked down at his hands where his ski mask had been twisted into a knot. "Yeah. Sure. Sorry. I'm in." He turned his big brown puppy-dog eyes on Mason and smiled, baring dimples that had had girls swooning ever since grade school. If only Dan had known what to do with them once they'd dropped at his feet.

"I need this money as much as you do." Dan nodded again. "Yeah. I'm in."

"Okay, then. Put on your mask."

Both men donned their disguises and began to creep through the darkened house. The place was a monstrosity, easily six thousand square feet if it was an inch. What two people without kids or pets needed with that kind of space eluded him. But, then again, everybody needed something to spend their money on. Perhaps Mr. Carrone could write off the ransom as just another household expense.

He grinned as he followed Dan up the solid oak staircase.

\* \* \* \* \*

Ray Carrone was cold. Halfway between the worlds of sleep and wakefulness, he became vaguely aware that he was uncovered. Silently cursing his wife who, despite the enormous bed, had a knack for hogging the covers, he gradually clawed his way toward consciousness. Without opening his eyes he reached out in search of the blanket but found, to his shock, that he couldn't move.

He tried harder but met with no success. His wrists were tied! When that realization hit, his eyes, at last, flew open.

"Finally," whispered a deep male voice. "Jesus man, you sleep like the dead."

Ray blinked, trying to bring the world into focus. He felt something cold against his temple and turned his head to try and make it out. He found himself looking into the barrel of a pistol that was the size of a small cannon.

"That's exactly what you'll be if you fuck with us, by the way. Dead."

He blinked, tried to speak and then realized his mouth was taped shut. He looked frantically around and realized the full extent of his predicament. Rope held him, spread-eagled, to the four posts of the bed. A man garbed in black, complete with ski mask, stood at his head with a gun, and another similarly clad stood at the foot of the bed with—he blinked again—with Kaley.

She was nude, tied and gagged, and held against the body of the second man. Her blond hair was a tousled froth, and despite her tall athletic frame and innately proud bearing, she looked vulnerable, helpless. Her blue eyes were wide and even in the dim pre-dawn light he could see the fear in them.

Despite the coolness of the room and his naked state, the heat of anger flushed his skin. No one threatened Ray Carrone, and no one treated his possessions that way.

"What do you want?" He tried to scream the words but of course, they came out as little more than a pathetic mumble.

The pistol nudged his cheek. "I don't really care what you're trying to say, *Mister* Carrone, I just need you to listen, and listen *good*."

His assailant motioned toward the foot of the bed. "You see that lady, there? The one with a gun to her head? You know...your *wife?*"

Ray merely glared his rage.

"She's a sweet little thing, isn't she? And very vulnerable. Well, it's your job to keep her safe, buddy, and it seems to me you're falling down on the job. A big, *fat* failure. Yup. That's how I see it."

Ray wrestled with his bindings but only succeeded in tightening the knots and making his captor laugh.

"You don't like that do you? Being a failure. Well, face it, *Mister* Carrone, we're going to steal your pretty little wife away and there's nothing you can do about it."

He motioned with the gun to the other man, who promptly dragged Kaley toward the door. She kicked and fought and tried to scream through the gag, but was no match for the six-foot thug who finally bent down and scooped her off her feet to carry her out of sight.

Ray turned fierce eyes on the man who remained beside him, waiting and watching.

"So now, the question is, how can you get her back? How can you redeem yourself and turn failure back into success?" A plain manila envelope landed on Ray's chest.

"Read this and it will explain everything." He got up, moved to leave, but hesitated at the doorway. "It's all there, Carrone. The time and place for the next contact, how much we want, and when. But there's one thing I want to make sure you are absolutely clear on. No cops. You so much as make one phone call to the police and not only will we fuck your wife until she's bloody and sore, and then dump her body in the bay, but the police will get all the information they need to turn your little money-laundering business inside out."

Ray felt his balls contract. How could they know about that? How could they possibly—

"Good," said the man in the mask. "We understand each other." He glanced at his watch. "I figure the cleaning service will find you in about three hours. So until then…" He made a mocking salute and disappeared down the darkened hallway, leaving Ray to stew in his own juices of impotent fury and righteous indignation.

# Chapter Three

Kaley flopped back on the bed and drew the lapels of the thick terry cloth robe in tightly about her. She closed her eyes and smiled. "Damn, I'm good."

"You?" laughed Mason. "I don't seem to recall you having much to do with it."

She opened her eyes and propped herself up on her elbows to better see her friend. He stood at the foot of the bed in this cheap little out-of-the-way motel that was going to be their home for the next three days. At least what little paint remained on the walls was mold-free and the sheets were clean. For now that was all that mattered. "I came up with the idea, didn't I? I planned the whole thing."

Mason stripped off his black turtleneck, revealing a rippling six-pack and shoulders that could give many a Greek god cause for insecurity. He dove onto the bed beside her, causing the ancient springs to groan and complain, and almost sending her sprawling onto the floor. He rolled onto his side and grinned as she scowled back at him.

"You had the *idea*," he said, "but we worked out all the nitty-gritty details. I'm the drive and the muscle and Dan's the technical-detail man. Right, Dan?" he yelled the last words loud enough to bring Dan running from the kitchenette. He had a half-eaten sandwich in his hand, and panic written all over his face.

"What? What's wrong? Why did you call me?"

Mason shook his head and laughed. "Dan, Dan the paranoid man."

"I'm not paranoid," said Dan, taking another bite and chewing. "Just cautious." He pointed the sandwich at Mason. "And you need me! If it weren't for me you'd go running off every cliff like some goddamn lemming looking for..." He shrugged. "Whatever the hell it is lemmings look for."

"I'm no lemming." Mason's tone was distinctly defensive. "I'm more of a..."

"Ferret?" offered Kaley.

He glared at her. "A what?"

"You know," said Dan, waving the sandwich vaguely in the air. "It's another word for weasel."

"I know what a fucking ferret is! I just—"

Both Kaley and Dan burst out laughing, and Mason's face flushed bright red.

Kaley was so lost in her good mood and her fit of the giggles that she was shocked to find Mason suddenly on top of her, pinning her wrists as his rock-hard cock nudged her pussy through the thick layers of terry-cloth. "Mason?" she breathed. "What the hell?"

"You know how I hate to be laughed at." His tone was harsh, but laughter twinkled in his eyes.

"We weren't laughing *at* you." She wriggled in a feeble effort to get away, but couldn't deny the effect of having Mason's well-formed pecs and rock-hard thighs pressed against her. "We were laughing with you." She turned her head. "Right, Dan?"

She blinked. "Where'd he go?"

Mason glanced at the door. "Dan's shy. Especially around beautiful women."

"Really?" she said, genuinely surprised. "That's too bad." Dan wasn't as broad or heavily muscled as Mason, and didn't have the same sort of chiseled jaw line, but he was fit and well-defined and his tousled hair and glasses gave him a warm, boy-next-door quality that many women found immensely appealing. Not her of course. She preferred rugged and dangerous, which was what had drawn her to Ray and, of course, to Mason.

She and Mason had hooked up in university after running into each other at numerous sporting events and finding that they shared a keen interest in athletics as well as an overdeveloped sense of competition and a love of adventure. They'd been friends and on-and-off lovers for a couple of years before she hooked up with Ray. It had been light and playful and fun.

Now she looked up at him, saw the lust in his eyes, and remembered exactly how much fun.

"Yeah," Mason was saying. "Dan sees himself as a sort of computer geek, I guess. Makes him skittish, especially around beautiful women."

"But you're not shy, are you Mason?" She shifted her hips in invitation. "Especially around beautiful women." Smiled coyly.

He arched one eyebrow, released her wrists and pushed back one lapel of her robe. "No. I'm not." He traced a circle around one sensitive nipple. "Your husband screwed around on you, eh? Man's a fool." He bent low to nip lightly at her skin.

She sucked in a breath. "Fool enough to fall for our scheme and give up the money he tried to cheat me out of with that damn prenup agreement."

His tongue traced the curve of her breast, sending shivers dancing over her skin. "He didn't know who he was dealing with." He laved her nipple, drew it into his mouth.

"No." She sank her fingers into his thick, dark hair and made her decision. Ray didn't deserve her fidelity, not anymore. In fact, it seemed he never had.

While she'd been designing killer ad campaigns and cooking romantic dinners for two... While she'd been dreaming up new and exciting ways to make her husband happy and make their marriage work—he'd been humping anything with tits and a shaved pussy.

After finding the CD in his pocket, she had sneaked into his office and, on a hunch, checked his private file cabinet. She'd found videos and CDs dating back years—dating back to before they were married. And then, out of some twisted need to torture herself, she'd made herself watch some of them. Too many.

Ray hadn't limited himself to sexy secretaries or desperate housewives. Some of those girls had been just that—girls. Young girls. Girls that she suspected Ray had sprung from Algebra class for a session in the back of his limo. And the "Office Fuck" video had been tame in comparison to some of the twisted games he'd played with those young things who were so vulnerable, so eager to please a man in designer duds.

It made her shudder to realize she'd shared a bed with him as long as she had. She'd saved some of the CDs to submit to the authorities at a later date, but she had wanted first crack at emasculating him.

She'd been taken. And now it was his turn

She pulled Mason against her. "No, he didn't know who he was dealing with."

He responded eagerly, devouring her breast like a starving man.

She arched her back and pulled aside the lapels of the robe in blatant offering.

"Mmm." He shifted to the other breast, his broad hands bracketing her rib cage. "You taste as good as I remember." He nipped her with his teeth and raised his head to look at her, his eyes gleaming. "Better."

And then he took her mouth. He fisted his hands in her hair and ravished her mouth, plundering her as surely and completely as a Viking taking his first virgin. His body was heavy, his scent thick with musk and sex, and the ridge of his erection against her cleft was driving her slowly mad. She slipped her hands beneath the waistband of his jeans and gripped his ass as she arched her hips in search of fulfillment. Her desire and frustration mingled, culminating as a low growl in the back of her throat.

He surrendered her mouth and she caught a glimpse of an impudent grin before he slithered down her body and settled between her thighs.

He parted the lips of her sex with his fingers. "You anxious for it, babe? You in the market for a good fucking?"

"Yes." She squirmed beneath his touch, anxious for his fingers, his tongue, his cock—anything to fill her.

His tongue tickled her clit. "And you think I can deliver."

"Oh God. I know you can."

"Ah, but is it me you want?" He tasted her, sucked her hard enough to make her start. "Or revenge?"

She sucked in a deep breath, lifted her head and admitted the truth. "Both. But does it matter?"

He grinned at her, two fingers inserted deeply in her pussy. "Not really, but if it's revenge you're after..." He pumped her, palpated her, made her senses spin. "I've got an idea."

* * * * *

Ray paced the length of his home office. He glanced at the printouts on his desk and scowled. "Goddamn stupid fucking bastards!"

"Actually," said Cyndi from her position at the computer. "I don't think they're that stupid."

"I didn't ask you!" he bellowed.

She flinched, returning to her task of searching for the information he'd requested.

"So, what do you want to do, Mr. Carrone?" Vince was wedged into a large leather wingback chair. One of the only pieces of furniture in the office large enough to hold him.

Ray's fists clenched reflexively. "What do I *want* to do? I want to rip both of their goddamn heads off and piss down the hole!"

"So you really want her back?" asked Cyndi, her eyes never leaving the computer screen.

"Of course I do. What kind of stupid question is that?"

Now she looked at him, her eyes a question.

He laughed. "Oh Jesus, Cyndi. Did you think *you* had a shot at taking over this household? Of becoming *Mrs. Carrone?*"

Her eyes narrowed.

"You're a decent secretary, a whiz with computers and a pretty good lay and that's it. Kaley is all class and style and she's exactly the kind of woman I need to go with my image."

Her face had gone red, but to her credit she kept herself under control. "So you're willing to pay two million dollars to get her back?"

He snorted. "Of course not. I'll just make it look like I am." Ray admitted to himself what he had no intention of admitting to his underlings. This was all about power and control. Kaley was *his* and he had no intention of giving her up without a fight. But he wasn't stupid. Even *his* ego wasn't worth two million dollars, and Kaley was hardly irreplaceable. He could find another one just like her if he had to. If she disappeared somewhere along the way — got caught in the crossfire, so to speak — then it would be regrettable but hardly cause for loss of sleep. His image was paramount. Ray Carrone couldn't afford to be seen as weak or incapable of looking after his own affairs.

"So no police?" asked Vince.

"Right. We'll look after things ourselves." The kidnappers' warning had hardly been necessary. "We'll follow their instructions for now, but in the meantime come up with our own — " The ring of the phone cut him off.

Before Cyndi could reach for it he snatched it up.

"What do you want?"

But to his surprise it wasn't the kidnappers. "Hello. Mr. Carrone?"

"Yes. What is it?"

"This is Dr. Mello's office. Is Mrs. Carrone available?"

He tamped down his temper. "I'm afraid she's not here at the moment."

"Oh. Well…"

*Jesus.* "Can I take a message?"

"Well, normally we like to speak to the patient directly, but I happen to know she was excited and would have wanted you to know as soon as possible. And considering how long you've been trying…"

Ray felt a twinge of dread. "Know? Know what?"

"Your wife is pregnant, Mr. Carrone. Congratulations."

\* \* \* \* \*

"Thanks, Trina," said Kaley, the cell phone snug against her ear. "I really appreciate it."

"It was nothing, Mrs. Carrone. I mean, a hundred bucks to make one phone call? And I really appreciate the job. Now I can get that new pair of boots I've been wanting."

Kaley batted away Mason's hand that had sneaked beneath the hem of her robe and was creeping up her thigh. "Glad we could be of service to each other. Now don't forget to throw that cell phone away when you're done."

"Right, Mrs. Carrone. No probs."

Relentless, Mason pushed aside the robe and began to nibble on her inner thigh. "Uh…Well, thanks again Sally."

There was some hesitation on the other end. "It's Trina."

"Oh." His tongue teased the edge of her pussy. "Right. I—" The phone was torn from her hand, clicked off and cast aside. "Hey! What do you—"

"Stop stalling." He pulled her to her feet and slipped the robe from her shoulders. "Let's do this."

"I wasn't stalling and you're just horny."

"Definitely. All the more reason." He raked his eyes over her nude body once before glancing at Dan who had been fiddling with the video camera. "You ready?"

"Sure." Dan's expression was distinctly uncomfortable, and if he hadn't looked so darn cute, she might have felt sorry for him. "You sure *you* are?" He was addressing Kaley.

"Ready?" She smiled reassuringly. "Don't worry, Dan. I'm something of an exhibitionist at heart. And I'm highly motivated."

Mason pushed her playfully onto the bed and reached for the handcuffs. He proceeded to secure her spread-eagled to the bed. "Translation—she's hot for my bod."

She rolled her eyes. "That's hardly the motivation I'm talking about."

"Whatever." He grinned down at her. "But considering that mouth of yours I certainly don't regret doing *this*." He gently applied a strip of duct tape to her lips and she tried to glare her outrage, but doubted she pulled it off.

His chore complete, Mason picked up his ski-mask and a flogger that had been laid out. He turned to Dan. "Ready?"

"Ready."

He pulled the mask into place and snapped the flogger against his palm. "*Roll'em!*"

\* \* \* \* \*

Dan focused the camera on Mason, who stood off to the side, away from the bed.

"Greetings, Mr. Carrone." Mason's tone was light but with a distinct edge. "Well, we've had your wife for approximately twelve hours now, and our hope is that you've begun to sweat. The conditions of the exchange outlined in the packet we left haven't changed, but since the *big moment* is still more than thirty-six hours away, we thought you might need a little reminder as to our intentions. A little added…incentive, if you will. Don't fuck with us Carrone, because if you do, your wife will pay the price."

On cue Dan swung the camera to the bed and felt himself grow hard.

"Beautiful, isn't she?" said Mason.

At this angle her face was visible, as was the fear that she was so good at portraying in her eyes. Her blonde hair was spread out on the pillow like a golden halo and her skin was the color of buckwheat honey.

However, the camera also had a good view of her pussy, spread wide, moist, pink and inviting.

Dan's already heavy erection became almost painful. He envied Mason, yet knew the boundaries. Kaley was

*Mason's* friend, and Dan had no business even fantasizing about being with her. And yet, he had. *God*, had he ever.

"And oh, so vulnerable," Mason was saying.

The snap of the flogger across her belly cut through the silence.

Kaley's head whipped around to face Mason and he laughed.

"So convincing. If I didn't know better I'd think you didn't like it." He raised the flogger and she shook her head vigorously. "Not that it matters one way or the other." He whipped her again, this time across her breasts and she moaned. She writhed on the bed, the movement ambiguous, conveying fear but stirring desire.

Dan knew the flogger was soft and not intended to cause pain. It was all part of the show, and both Mason and Kaley had voiced their intentions to enjoy every minute of it. Dan would make do with enjoying the performance.

The flogger fell again and again, across her breasts, ribs, belly, hips. Her skin became flushed and her nipples grew erect. She continued to writhe and moan, her body jerking with every blow, the scent of her arousal filling Dan's nostrils.

Mason snapped it across her thighs — and stopped. "Well now, ain't this interesting." He allowed the tails of the flogger to trail across her pussy. "Your wife is wet. Maybe she wants it more than she's letting on."

Again Kaley shook her head vigorously and again, Mason chuckled. "Why don't I believe you?" He swished the tails slowly across her pussy and they came away damp. "Hmm." He leaned down, used his fingers to spread the lips of her sex. "Let's get a closeup here, shall we?"

Dan swallowed thickly as he zoomed in on her swollen pussy.

Mason smoothed his fingers over her clit and she writhed in what appeared to be an effort to get away. "You keep still." He hopped onto the bed and straddled her hips, facing the camera. "That should do it."

He used both hands to part her sex, and proceeded to massage her clit between two fingers. There was no mistaking the groan of pleasure that reverberated through that room, or the way her juices flowed onto the sheets.

Mason pushed two fingers inside her, all the while continuing to massage her clit with his thumb.

"Oh yeah." Mason's voice had grown thick. "You want it, don't you?" He thrust his fingers into her again.

She groaned what was no doubt intended to be perceived as a protest, but it only served to enhance Dan's already painful erection.

"Christ," moaned Mason. "I'll be you're sweet." Abruptly he hopped off her and crouched between her legs. He lifted his mask to expose his mouth and bent down to taste her.

It took Dan a second to adjust his position in order to get a decent view of what was happening. He was quite impressed with his ability to hold the camera steady in light of what he was observing.

Mason was lapping her up like a cat starved for fresh cream. His tongue dipped inside her and then he moved on to suckle her clit. "You want me to fuck you, baby?" he asked his lips against her sex.

Dan pulled back far enough to catch the shake of her head.

Mason's tongue continued its assault. "Oh, so you want to come in my mouth?"

Another shake of the head, but her chest was heaving, her breasts gleamed with sweat.

"You're gonna come whether you like it or not, babe." He moved up her body until his eyes were level with hers. "Cock or tongue. Your choice."He ripped the tape off her mouth.

She sucked in a huge lungful of air. "No, please," she said at last, playing her role. "Please stop."

He kissed her then, thrusting his tongue deeply into her mouth, forcing her to taste herself, even as he toyed with her already straining nipples.

She accepted the kiss this time, arching her back in what could have been either pleasure or protest. He laughed, ending the kiss and sitting up, straddling her hips. "Cock or tongue? How do you want your hubby to see you come for me?"

"Cock," she breathed, licking her lips that were coated with her own juices.

He reached for the button on his jeans. "You want me to fuck you?"

She closed her eyes, turned her head away.

His jeans pushed past his hips and his cock jutting out before him, Mason grabbed her chin and forced her to look at him. "Say it, babe or I'll flog you 'til you bleed."

"Fuck me," she said, her voice a rasping whisper. "Please."

And he did.

* * * * *

Kaley arched her hips to meet him as he thrust into her. His cock was as thick and strong as she remembered, but the excitement had never been so intense.

He didn't bother with gentility this time, but took her like a kidnapper would, like a man accustomed to violence. Like a man possessed. And that was exactly what she wanted.

She wanted to lose herself in the act, to be taken and be taken hard, but taken by someone who she knew loved her as a person rather than a possession. By someone who would make sacrifices for her, and take risks on her behalf. Why had it taken so many years to figure out that Ray was none of those things?

Damn it, but he hadn't even been that great of a lover. He was far too selfish for that. Well, his selfishness was coming back to haunt him. In spades.

When Mason's lips joined with hers again, she accepted his tongue eagerly, just as she accepted every thrust of his cock. She allowed it to fill her, allowed her body to respond as it was meant to.

His lips were hungry and exciting, his assault strong. The ache built low in her belly and spread to her clit until she thought she'd burst. And when she finally did, she turned her head away from the camera, but didn't bother to hold back the cry of satisfaction that was burning in her chest. Perhaps Ray would think it a cry of pain.

And perhaps she didn't really care what he thought.

Her pussy clenched and squeezed, draining every ounce of energy she possessed, and drawing Mason to his own explosive climax.

"Jesus," he said, collapsing on top of her. He turned to the camera. "Two million is a small price to pay for this, Carrone. As much as I'd like to keep her though, I *will* make the trade." His voice turned hard. "But if you choose to screw with us, and *not* do as we've instructed, rest assured next time I won't be nearly as gentle, and I'll be using a real whip. You'll barely recognize what they pull out of the bay." He leaned closer to the camera. "So *don't fail!* It's as simple as that."

She heard the camera cut out and allowed herself to relax

# Chapter Four

Kaley pulled on her jeans and tucked in her T-shirt, but never once diverted her eyes from the window. The hotel may be cheap and in poor condition, but you couldn't beat the view, and tonight's sunset was spectacular. Bands of fuchsia and gold sliced across the sky, reflecting in the water and searing her eyes with their intensity.

"Do you want some tea?"

She turned to see Dan come into the room with a small tray and two mugs.

"Sure. Thanks." She plopped down on the bed and crossed her legs, watching him intently as he set down the tray. He wasn't as broad or muscular as Mason, and his hair was always sticking out in a half dozen directions, but his smile was sweet, his brown eyes sincere and—she sighed—his ass in those jeans could have a woman on her knees and begging in a heartbeat.

"Kaley?"

She blinked, noticed the mug hovering before her eyes. She chuckled and accepted it, warming her hands on the earthenware. "Oh, sorry. Guess I'm a little distracted."

"Understandable." He reached for a chair, pulled it out and noticed the seat was cracked.

Kaley patted the bed beside her, and after a moment's hesitation he complied. Although he sat perfectly still,

Kaley had the distinct sense that he was squirming inside his skin.

She took a sip of her tea. "You're not terribly comfortable with all this, are you?"

His shoulders slumped. "Is it that obvious?" He looked up at her then, his eyes imploring.

She laughed. "Oh God, Dan, it's like watching a cat dip its feet into cold water."

He blew out a breath. "Yeah, and that's pretty much how it feels. The whole kidnapping thing is crazy. I don't know how the hell I let Mason talk me into it."

"I don't think it's so crazy," she said softly.

His eyes snapped to hers. "I-I'm sorry. I know you have your reasons, and I sure went into it with my eyes wide open, but being in the middle of it is…" He blew out a slow breath.

"Daunting?"

He stared into his mug. "Try terrifying." He took a sip and Kaley continued studying him.

"That's not the only thing you're uncomfortable with, though. Is it?"

He looked at her over the rim of his mug. "What do you mean?"

"Come on, Dan. It didn't take a psychic to see how uncomfortable you were with filming our little simulation."

He shrugged, tapped his mug with his index finger.

"I'll admit I'm surprised. I figured anyone who's hung around Mason as long as you have, would have been exposed to all kinds of sexual…" Dan looked at her and she tilted her head as she considered. "…misadventures."

She could tell he was working to suppress a grin. "I've always just heard about them after the fact. I've been lucky that way."

She covered her mouth in mock consternation. "You mean *my* Mason has been known to kiss and tell?"

Dan let out a loud guffaw. "Trust me. I'm sure I only hear *half* of what he's been up to."

"And what about you, Dan? Surely you've had a few misadventures of your own. Do you kiss and tell?"

The mood shifted as quickly as if she'd flipped a switch. He stood and motioned to her mug. "Do you want more tea?"

"No. I've barely touched what I have, thanks."

"Oh. Right." He stood there, apparently at a loss for how to proceed, and Kaley had a moment of regret.

"I'm sorry. I didn't mean to make you uncomfortable. I'm just so used to talking and joking about sex with Mason, and most of my friends for that matter, that I just take it for granted that everyone else feels the same way. Besides, it's none of my business."

"No, no. It's not that." He let out a nervous chuckle and sat down again. "It's not that I'm uncomfortable talking about sex. And I don't mind you asking."

"No? Then what is it?"

"I—it's just." He dropped his gaze. "You'll laugh."

"I won't laugh," she said sincerely, although her curiosity was piqued. "I promise."

He cleared his throat. "I...uh...God, I've never told this to anyone else before." He hung his head. "I think I feel sick."

"Dan!" She reached for his hand, and was relieved when he didn't pull away. "What is it? Nothing can be that bad. Whatever it is, surely—"

"I haven't slept with a woman in five years."

Kaley's next words died on her tongue. She blinked. And then blinked again. "But you're twenty-five years old."

Impossibly, his head hung lower. "Twenty-six."

"But I don't get it." She grasped his chin, lifting his face so she could see his wide brown eyes. "You're an intelligent, attractive man. How is it that you have trouble finding women who want to sleep with you?"

He shrugged.

"Are you waiting until you get married? Is that it?"

"No. It's not that." He shrugged. "Don't get me wrong. In college I went a little wild." His cheeks flushed a bit with the admission. "But I guess, since then—since I grew up—I just haven't met anyone that I really *wanted* to sleep with. I've dated some very attractive women, but there always seemed to be some reason not to." He squeezed her hand. "Please don't tell Mason."

Kaley was still reeling. "You mean he doesn't know?"

"Well, I think maybe he suspects. I think that's part of the reason he pushes me into all these extreme sports and things. He thinks I'm shy and introverted and that if he gets me to come out of my shell I'll be more confident with women."

"But that's not it."

"Well, maybe," he admitted. "Part of it."

Kaley suspected it was quite a bit more than "part" of it.

"Has Mason ever set you up with anyone?"

"Yeah. But it never worked out."

*Why?* She wondered, but didn't ask. She also wondered if being exposed to Mason who was so flamboyant and sure of himself, especially where women were concerned, could be a little intimidating. It could be an impossible image to live up to.

Kaley pulled her knees up and rested her chin on them, considering. "So how did watching us make you feel?"

He cleared his throat. "Uh...what do you mean?"

"Well, did you like it? Watching, I mean. Or was it a turn off?"

He laughed aloud. "No. Definitely not a turn off."

"But it did make you uncomfortable."

"Well, it's not like I don't watch a little porn now and then, but being so close to it..." He shifted in his seat. "Yeah, I guess it did. A little."

She set her feet on the floor and shifted closer. "Because it felt like an intrusion? Or was there some other reason?"

He licked his lips. "Maybe."

She had a hunch. "It made you uncomfortable because you wanted in on it, didn't you?" She shifted still closer, laid a hand on his knee.

He didn't move. He went very still, his gaze dropping to her hand and his throat working as he swallowed. "I...uh..."

She slid her hand a little further up his thigh. "Is that it, Dan? Did seeing that make you hot? Did it get you thinking about sleeping with *me*?" In an effort to emphasize her point her hand crept up to his waist and slipped beneath the hem of his shirt. His skin was warm and firm, and it quivered beneath her touch.

He stayed very still, but his breathing was choppy. "But I hardly know you."

"Does it matter?" She slid her hand a little higher, across ridges of abdominal muscle and ribs until her thumb stroked a straining nipple. "If it's love you want, I don't think I can help, but if it's friendship, trust, and simple sexual satisfaction then—"

He grabbed her wrist with enough force to startle her. "There's nothing simple about it."

She smiled. "Is that a yes or a no?"

He reached for her other hand and guided it beneath his shirt. She had her answer. And that pleased her.

She couldn't say why, exactly. Dan was nothing like the men she had dated in college, and he was certainly nothing like Ray. He had a sweetness about him, however, that she found oddly appealing, despite the fact that she had always steered clear of men like that. But then again, he also had an intensity, an...*earnestness* that captured her attention and held it. It radiated out from him, the effect subtle but unmistakable. Quiet yet powerful. Like the feeling in the air just before a storm.

She skimmed her hands over his skin and enjoyed the tiny shivers that accompanied her touch, and when she looked up at him, and met his gaze—felt the force of it—a little bolt of lightning zinged through her gut. The suddenness and forcefulness of his kiss stole her thoughts. His lips were firm and insistent, his tongue hot and eager. It startled her, but perhaps it shouldn't have.

He sank his fingers into her hair and held her there as he crushed her lips and ravished her mouth. She wrapped her arms around him and pulled him closer, digging her fingernails into the flesh of his back.

Abruptly he stopped, abandoning her mouth and leaving her breathless and wanting.

"Sorry," he whispered, her arms still latched around him. "I don't know where that came from."

"Does it matter?" She nibbled on his jaw, traced a line along it with her tongue, found trace of stubble "As long as you can find it again."

"You mean you didn't mind?"

In response she held him tight and flung herself back onto the bed, dragging him with her. He landed on top of her, his body between her splayed legs, his laughter echoing through her mind.

"You surprised me." He was still chuckling as he looked down on her.

"Ditto."

He continued gazing at her, the smile remained, but the nature of it changed. It took on a hungry edge that made her skin quiver. He drew a fingertip along the line of her T-shirt, over the curve of her breast. "What about Mason?"

She blinked, focusing on his words. "Mason? What about him?"

"I thought you two…" He shrugged.

"You mean because of what we did here?"

He said nothing, but the question in his eyes was clear.

"Mason's a very talented lover, and a good friend. But that's all he is, and all he'll ever be. That was a show for my slime-ball husband's benefit. Nothing more."

"You enjoyed it, though."

She traced a finger over his cheekbone. "Yes. Of course I did. I'm human. If that makes me easy, or a whore, then we can just—"

"No!" He covered her mouth with his hand and then said more softly. "No. That's not what I meant. I just wanted to make sure—"

"You weren't horning in on Mason's territory?" She chuckled. "Have no fear. Mason has no claim on me."

"Hey," called a voice from the doorway. "I take exception to that."

They both turned their heads to see Mason, a stack of Chinese takeout boxes in hand, as he stood, grinning, in the doorway.

"So what's going on, Dan? Movin' in on my woman?"

"Ah come on, Mason." Kaley wrapped her arms around Dan's waist and held on when he tried to slip away from her. She winked at Dan, grinned at Mason. "A little competition would do you good."

"Competition? Dan?" He snorted, stepped into the room and set the boxes on the table beside the bed. "Who're you tryin' to kid? I could blow him outta the water with both hands tied behind my back."

Kaley slipped her hands underneath Dan's shirt. "I don't know about that. I think you might be surprised."

Mason opened a carton and pulled out a chicken ball. "Yeah. Right." He popped it into his mouth.

Dan, finally getting into the spirit of things lifted Kaley's shirt and traced a tongue along the curve of her breast. He murmured against her skin. "Is that a challenge, Mason?"

Kaley watched Mason out of the corner of her eye, saw his left eyebrow arch with interest. "A challenge? What does that mean?"

Dan peppered kisses along Kaley's rib cage, drew a line down her belly with his tongue, suckled her navel. He murmured against her skin. "Exactly what it sounds like." He turned his head. "Are you up for it?"

Mason narrowed his eyes. "*Up* for it?" Abruptly he dropped the box of chicken balls onto the table and whipped his shirt off over his head. "You bet. I never pass up a challenge. You know that."

Kaley laughed. "Hey, hey. Hang on there a second. Don't I get a say in this?"

"Nope." Mason's jeans dropped to his ankles. "You're going to enjoy it whether you like it or not."

Dan climbed off her and began working at his own jeans. She propped herself up on her elbows. "So what is this? A threesome where you guys compete to see who can make me come the most?"

Dan and Mason stopped what they were doing, exchanged a look and grinned. "Works for me." Dan's jeans hit the floor. He looked at her. "Does it work for you?"

She lay back on the bed, gazed at the ceiling and considered. Maybe a little "contest" like this was exactly what Dan needed to boost his self-confidence. If he could match Mason, or possibly even outshine him in this kind of sexual forum, then maybe he'd get over his insecurities. She'd do it for Dan. Her motives were purely selfless.

Purely.

She grinned. "Sure. But I have one condition."

"Yeah?" Gloriously nude, Mason crawled onto the bed and knelt beside her. "And what would that be?"

Nude as well, and showing off a remarkably well-defined six-pack not to mention a startling hard-on, Dan knelt on the opposite side. She looked from one to the other. From light and sweet to dark and dangerous and back again. "Set up the video camera, boys. And I'll explain everything."

# Chapter Five

Kaley leaned back against a rock hard chest, and dug her fingers into Mason's well-toned thighs. He was leaning against the headboard, with her nestled between his legs.

He nuzzled her neck, skimmed his hands down her arms. "For God's sake, Kaley, lose the bra."

She'd stripped as well, but only down to bra and panties. "Come on, Mase. You guys gotta work for it a little. Right Dan?"

"Definitely."

She glanced up and sighed.

Dan stood at the tripod, fiddling with the camera, his back to her affording her an unobstructed view of his well-developed *assets*.

Apparently finished, he turned to face her and she sighed again.

Dan puffed up visibly, standing there, soaking in her adoring gaze.

"Hey," complained Mason. "You're gonna give me a complex."

Kaley dug her nails into his thighs. "Are you kidding? You've got an ego the size of the Roman Empire."

Dan crossed the room and crawled onto the bed. "Didn't the Roman Empire fall centuries ago?"

"Exactly."

Mason made a low growling noise in the back of his throat, but Kaley took no notice. She was far too absorbed in the way Dan's fingers were working their way across the balls of her feet.

"Mmm." Her head lolled against Mason's shoulder. "A foot rub. I'm a foot-slut from way back."

"Hmm. How about this?" Mason countered by running his fingers through her hair and massaging her scalp. Her head rolled forward to allow him better access as his fingers worked out tensions she hadn't even realized were there.

But then she felt the soft, moist warmth of Dan's tongue. It circled her toes, drew them into his mouth, suckling each one in turn until her insides melted.

Mason's hands moved to her shoulders. He slipped the bra straps down her arms and pushed aside the cups of her bra. He caressed her breasts, tweaking her nipples until she arched her back in agonized pleasure.

Dan, however had abandoned her feet and moved on to her legs. Fingers and tongue cruised up her calves, massaging muscles and teasing senses. He nibbled on the inside of her knee and she giggled, but when his mouth moved on to the soft flesh of her thigh the giggle turned to a moan. He pushed her thighs apart and she complied, making note that her bra clasp had been popped and the lingerie had joined the rest of their clothes on the floor.

Mason's hands coasted over her breasts and down her belly, stopping only when they reached the barrier of the top edge of her panties.

She felt his breath on her ear even as Dan's tongue tickled the lower edge of her underwear and traced the crease.

"Who do you want to touch you?" whispered Mason, his breath as hot and thick as his cock that nudged her ass.

She just shook her head, unable to form coherent thought, let alone words.

So when two sets of fingers slipped beneath the satin, she almost rocketed out of her skin.

Dan pushed aside the material and eased inside her. Deeply. "Damn, she's wet."

"Oh yeah?" asked Mason, working her clit between two fingers. "Let's see." His fingers joined Dan's, and together both men pushed so deep she cried out from the pressure of it. And the pleasure.

"Please," she breathed, arching her hips and seeking something she couldn't quite define.

"Please what?" asked Mason, the grin evident in his voice.

"I...I don't know."

"Fuck this thing," said Dan, and she felt him rip away her thong as if it were made of nothing more than spider silk.

She opened her eyes and looked down, marveled at seeing two different hands playing with her pussy.

"Damn," said Dan, pushing Mason's hand aside. "I want those lips." And, with two fingers still buried deeply inside her, he bent his head and tasted her.

"Hmmm. Not a bad idea." And with that, Mason eased out from behind her and shifted to the side. His lips had fused with hers, even before her head hit the pillow.

Dan's tongue was slow and languorous as it circled her clit and licked her juices. The pressure from his fingers was deep and exquisite, a pleasure that was so intense it verged on painful.

Mason's kiss was soft at first, teasing and sweet, but as the intensity built in her pussy his kiss grew more eager. Hungry. Voracious.

The climax built deep within her womb and she arched her hips against Dan's mouth, in search of what she needed to put her over the edge.

"That's it, babe," he said, his fingers working toward her G-spot. "Let it go."

Mason cupped a breast and squeezed, tweaking a nipple, even as Dan's mouth ravished her sanity.

His fingers were buried deep inside her when the orgasm struck, washing over her like a tidal wave of pleasure.

She tore her mouth away from Mason's and had to tamp down the scream that swelled in her chest. The climax pounded her, and she was just catching her breath when Dan gripped her ass, lifted her hips and thrust his cock inside her.

"Is this okay?" he asked, his voice low and breathless.

She wanted to smile at the little show of insecurity, but was far too caught up in the roller coaster these men were putting her body through. "Yeah," she breathed. "That's —"

His sudden, fierce thrust startled her and stole her next words. She let out a little yelp of surprise, which must have concerned Mason.

"Hey, babe. You okay?"

She reached out and wrapped her hand around his throbbing cock. "I. Want. You." She stroked the moist tip with her thumb.

Mason's grin was devilish. "Oh yeah? How?" And then he straddled her, offering himself to her mouth. "Like this?"

In response she parted her lips and took him into the moist heat of her mouth. He tasted at once salty and sweet, hot and wicked. He gently gripped her head, sinking his fingers into her hair and slowly fucking her mouth, even as Dan fucked her pussy.

Dan's cock filled her. Mason's excited her.

Such intense intimacy with two sculpted male specimens worked together to build her excitement again.

Dan's thrusts accelerated and she could sense his climax building, along with her own. She caressed Mason's balls and his groan of pleasure added to her excitement.

When Dan's hands crept around her ass and touched the sensitive skin around her anus, it was enough to send her spiraling out of control. A fresh orgasm racked her body and pulsed around Dan's cock, sending him crashing toward his own climax.

Unable to withhold her cry of pleasure and in desperate need of oxygen, she relinquished her mouth's hold on Mason's cock and collapsed back onto the pillows. It only took a few movements of her delicate fingers to bring him to his own devastating climax.

He cried out in ecstasy, his cum splashing over her chest and trickling around her neck, and at last all three collapsed in a collective heap on the mattress, Mason on one side, Dan on the other.

"Hey," said Mason, trailing a finger across her chest. "Don't say I never get you anything."

"Huh?" she asked.

Dan propped himself up on an elbow and grinned. "It's the famous pearl necklace."

"Oh. That." She waggled her eyebrows. "Actually, if it's from Mason, that would have to be *in*famous."

"Ha ha," chortled Mason. "Very funny. You're usually much wittier."

"I'm too hungry to be witty. Where the hell is that Chinese food, anyway?"

"Right here." Mason picked up a box and popped open the tab. "But it's cold."

"Hmm," said Dan as he plucked a chicken ball out of the box. "I think I have an idea about how to warm them up again."

\* \* \* \* \*

Kaley felt silly and slightly ridiculous, but she couldn't remember ever having quite so much fun.

She was laid out on the bed, a row of sweet and sour chicken balls arranged on her chest and belly. Plum sauce had been drizzled over the delicacies, and now Mason and Dan were arranging bits of beef, broccoli and almonds over the remaining portions of unclaimed skin.

"Hey." She giggled. "That tickles."

"Just wait," muttered Mason. "You ain't seen nothin' yet."

"You're going to feed me, too, right?"

In answer to her question, Dan picked up a spare chicken ball, dipped it in sauce and held it between his teeth. He bent down and offered it to her.

"Oh Dan. You really are coming out of your shell."

Unable to speak, he merely waggled his eyebrows, coming close enough that her lips touched the morsel. She nibbled tentatively at first, savoring the flavors as well as the soft brush of Dan's lips against hers. "Mmm," she said when the last of the chicken found its way past her lips.

"Mmm," she groaned again when Dan's mouth joined with hers, the flavors of saucy sweetness mingling with her own juices that lingered on his lips.

His kiss was languorous and decadent, his tongue soft but insistent. For just a moment she lost herself in him, and wondered if she'd ever find her way out again.

"Hey, hey, you two," complained Mason. "I'm starting to feel left out here."

Dan pulled away, but held her gaze for a moment before turning his attention on his friend. "It's your own fault. This whole contest thing was your idea."

"Not much of a contest," said Mason, licking some plum sauce out of Kaley's navel and making her giggle. "More of a cooperative effort, I'd say."

"Right. I guess it was." Kaley plucked up a piece of beef and popped it into her mouth. "But that's better anyway. Just like this whole kidnapping scheme. A cooperative effort that will net us a nice profit and make Ray Carrone regret every time he screwed around on me or took advantage of some poor innocent girl."

"Speaking of which…" Dan licked some teriyaki sauce off her nipple. "You delivered the tape without any problems?"

"Uh huh." Mason's tongue swirled across a rib and picked up a piece of broccoli. "And the stage is set for tomorrow night."

"Good," said Kaley, accepting another chicken ball and another deep, lingering kiss from Dan. "I wish I could see his face when he realizes what he's lost."

"You'll just have to imagine, I guess," said Dan.

"Yeah." She sucked in her breath when Mason drizzled some extra sweet and sour sauce over her pussy and proceeded to lap it up. "I guess I will."

# Chapter Six

Ray stood on the dock and gazed out toward the ocean. The sky was overcast, the clouds allowing absolutely no starlight to seep through and giving the illusion of looking out into a thick, black void. The warehouse behind him listed to the side, as if it might collapse and drop into the water at any moment. And the one lone street lamp cast the entire scene in eerie cartoon-like shadows.

The whole thing gave him the creeps. "Jesus H. Christ," he mumbled, glancing at his watch. On top of it all, the kidnappers were late. "I can't believe this."

His radio crackled. "Huh? What was that, boss?"

"Dammit." He'd forgotten about the two-way radio hidden in his suit. "Jesus, Vince, you idiot. Shut up already. Don't you remember the signal?"

"Oh." There was a moment's hesitation. "Sorry, boss. I forgot. What was that a—" Vince grunted something unintelligible.

Ray rolled his eyes and whispered into the microphone. "Dammit. Can you speak *English?*"

"Actually," whispered a voice in Ray's ear. "At the moment, he can't."

Ray would have whirled around and taken a swing at the man whose body was pressed up against his back, but the distinctive pressure of cold metal at the base of his neck acted as an effective deterrent. "Fuck. What did you do to him?"

"Have no fear. He's merely incapacitated, but you reneged on our deal, Mr. Carrone."

"I brought the money." He motioned to the briefcase at his fee. And I didn't talk to any cops."

"Perhaps. But you didn't come *alone*."

Ray felt a sharp prick in the flesh of his neck. His hand flew up to ward off whatever was piercing his skin, but too late. The syringe was already embedded deeply in his flesh, the plunger depressed.

He yanked it out and stumbled away, glaring at his attacker. "What the hell?"

The man stood there, his face bare, his expression smug. "Don't worry, Mr. Carrone. It's not lethal. Merely a paralytic. A bit of…insurance."

Ray swallowed, blinked, and dropped to his knees, all under the watchful eye of his attacker. "Where's Kaley?" was all he managed to say before he fell to the concrete, his lips unable to move, breathing the only movement he seemed capable of.

He watched the man pick up the briefcase and pop it open, giving the contents a quick once over. "Good." He snapped it closed. "I'll have to trust you that it's all here."

He turned to go, and Ray wanted to scream. Helpless rage clogged in his throat. He hated being helpless and out of control. He needed to control his destiny. That was why he was here, after all. He had to remember why he was here and what was important. He had a son to worry about, his name and his progeny to protect. He had to have someone to follow in his footsteps, to take over the business when Ray's interests turned to tropical women and exclusive golf clubs. A child validated him, made him a man. Hadn't his own father drummed that into him from the time he was old enough to walk? Until he had a son a man hadn't truly grown up, he hadn't "made his mark". And Ray *needed* to make his mark. It was worth his entire empire if necessary. For Ray it was worth everything.

But he couldn't verbalize any of that. All he could do was watch in mounting fear as the kidnapper turned to go.

And then, abruptly he stopped and turned around. "Oh yeah. I almost forgot. You wanted your wife back."

Ray tried to glare his hatred.

"Don't worry. She's right there." The man motioned with his hand, and Ray was able to move his eyes enough to see. She stood at the edge of the dock, looking pale and fragile, and very alone in the watery lamplight.

She wore tattered sweats, her hair hung limply around her face, and her hands and feet were bound.

He breathed a sigh of relief, but felt a fresh surge of fear when the kidnapper, briefcase in hand, crouched down beside him. "She's beautiful, isn't she? And, as I'm sure you noticed from that video, a damn good fuck."

Mention of the video that he'd received the night before kindled a fresh rage inside Ray. He managed to make a low growl in the back of his throat, but it only served to amuse the other man.

His smile was tainted, however. "I can understand why you want her back so badly, but what I can't understand is why you would jeopardize her with your stupid stunt." He shook his head. "Bringing along a bodyguard. Really, Mr. Carrone. How cliché is that?"

"Ray?" It was Kaley's soft voice from the far side of the dock. "Are you all right?"

Ray kept his gaze trained on his tormentor.

"You didn't listen," he continued. "You didn't follow *instructions*. And I'm afraid you'll have to learn your lesson the hard way."

Those words echoed in Ray's brain. They echoed inside his head, filling his heart with fear and reminding him of…something. He felt as if he should recognize those words, as if they held some significance.

"Right?" said the kidnapper, standing. "Right." And suddenly he turned, lifted the gun and fired.

Out of the corner of his eye, through a veil of horror he saw Kaley's body jolt, saw her face contort as she staggered backward. And then he saw her drop off the edge of the dock.

The scream inside Ray's throat was silent, but even if he'd been able to make a noise there would have been no one to hear it.

He was completely alone.

# Chapter Seven
## *One year later*

"Hello," said the voice at the other end of the phone. Thanks to the untraceable internet hookup, the voice was a little fuzzy, but it would have to do. "Ray Carrone's office."

Kaley giggled as Dan traced a finger down her thigh. The soft tropical breeze toyed with her hair, and in the background she could hear the clink of ice as Mason prepared a pitcher of Margaritas.

"Uh...could I speak to him, please?"

"Certainly. Whom shall I say is calling?"

"Actually, I'd rather not. I'd like to surprise him."

The hesitation was minimal and a moment later the phone in her slimeball husband's office rang.

"Ray Carrone." Was it her imagination or did he sound tired? She wondered if his lawyer was keeping him up late going over the defense for his statutory rape case. Correction: *cases.*

She grinned. "Ray, *dahling.*" A chilled Margarita glass was pressed in her hand and Mason sat down beside her on the love seat, snuggling her in tightly between two warm, firm bodies.

The three of them had originally decided to just hang out together here in Bermuda for a while. It had seemed logical, safer and smarter. But they'd quickly realized what they should have already known. They were good together. Damn good. They made good friends and great partners.

The idea to pour some of their capital into starting a beach-side fitness facility for tourists had really taken off. They'd each slipped so naturally into their own niche in running the operation that they'd laughingly admitted they were destined to be together. The fact that they made even better lovers than they did partners merely cemented their decision.

She spoke to her ex-husband. "So, how are you?"

Silence. "What the hell is this?"

"This, my dear, is your long lost wife."

"What the fuck—"

"For once in your life, Ray, shut up and listen. If you want answers, you'll do as I say."

He cursed and ranted a few more minutes, but eventually heard enough to understand what was expected of him. Two minutes later the trio saw Ray Carrone's name flash on the computer that sat on the coffee table in front of them.

They turned on the speaker phone and webcam. And waved. "Hi Ray!" She lifted her glass in a mock salute. "So good to see you again. How've you been?"

"You're supposed to be dead, Kaley! And—hang on a second. Who are they? Isn't that—"

"Meet my kidnappers, my co-conspirators and..." The men leaned in and planted a kiss on each cheek. "...live-in lovers." She sipped from her glass and nodded to Dan, who hit a button on the computer. "If you watch the corner of your screen you can watch a tape of some of the...activities that transpired during my captivity." She grinned. "It was sheer hell, Ray, I don't mind telling you. Sheer hell."

"What the—You *bitch!* You set me up! Do you have any idea the shit I went through with the cops after you disappeared? For a while they thought *I* had something to do with it."

She tisked, pleased and not altogether surprised by this new information. Nor was she surprised to hear that he had expressed no sense of loss or relief that she was indeed alive.

"And you screwed around on me, Ray. You should know I don't take kindly to being used and lied to. You paid the price and learned the lesson." She shrugged and laid her head on Dan's shoulder. "And we both got what we deserved."

The silence on the line was thick and when he spoke his voice was low and measured. "What about the baby. I want my *son!*"

"Oh Ray, there was no baby. Never was. Never will be. It was all part of the sting. I had to make you suffer, after all. I had to—" The line went dead.

Dan leaned in and nibbled on her ear. "Well, I'd say that went pretty well."

"Better than well," agreed Mason. "He got exactly what—"

The wail of an infant cut through the moment.

"Wow." Mason blew out a breath. "That was close."

"Fuck!" exclaimed Dan, moving to get up. "She barely slept ten minutes! It took me three times that long just to get her to sleep. I thought all newborns did was sleep."

Kaley grabbed his hand and dragged him back down. "She's not a newborn anymore, hon. She's six weeks old."

The fact that she'd conceived so quickly with Dan and Mason had confirmed Kaley's suspicion that Ray was the source of their infertility problem. Whether it was Dan's or Mason's sperm that had actually done the job, however, was irrelevant. Jasmine had two fathers. It was that simple.

"Right," said Dan, his eyes misting up a little. He was such a softy when it came to their daughter. "I can't believe how much she's grown already.

"I'll get her. She might need to nurse." She squeezed his hand. "And you guys do too much already."

"That's impossible. We can't do enough for our ladies.," said Dan, his smile warm and his kiss whisper-light. "Right Mace?"

"Uh...I dunno. There's definitely such a thing as 'enough' dirty diapers."

Laughing, Kaley wrapped an arm around each of them and squeezed. Damn if they didn't make great parents, too. "Sorry guys. You share in the giggles and kisses, you gotta share in the crap."

"Are you talking about little Jasmine or yourself?" asked Dan with a twinkle.

"I think you know the answer to that already, babe." She kissed his cheek and winked. "I think you know already."

# About the Author

Nikki lives in a small town in Ontario, Canada. In the midst of the chaos that comes with raising three small boys, working part-time as a lab tech in a hospital blood bank, and caring for her ever-adoring husband, she dreams up her stories. Nikki's work is an eclectic combination of romance, mystery, suspense and humor with characters that have plenty of room to grow. To learn more about her and her work visit her at www.nikkisoarde.com.

Nikki welcomes mail from readers. You can write to her c/o Ellora's Cave Publishing at 1056 Home Ave., Akron OH 44310.

# Also by Nikki Soarde

And Lady Makes Three *anthology*
Duplicity
Jagged Gift
Phobia

# CLOSE ENCOUNTERS OF THE CARNAL KIND

Delilah Devlin

# Chapter One

Through the swaying branches of the cypress trees that nearly choked the night sky, Etienne saw a light — a yellow-orange ball of fire — so bright he wondered how the air he breathed wasn't singed.

He stiffened against the instinctive need to dive for cover.

"*Ooo-eee*, we know where Uncle Jacques be tonight," Arnaud said, popping the top of his beer can and taking a long draw, his gaze following the light as it slowly passed from north to south.

Etienne looked down on his brother, who sat in a wicker chair, his feet propped on the porch rail, and he smothered a curse. "So long as he doesn't go blabbing to the *National Enquirer* again about seeing aliens, I don't care what he does."

"Does seem to be all dat man can talk about. Bad enough he tol' them 'bout the aliens takin' him away, but to tell da world what dey did after?" Arnaud's expression turned glum. "Family still hasn't lived dat one down."

Etienne winced at the reminder. "No doubt he'll be in his pirogue all night on the bayou, looking for them. You'd think he'd be hiding."

"*C'est vrai!*" Arnaud shook his head. "Any man gets his ass probed and talks about it to everyone after — dat man has no shame at all. No wonder Leticia left him."

Etienne nudged Arnaud's chair with his good foot, nearly unseating him. "You make it sound like you believe his story. Uncle Jacques is crazy as a loon. Always has been."

Arnaud shrugged, looking sheepish. "Yeah, but you weren't here. You didn't see him—all sunburned on his face and lookin' rumpled and tired—like he'd laid a dozen whores. He couldn't stop talkin' 'bout it. Don' think he slept for days afterwards."

"But what exactly did he say? I found an *Enquirer* in the PX after I spoke to you. He didn't say what the aliens looked like or anything about the ship."

"Yeah," Arnaud snorted. "Only dat dey wanted babies—wanted to mate wit' him." Arnaud gave him a look full of wicked mischief. "But your name did come up, big brother. Dem aliens be lookin' for you, now!"

Etienne gave him a searing glare. "Fuck! That's why I haven't been to town. It's a good thing he didn't share that part of his story with the reporter. I might shoot anyone who showed up on my porch uninvited."

"You see? Dat's your problem. You lost your sense of humor. Did the Army knock it out of you?"

Etienne slumped onto the chair beside Arnaud and set his cane against the porch rail. "Something like that," he muttered, wishing his brother were anywhere but here, but the man hung around him like a hungry mosquito.

"You know, you come back from dat desert and you don' say nothing 'bout what you seen—what happened. *Maman* is worried for you."

Etienne glanced out over the still, stagnant water. The words were there, right at the tip of his tongue, but he couldn't push them out. Instead, he shoved away the bleak memories. "It's over. I'm back. Leave it at that."

"Are you?" His brother's dark eyes glittered with concern in the dim light cast by the single bulb hanging from the rafter above. "You ain't the same man you was before. Hell, you don' even talk like one of us no more."

"I've been out in the world, Arnie. Took advantage of the Montgomery GI Bill. Maybe you should try it sometime."

"No thanks. Not if it means I come back grumpy as an alligator. Speakin' of which…"

The wicked gleam returned to Arnaud's eyes, and Etienne stiffened. He knew his brother well enough to know he planned mischief.

"Tell you what. How 'bout we go down to da Possum Palace and wrestle us a gator? The tourists love it when we strip down and get dirty." He waggled his eyebrows. "Maybe get us some Yankee tail tonight."

Etienne stared down at his leg, stretched straight in front of him.

"You could sit at poolside—just take off your shirt and show da girls those muscles you got. Dey take one look at you and your bum leg—you get all da pussy you need to make you happy again."

"Pussy isn't what I need. I need rest," Etienne said, gritting his teeth.

Arnaud sighed. "You rest—and *mope*. You just got back and now you hide in da swamp in your cabin. I'm not goin' to let you do dis to yourself for long."

"Give me a few days, Arnie," Etienne said, keeping his tone even and quiet, when all he wanted to do was rail—at Arnie, at his shattered leg, at the bastards who'd taken his friends out with a pipe bomb.

His brother stood and stretched his arms above his head, still staring at the light, when suddenly it blinked out. "What you think it is?"

"Fuckin' swamp gas, if anyone asks!" Etienne shrugged. "I know what it isn't. It's no alien spaceship."

\* \* \* \* \*

Etienne leaned forward, cuddling his beer between his hands, letting the silence wrap around his jangled nerves. Here in the swamp, in a hunting cabin filled with happy childhood memories, he hoped to finally shrug off his soul-deep sadness. He loved his brother and family, but he didn't want to invite them into the dark place he'd been forced inside ever since Tekrit.

Arnaud had left half an hour before, frustrated and hurt—Etienne knew it, but couldn't reach out to him, not yet. Maybe a few more days of staring out at the green, wet world around him would drown the memories of the sun-baked dirt that drank his buddies' blood like a thirsty sponge.

He needed time to fit back into his old life. He snorted at that thought—like he'd ever really fit in to begin with. Taller by a foot than his brothers and swarthy-skinned to their olive, he'd often wondered if he hadn't been traded in the bassinet at birth. And he'd never been satisfied with what life offered him in the bayou—it's why he'd enlisted in the first place.

A twig snapped nearby, and Etienne froze. As if he'd never left Iraq, time slowed, and in one long moment he realized the crickets had stopped their raucous chirping, the owls no longer called to one another—he had a visitor.

Etienne eased from his chair, ignoring the cane, and slid into his cabin. The gun, already loaded with shot to pepper any reporter's ass, stood next to the door and he reached for it.

Footsteps crunched closer, then climbed the wooden steps just as he swung back around with the shotgun cradled in his arms. But the woman who strode toward him wasn't like any reporter he'd ever seen.

Her smile was tentative as she stopped in front of him. Her gaze was wide and curious as she stared up into his face for one long moment. Then she drew in a deep breath, lowered her gaze and knelt at his feet, pressing her forehead against his thigh.

Etienne felt a frown furrow his forehead, wondering what the hell was going on. He tried to nudge her away, but she grasped his calf and clung, speaking softly, the words guttural and lilting at the same time. Definitely not English, not like anything he'd ever heard in his travels.

When she rose, her eyes glittered with moisture, which she quickly blinked away. This time the smile she flashed was joyous.

Etienne's suspicions roused and he glanced out into the darkness, wondering whether he was the butt of a joke and not liking it one damn bit.

The woman in front of him was too fresh-faced, too innocent-looking to be real. His glance raked over her body. She was clothed from her neck to the tops of her shiny brown boots in a skin-hugging material that looked soft as sueded leather, as soft and golden-brown as the large eyes she raised to stare up at him.

Color crept over his cheeks as he realized he'd stood frozen in place, transfixed by the woman's beauty. Beautiful or not, innocent or not, she didn't belong here. "*Cher*, you can turn right around and go back where you came from," he said, the words coming out less harsh than he'd intended.

She smiled and started to speak again, and then rolled her almond-shaped eyes. Her hand lifted to her ear, and she tugged at the shiny stud stuck in her left lobe. "Sorry 'bout dat. I forgot to turn on my translator," she said in a Cajun accent.

Not a reporter, not with that accent. A Creole girl by the look of her. Etienne sighed and propped the shotgun beside the door. "All right, who put you up to this? Arnaud?"

She shook her head, which shivered her long, dark hair around her shoulders. "Didn't Jacques tell you?" she asked, her expression falling. "He was s'posed to give you a message."

His eyes narrowed. "I haven't seen him since I returned. But you can tell him, thank you very much, but I'm not interested—however attractive you are, *cher*." He turned to reenter his cabin.

A small, slim hand clamped on his forearm. "But you don' understand how important dis is—"

Etienne shrugged her off, ignoring the plea in her large doe-like eyes. "Look, I'm sure you're very good at...whatever it is you do—"

"I'm da best!" she said, eagerness shining in her face. "Dat's why I'm here."

"Fucking hell! I can't believe he thought I needed a whore," Etienne muttered under his breath.

"A whore?" The woman's face screwed up with a look of confusion. "Wait, I think I'm not translatin' dat word correctly."

"This is a joke, right?" Etienne blew out the breath he'd been holding since she appeared. "He sends you in that *space costume*, and you're supposed to do what? Give me a ride?" His eyes widened, and he jerked back a little. "You're not expecting to probe my ass, are you?"

"Only if you won' surrender your sperm, Sire," she said, a blush rising to her cheeks. "I can assist you…" Her voice trailed off, and she nibbled at the edge of her full lips.

"I just bet you can," he murmured, wondering why he was fighting this so hard. The woman was a knockout. She was tall and slim-hipped, with small, round breasts. Any one of his old buddies would have given a month's pay to slide between her thighs.

As he appraised her attributes, her nipples beaded beneath the soft, thin leather. "Perhaps you need a little foreplay before you give me your semen?" she asked, with a flirty tilt of her head. She straightened and thrust out her chest, but the effect was robbed of vampdom by her girlish smile. She was one hell of a confusing, yet alluring, package.

Jacques knew what he was doing. If she'd carried the odor of the streets on her, he'd have sent her on her way in a heartbeat.

Etienne felt his anger waver. Her skin was dusky like milky café au lait, her pores so fine he knew her cheeks would be as soft as a baby's. He wondered if the rest of her would be as soft. This close, he could smell the fragrance clinging to her skin—like almonds mixed with a musky floral scent that tugged at his cock.

The woman shifted on her feet as he stared, then she squared her shoulders. "We'll never know until we get dis done." She reached for the fly of his jeans.

"Wait a minute…" His hand closed over hers to halt her.

She looked up, a question in her guileless gaze.

"Where the hell did he find you, sweetheart?" he murmured, staring down at her.

A dimple dented one cheek. *A damn dimple.* "Oh, I found him."

Her grin was childlike, and it angered him that she was playing with him. "Was he drunk when you fed him that line about surrendering his semen?"

She tilted her head to the side, her smile faltering. "Line?"

Etienne swore beneath his breath, patience at an end—restraint beyond his control as angry anguish exploded inside him. He gripped her waist hard, pulling her toward him. If his uncle thought a prostitute would prod him from his blue funk, who was he to argue? He certainly hadn't managed on his own. Maybe this was what he'd waited for…

Her mouth opened around a startled gasp, which he breathed in as he sealed her mouth with his.

But her lips didn't move beneath his, and he opened his eyes to find her wide-eyed gaze staring back at him. He pulled his head back. "Kiss me," he said, his voice gruff. "This is what you came for, wasn't it?"

"I came for your sem—"

He didn't want to hear her "story" again and slammed his mouth down to shut her up.

This time she pressed back, sliding her lips beneath his. Her kiss was soft and tentative, drugging to his jaded senses. Her breaths came quick and excited, puffing into his mouth. Despite the fact, or perhaps because she wasn't very good at kissing, an electrical charge of heat pulsed throughout his body, tightening his loins.

Etienne groaned and pulled her body flush with his, grinding his cock against the soft cleft he found between her legs.

Her hips jerked then pushed forward, finding his rhythm, sliding her sex against his as she moaned into his mouth.

With her breasts mashed against his chest, his shaft riding her mons, Etienne drank from her lush, feminine mouth. The softness trembling against him soothed and excited his soul. He hadn't known how badly he needed this—needed her—until this moment. He sank into the kiss, spearing her mouth with his tongue, sweeping inside like his body ached to burrow into her sweet flesh.

But she wasn't the answer to his problems—she wasn't even here because she wanted it. Good old Uncle Jacques had sent her.

Etienne realized he was only fighting himself. He'd wanted solitude to lick his wounds, but his family seemed to understand that deep down he needed to be touched.

This woman's soft hands were as good as any. At least she wouldn't be expecting him to spill his guts. He broke the kiss and pushed her back. "Go ahead," he said, releasing her hand. "Take my semen," he bit out, bitterness licking the embers of his anger into flame once more.

She swallowed, looking a little frightened by his anger. If she was scared, fuck her. This was what she'd been paid to do.

Eyeing him with caution, she flicked open the snap at the waistband of his jeans. Then she drew down his zipper and knelt in front of him to ease his jeans past his hips.

He wasn't wearing any underwear, so his sex pushed into the widening gap until it sprang free. The warm breeze blowing over his flesh and the woman's intent stare did the rest. His cock quickly filled and rose.

Etienne sucked in a deep breath and raised his hands to brace himself within the doorframe as the woman bent over him.

She licked her lips. "I'll make dis quick."

"Don't rush on my account." Now that he'd decided to enjoy his "gift", he wasn't in any hurry.

The woman cleared her throat then opened her mouth and swallowed the head of his cock.

Etienne groaned and his toes curled inside his boots. The sensation of her hot, moist mouth drawing on his sex was so exquisite it hurt.

Her gaze never left his as she drew back and licked around the soft head. The sight of her pink tongue darting out to lap at him tightened his groin. She followed the ridge all the way around, then licked down his length, caressing him with firmer strokes as she went.

Etienne gritted his teeth as she took her time, priming him. Her head dipped and her dark hair shimmered in the moonlight as she worked his flesh.

She returned to the head and suctioned it into her mouth, her eyes closing as her lips drew hard, her cheeks hollowing with the effort. Then her hands glided up his thighs.

One cupped his balls, already drawn taut and close to his body. She kneaded them gently with her palm and fingers, rolling and tugging until he pulsed his hips, beginning the drive toward release. The other hand circled the base of his cock and squeezed, twisting up and down his shaft.

A throbbing started in his injured leg, interrupting his upward climb, and he eased his weight to his good leg, then clamped one hand on the back of her head to encourage her to take more of him, deeper into her throat.

Her jaw opened wider and her teeth skimmed his length as he pushed his cock along her tongue until he butted the back of her throat. With his body wound tight as a coil, he closed his eyes and let his head fall back, groaning as she dipped and bobbed faster—sliding down him, sucking hard on the upstroke. Christ, she had a talented mouth after all!

Just as he was ready to let her sweep him along in a frenzied tide, the hand cupping his balls slid further back, her fingers tracing the cleft of his buttocks.

Before he could utter a protest, one finger eased inside his ass, tunneling, manipulating his prostate. With a shout of protest, mixed with anguished release, his hips bucked and his body exploded, cum jetting inside the woman's mouth.

Etienne bit back a curse and pumped twice, weak thrusts now, his body trembling in the aftermath. He curved his fingers around the wooden doorframe and opened his eyes to glare down at the woman. "I said my ass was off-limits."

Her lips pursed, and she reached for the belt cinching her small waist, pulling a small vial from beneath it.

While he watched, furious, she spat his creamy cum into the vial, and then held it aloft and tugged her ear. She murmured something unintelligible and light glimmered around the small bottle before it flickered and blinked out. When the light disappeared, so did the vial.

"What the hell?"

The woman rose and tugged up his pants, but he shoved her hands away and tucked his cock inside. Pulling his clothes together, his gaze never left her.

As soon as the snap of his jeans closed, he grabbed her wrist and pulled her inside the cabin, into full light. "What the hell just happened?"

Her gaze met his, her chin raised in defiance. "I sent your sperm to my ship. We need to know if you are potent."

"Ship?" His mind skipped over that detail for the moment to return to the one blaring a warning in his mind. "Why the hell do you need to know I'm not shooting blanks?"

"If you're potent, Sire, I'm here to take you home."

"My home is here. I'm not going anywhere." He raked his hand through his hair, still rattled at seeing his cum disappear into thin air. Perhaps Uncle Jacques hadn't been drunk after all.

"Sire, if you're potent you must return to fulfill your destiny."

"And what might that be?" he asked, half afraid to hear the answer.

Her wide-eyed gaze filled with dreamy fervor. "To assume the mantle of kingship and lead our forces in the war against the Gracktiles."

He snorted, wondering what rabbit hole he'd just fallen into. "Is that all?"

"Oh, and to beget the next generation of our ruling caste."

"Fuck me!"

# Chapter Two

"You! Sit!" The man towering in front of her pointed to a sagging couch.

Knowing now was not the time to press her point, Mariska flounced down on it. Every king was entitled to a rant every now and then.

"Not another damn word!" he spat at her, anger staining his regal features a magnificent red.

Mariska pressed her lips together, hugging herself with excitement. His Royal Highness, Emperor of the Sister Planets, High Commander of the Kathar Forces, was a fearsome sight to behold as he stomped across the wooden floor.

Admittedly, his stomp was hampered by his limp, as he seemed to favor his left leg. But the fault only raised his stature in her eyes. A damaged warrior. A scarred but still powerful knight of the court. His wives would be very blessed. She sighed dreamily, a small ache of envy dampening her exhilaration.

The savior of her species stalked just paces away—so near she could reach out and touch him with her fingertips, if she were foolish enough to try. At the moment he looked angry enough to eat a *crote*.

To think that she, fightership commander *ordinaire*, had had his most Glorious Highness's cock in her mouth! And any moment now, Carillon would transmit the message that would turn the tide in their war with the

Gracktiles. The test would only confirm what she already knew.

The man *reeked* of potency.

From his broad, heavily muscled shoulders to the tensile strength of his trim abdomen, power radiated from his majestic form.

And he was handsome as a god! His dark hair, worn close-cropped like a warrior's, shone blue-black under the light. His skin was burnished brown, his eyes dark, his nose a sharp blade, his mouth…

Mariska shivered. When he'd grabbed her and blessed her lips with that odd, breath-stealing caress, she'd felt like she'd sprouted iridescent *Glimyr*-wings and floated away.

Her body still hummed with the wicked way he'd pressed his body against hers. *Stars!* Her clothing felt too tight, and the room warm. But it was best not to linger over those memories for long. The joys to be found within his arms were not intended for the likes of her. Besides, he looked anything but amorous at the moment.

Magnificently enraged was a more apt description— and she was the cause.

She shrugged philosophically. He might be muttering obscenities and casting veiled insults her way now, but she understood his anger. He couldn't grasp his importance, and he wasn't in the mood at the moment to hear about it.

She tugged her translator and switched from Cajun to Katharian. Better to give him a little privacy for his rant— besides, she tended to have this effect on men. Why should His Royal Highness be any different?

For the moment, however, the sight of him was hers to savor. Her reward for his return would be enormous—

her wealth would eclipse many a landed family's, her name would be recorded in the tombs of future kings.

She had done what trackers, seers, and mages had been unable to do—find the last reproducing male in the ruling line.

Her destiny had begun so humbly with a transport mission to deliver an aged mage to the Queen's palace. A mission she'd resented because it was far beneath her fighter's status.

The old man had muttered to himself throughout the flight about something he'd misplaced. Mariska hadn't paid him any mind until he'd mentioned the Gracktiles and their plot to render every heir impotent, knowing that while technology could reproduce replicas of the ruling class, their beliefs would forever deny them its use. The Gracktiles had succeeded with their plot, poisoning each of the male heirs, destroying their seed and the future of the Empire. The Gracktiles had only to wait until the last of the ruling class died out to recapture the worlds they had once ruled over themselves, before the Revolution, which had cast them off the Sister planets.

Once she'd grasped the significance of the old man's mutterings, she'd pressed him for details, recording every clue that surfaced from his age-diminished mind. Working with her aged science officer, Carillon, she had pieced together his journey, which had spirited away the Queen's newborn son to the Mother Planet, to hide him until the danger had passed.

With the old mage's influence in the Queen's court, she'd managed to depart, her ship fully provisioned, and without having to file for approval. For all she knew, her command believed she'd deserted her post.

But other than the one embarrassing misstep with Jacques, her treasure hunt had succeeded beyond her dreams. The embodiment of all that was precious to her worlds stomped just feet away.

She should have known Jacques was not the king. No matter he had swum his little boat right past the very cabin where the foster mother said the king would be upon his return. Jacques had screamed like a woman when she'd transported him to her ship, had fought off her attempts to convince him to give her his sperm voluntarily. Not until Carillon had strapped him to a gurney and she'd used the little trick the mage had told her to ignite his passion had he rendered her his sperm. But she'd stuck her finger up a commoner's ass for naught.

"Riska? Are you sitting down?" a voice broke into her reverie.

"Yes, Carillon." She closed her eyes, wishing with all her might the news would be what she hoped.

"My girl, you've done it! It's him! And he's potent!" His voice held such glee she could almost see him dancing his doddering jig as he read the results from the ship's assimilator.

Tears filled her eyes, and she blinked to rid herself of them. She was a fightership pilot for *stars* sake!

She realized the stomping had halted, and her King was glaring at her again. She tugged her ear and switched back to Cajun.

"You haven't heard a word I said."

"Forgive me, Sire. Dat was my Science Tech. He was deliverin' the results."

"Stop it!"

"You must let me speak, you don' understand da importance of my mission."

"Stop with the Cajun-speak! Why are you using it?"

"Oh," Mariska shrugged, caught off guard by his comment. "I thought you'd be more comfortable hearing it."

"Get rid of it, now."

"Yes, Sire." Whew! The man just found out he was royalty and already he was slinging commands. She tugged her ear. "Replace Cajun wit' middle continent dialect." She schooled her face to hide her irritation. "Is this better?"

"Now get out," he said, his body held rigid.

"I can't do that."

"Get out, or I'll throw you out."

Mariska rose from the sagging sofa and faced him. "Sire, you aren't safe here any longer. I'm only the first to find you. Others may follow. You and the family that raised you will be at risk if you don't come with me now."

His chest rose and fell rapidly, his fists clenched by his sides. "I'm not who you think I am. I'm Etienne Lambert. I was born and raised here."

"Raised, yes. But you were born far from here." Mariska added softly, "Call your mother. She will tell you." She walked to the door. "I'll wait outside."

Beneath the shelter of the crude awning, Mariska listened to the faint rumblings inside as *Etienne* spoke with the woman who had raised him.

While her heart went out to the man for the shocking news she had delivered, she couldn't still the impatience tying her stomach in knots. She had to get him to the ship quickly.

The door opened behind her, and she turned. Light spilled from the interior, revealing his strained features. His mouth was a straight, stern line. "So, you were telling me the truth." He stared out over the dark water. "I don't give a damn. I'm not going."

Mariska made a decision. One she knew could have severe repercussions in the coming weeks. She walked to him and gazed into his impassive face. She reached up and ran her hands across his chest. He had seemed to soften toward her the last time she touched him. Perhaps it would work again.

"Look, I know this is important to you, *cher* — "

She shook her head, but didn't reply. Instead she stepped closer and encircled him, sliding her arms around his back. "Would you give me another…kiss, before I leave?"

Etienne's expression didn't change — but he growled deep in his throat as his mouth descended toward hers.

At the last possible moment, Mariska turned to give him her cheek and tugged her communicator. "Carillon, transport now!"

✦ ✦ ✦ ✦ ✦

Hours later, His Highness, *Etienne Lambert*, was still in a royal snit.

Mariska had given him a wide berth, leaving it to Carillon to acclimate the king to his new situation. She'd locked herself away on the ship's bridge, checking and rechecking their coordinates and flight plan — any excuse not to think about what had transpired between them at his humble cottage.

For weeks she'd been so focused on the task of finding the king, that when she'd finally been confronted with him, she'd acted like a *Glimyr*-monkey. He'd thought her a Pleasure-Giver! When she'd returned to the ship, she'd immediately accessed the on-board computer to verify the translation of that hideous word, only to be mortified when its true meaning was confirmed.

And how had he come to that conclusion? Had it been her immediate insistence that he surrender his seed? Or had she betrayed the instant attraction she'd felt for him?

Somehow, bedazzled and nearly tongue-tied with star-struck awe, she'd managed to make him believe she'd been after sex! Mutual, consensual, sweaty sex. Something she was denied as a fighter, due to the direct correlation between sexual activity and the loss of reflex and focus under the dizzying influence of an overstimulated libido. Ridiculous!

Already she suffered the aftereffects. Her mind was consumed with that…kiss. She replayed it over and over—how his lips had felt and tasted as he slid them over hers, how his body had rocked against the cradle of her thighs, and how she'd *flowered* beneath his attentions.

Only she wasn't feeling so fragrant now. He'd thought her a *whore*!

A sharp rap sounded on the door panel. "Open the door, Mariska."

She froze and her heart skipped, and then galloped inside her chest. Oh why couldn't he just accept his destiny and leave her to her own!

She stood and waved her hand in front of the lock and the door slid silently open.

Immediately, he filled the narrow doorway with his broad shoulders—she wished she hadn't noticed that.

His dark gaze bored into hers. "Your *Science Tech* has told me everything I need to know."

Mariska nodded. "Good. That's good." She cleared her throat. "Then you understand now why I had to—"

"And since I'm not getting off this ship anytime soon, it's time to get to work on the primary mandate of my rule." He stepped further into the cabin, crowding her back against her chair.

Swallowing the panic his proximity aroused in her, she squeaked, "Which mandate would that be?" She didn't like the feral smile that stretched his lips—not one bit! Nor the gaze that seemed to strip her of her clothes in a single glance.

"Why, the begetting of heirs." He leaned closer, his chest brushing hers.

"Oh... Oh!" Feeling a little giddy and very out of her depth, she continued, "Well, we do have receptacles aboard the ship for that purpose, but gentlewomen really do prefer going about the...begetting...the old-fashioned way. It builds bonds of affection." *I'm babbling! He's going to note the similarity between a Glimyr-monkey and me when he finally sees one!*

"Do you really think we have time to wait to reach your planets?" His head lowered, and his mouth hovered over hers.

Drugged by the musky scent of his skin and the heat that rolled off his body in waves, she managed a breathy, "No?" She shook her head. What was he saying? "Yes!"

"And I'm afraid I won't be sufficiently stimulated squirting into another vial."

"Squirting?" Her cheeks burned as she realized his meaning. "Do you require…assistance? Carillon is knowledgeable…"

His smile turned into a smirk, and he tsked. "As charming as he is, Carillon's assistance would have an adverse effect on my success." He nudged a leg between hers. "I need you. Beneath me." He pressed his lips to hers, a kiss so brief she moaned. "Now."

He'd framed his desires in a command. How could she refuse? His mouth slid along her jaw. "For the sake of our species…I suppose…"

"Not for our species…for me. *I* desire it." He raised his head and glanced around the cramped confines of her cockpit. "If you're otherwise engaged, perhaps you could grip your controls while I carry out my destiny."

The picture he drew was one she'd rather never have seen. For the rest of her life, she'd view a captain's chair in quite a different light. *Stars!* How was she ever to regain her focus? "The ship's on autopilot. Here would be a little awkward, I think," she said her voice thin. How was she expected to breathe when every inhalation rubbed her nipples against his chest?

"Then in the science lab?" He raised a wicked brow. "Carillon could take notes, estimate trajectory, count the minutes between regenerations—"

He intended multiple *regenerations*? "Not the lab," she said, feeling dizzy from lack of air. When had the bridge become so hot?

"Then where?" he asked, his voice silky and so deep her body wept.

"My quarters—" He pulled away so quickly she grabbed for the chair to steady herself.

"After you," he said, with a sweep of his brawny arm toward the door.

Shaken, her tummy trembled like a thousand little *argnats* beat their wings inside her. She slid past him into the corridor, achingly aware of him following closely on her heels. Her pace picked up—she needed space, a moment to review what had just happened and regroup her failing intellect. *Think!* "You know, this really isn't a very good idea. Few children are born out of wedlock—"

"I'm not asking you to marry me—only to receive my seed. But who am I to buck a tradition? When we arrive at whatever the name of your planet is—"

"Euphrazha?"

"—we'll take care of the formalities."

He couldn't mean to marry her! "But you already have a stable of wives available to provide you service—handpicked by the Queen Regent herself."

"I choose my own *vessels*. And right now, you're *convenient*."

*Convenient?* Mariska's head jerked back, and she halted in mid-step. Unfortunately, too close to the Royal Menace to avoid collision. Only he didn't slam into her, it was more a steady slide, which pushed her against the bulkhead next to her cabin door.

With her chest flattened against the wall, she was all too aware of what prodded her bottom.

"Here, then?" he whispered, his breath feathering her cheek. "How do I open this outfit?"

Could her wardrobe provide her the means of averting his intentions?

"If you don't tell me, I'll just rip it, *cher*."

*Stars*, did he have to say it in that sexy rumble? "It stretches, just slide it—"

He tugged at the neck, slipping it down, and then he pressed a kiss to her bare shoulder. "Your skin's soft as a baby's," he said, sliding his lips over her shoulder, up her neck, then tugging her earlobe with his teeth.

Mariska closed her eyes and leaned her forehead against the bulkhead, glad he pressed against her body to hold her there, because she would have melted to the floor.

He pushed her uniform lower, until the opening slipped beneath her breasts. His hands reached around and cupped her.

Her nipples tightened into pointed barbs, stabbing at his palms. The scrape of his roughened skin sent a shudder through her body.

"You're so good, *cher*, so responsive." He pushed the fabric lower and her arms were trapped against her sides, while her upper chest and belly were exposed to his roving hands. He leaned her back and her head fell against his shoulder. "Lovely, coffee-colored nipples." He twisted the tips with his fingers and then flicked them with his thumbs. "Will you taste bitter? Or are you sweetened with milk?"

"Aaah," she moaned. Why did he have to talk? His words tightened her belly, drew moisture from her body to dampen the crotch of her uniform.

He shoved her clothing down, past her buttocks, cinching her legs closed. His palms smoothed over her ass and around to her...

She struggled to free her legs, to widen them. She needed his touch there. Needed him to soothe the fire licking at her pussy. She wriggled against him. "Please..."

"I will." So quickly she swayed on her booted heels, he turned her in his arms. "But first, I get to play." He quirked an eyebrow. "Tit for tat."

Whatever that meant, it couldn't bode well for her — not accompanied by the wicked smirk that twisted his sexy mouth. With his arms encircling her to hold her arms close to her sides, and her uniform binding her legs, she yelped as he hoisted her over his shoulder and entered her cabin.

Dizzy, breathless with alarm and something a great deal more thrilling, she wondered when he'd learned to use the identi-locks. And who had programmed them to accept his palm prints?

# Chapter Three

Etienne strode into Mariska's quarters and flung her onto the narrow mattress, ignoring her yelp of alarm. Anger had built inside him for hours—surprisingly free of pain or regret. Instead, it was an empowering fury that found its target in the form of one slim girl—a vexing creature who stared up at him, wide-eyed and huffing.

Good! He hoped she was also a little worried about the direction of his thoughts. He grabbed for one foot and tugged off a boot, then quickly stripped her of the other.

She shimmied on the mattress, elbowing her way to a sitting position. "I'm captain of this ship—a fighter, not a pleasure-giver!"

"*Cher*, I know you're not a whore. Carillon filled me in on just exactly who and what you are. Also told me where you learned that nasty little technique for extracting semen." He pulled her uniform off her long legs and tossed it over his shoulder. "You don't want to remind me now that you used it on my uncle, too."

"Jacques wasn't cooperating...desperate measures—"

"I said don't remind me. Kinda takes the nice off my edges."

"What nice?" she bit out.

He smiled at her tart response. "Exactly."

"You're insufferable."

"First time I've been called that—but it's better than some insults." He knelt on the mattress and crawled on his hands and knees until he was poised over her. "Let me look at what I'm getting."

Her gaze tossed daggers his way. "You haven't gotten anything yet."

"Glad you added that last word. Tells me your mind is headed down the same road."

"We're in deep space," she replied, her tone resentful. "We don't have roads — we have azimuths, coordinates — "

"Shall I map your coordinates?" he growled, his gaze honing in on the delta of her honeyed thighs before he glanced back up to catch her stare. "Make sure I can find my way?"

Her mouth opened, but only a weak gasp escaped. Her eyelids dipped, and her lips trembled.

"That's right, I need to reconnoiter," he said softly. He glanced down again, amused when she clamped her legs shut.

The girl was one long, cool drink of water to his parched senses. Creamy coffee-colored skin, dusky brown nipples, a thatch of dark, crinkly curls between her legs. Would her pussy's tender flesh be pink — or darker? He shoved away the need to find out now. First, a little "tit"…

With new appreciation for his mother's quaint saying, he slid his knees along either side of her hips and sat down.

Her eyes rounded, and her hands covered her breasts. "S-sire?"

"*Etienne*, when you're naked."

A small frown furrowed her brow. "And when I'm not?"

He smirked. "Lord and Master." Not for the first time, she betrayed a hint of annoyance. He liked that. All that wide-eyed adoration made him uncomfortable. "Now remove your hands from your breasts, *cher*."

"Because you command it?" she asked sulkily.

"Got that right."

Her hands slid away and fluttered like she didn't know where to put them.

He guided them down to the pillow beside her head. "When you figure out what you want to touch, go right ahead."

She mewled, then. A little throaty moan that told him everything. He leaned down and kissed her mouth, a soft brush of lips.

Hers opened immediately—she'd learned. He'd taught her something new. Now, she asked wordlessly for him to deepen the caress.

Etienne was more than ready to oblige her. He slanted his head and probed her mouth with his tongue, licking the rim of her teeth, stroking deeper to lap at her tongue until hers joined the dance.

His body hardened, all his male parts cramming against the fly of his jeans, his thighs tensing, his belly clenching with the need to get to the fucking part as fast as he could fly out of his clothes.

He broke the kiss and took a deep breath to slow his thudding heart, avoiding her sloe-eyed gaze.

"Tit" first, he reminded himself and scooted lower down her body.

At the first touch of his tongue to her pouting nipple, her fingers threaded through his hair and clutched him tight. He smiled against her breast and swallowed the nipple, tonguing the tip while he suckled.

Her hips bucked beneath his spread thighs, and he growled, deep in his throat. Her voice broke on a strangled moan. "Please, harder."

He bit the hard button of her nipple, and then licked it to soothe away the little pain.

Her head thrashed on her pillow, and he looked up to see the tangle of her hair brush her cheeks, her nose. Her mouth opened around a soundless moan.

Growing harder by the moment, he moved to her other nipple and tortured it in like fashion until her body writhed beneath him. He dipped his hips and rubbed his clothed cock against her soft belly, rutting to ease the ache swelling his loins.

"*Etienne,*" she groaned.

"I know, sweetheart," he said, pressing his lips against her ribs and sliding lower. "Just a little more reconnoitering." He sat up, now riding her closed thighs. His fingers raked the wiry hair on her mons.

Her back arched and her eyes glazed over. "I can't stand it."

He slid a finger between her tight, closed lips and drew moisture to rub against the hard little knot buried at the top of her cunt.

At his first touch, a high, thready keening erupted from her.

He circled her clitoris, watching her writhe, his thighs fighting to keep her legs anchored to the bed. When her fists bunched the bedding and her back arched high, he lifted his injured knee and nudged open her thighs.

Eager now, she spread her legs, making room for him to climb between. He slipped his hands beneath her ass and knelt low, inhaling the fragrance of her arousal. Arnaud had been so right. This was what he'd needed— feminine cries to lift his soul out of the darkness, glazed passion to coat his tongue and lips, a woman's softness to sink inside.

Her pussy lips were dark like melted chocolate. He sucked them, wringing shallow sobs from her. Then he licked lower, stabbing into her channel as far his tongue could reach to lap at the salty dew he'd inspired.

Her thighs trembled against his shoulders, and her cries grew harsh. She was nearing her release.

He rose and stripped his T-shirt over his head, flinging it to the floor.

Mariska watched him, her chest rising and falling so fast her breasts shivered.

"Will you deny me?" he asked, toeing off his boots.

"Sire, I'm yours to command," she said, her voice shaky and small.

He gave a sharp shake of his head and flicked open his pants. "Do you want *me*?"

She swallowed and drew in a ragged breath. "Yes, Etienne."

He shoved his pants down, stripping them off, and then returned to her, settling his sex between her legs. "Touch me, Mariska." He lowered his head to her shoulder, waiting for her soft hands to draw him closer.

She smoothed her palms over his shoulders and higher, lifting his face, then bracketing it between her hands. "Give me your seed," she whispered, and reached up to take his lips.

Etienne groaned into her mouth and prodded her sex with his, until he found her moist entrance and thrust hard inside her.

Mariska tensed beneath him, emitting a scratchy scream.

Too late, he realized he'd torn her hymen. *Christ!* He reared back, his cock still impaling her tender flesh. "Dammit to hell! Why didn't you tell me?"

"Tell you what?" she asked, her body shuddering beneath his. "Why did you stop?"

"You're a virgin!" he gritted out, still so hard he felt ready to burst from his skin.

"Was...a virgin," she said with a shaky laugh. "I'm a fightership commander. Sex is detrimental to our performance." She smoothed her hands down his back and squeezed his buttocks. "Are we finished?" She sounded disappointed.

"If I were a stronger man...ah hell!" He pumped, a shallow preliminary thrust. He watched her expression, gauging for discomfort or pain.

Instead, she sucked in her breath, and her eyes half-closed. Her hands squeezed harder, pulling him closer, deeper.

His jaw set hard as stone, he pulled out a little way and slid back inside. Then he repeated the motion, keeping the pace slow and steady.

Mariska planted her feet in the mattress and countered his motion, learning his rhythm.

"That's it, baby," he praised her, dropping a kiss on her lips. "Slowly now, when we meet, grind your pussy against me."

She blinked at the suggestion, but she was a fast learner, tilting her hips up when he drove deep, rubbing her clitoris against his groin, their hair producing a scratching sound that grew sharper, harsher as the friction built between their bodies. Soon, her breaths became more jagged. "Etienne?"

He leaned down and kissed her forehead. "It's all right, *cher*. Go with it, I'm here."

Her eyes squeezed closed and her mouth opened around a silent scream, and suddenly her hips bucked beneath him, awkward jerky bursts, out of sync—pulsing faster.

Etienne hooked his arms under her knees to control her movements and slammed into her, delivering powerful, full-throttled thrusts. When her orgasm clamped around his dick, he hammered at her cunt, his own release intensified by the loud, long scream that ripped from her throat.

When his hips finally slowed, he sank down onto her body until the trembling that shook his belly and legs came under his control. He lifted his arms to disengage with her legs and pushed her thighs down to lie alongside his. Then he rose on his elbows to look into her face.

Mariska's eyes were still closed. Perspiration dotted her forehead and upper lip. Her expression was so peaceful he might have thought her sleeping, but for the hands that swept lazily up and down his back.

Loath to move away from her, Etienne settled his head into the crook of her neck and let her soothe him with her soft hands. Beneath his ear, her heart beat slowly and reassuring. Her body's warmth, made more so when added to his, soon had his eyelids drooping. He snuggled his face closer, feeling more relaxed than he could ever remember.

Only he wouldn't give Arnaud credit for being right about what he needed. Arnaud, horndog that he was, wouldn't have understood it took one special woman to annihilate the darkness in his soul. No one else's pussy would have done. Only Mariska's. Etienne smiled against her neck.

"Etienne, are you sleeping?" she whispered.

"Am I too heavy for you?" God, he hoped not. His cock was still burrowed in her heat, and her body was softer than any mattress. Their contact—skin-to-skin—wasn't something he was ready to give up. Not yet. Maybe not ever.

"No. I like this," she said, stroking down his back, then stopping to cup his buttocks and squeeze. "Will you want to do it again?"

"When I have more sleep, I promise. But I've been up all night."

She was silent for a long moment, and he started to fall into slumber, when, "How long will you sleep?"

He groaned. "Are you eager for me, *cher*?"

"I was hoping for more regenerations," she said slowly.

The cobwebs lifted with a single snort of laughter. "We're going to work on your vocabulary."

"Regenerations isn't the correct word? You used it."

"I was being sarcastic."

"Then what would you call it?"

"Fucking."

"But that doesn't sound as pretty—it doesn't roll off the tongue."

"No, it's blunt, descriptive—a little nasty."

"So fucking as a noun—does it encompass everything we did?"

"No, fucking was just the part where I put my cock into your cunt. Do you need explanations for those terms, too?"

"No, cock is in the translator's dictionary. Cunt I can guess from the context of the sentence." Her cunt pulsed around him, as if the mention reminded her body how it was currently employed. Mariska's legs moved restlessly along his. "I would have used pussy. It sounds softer."

"Good point, yours is...cuddly, like a pet. But cunt is nastier, gets my engines burning faster."

"Then by all means, call it cunt." She sighed and rubbed her cheek against his. "So, fucking was only that last part. What do you call the rest?"

"Reconnoitering."

"Ahhh..." She kissed his ear. "I thought you were being clever." He heard the smile in her voice.

"I am. Now, go to sleep."

Her cunt pulsed again, and he realized she squeezed him on purpose. Already, she was learning to use those sexy little muscles to arouse—the girl was anything but slow.

Slowly, his dick *regenerated*, filling, stretching her channel as it nudged its way to full arousal.

Her body reacted, coaxing him with a wash of fresh encouragement that surrounded him with moist, fragrant heat.

"If you are tired..." she began.

"Too late to change your mind," he growled. "Something's awake."

"Thank the gods!"

\* \* \* \* \*

Mariska woke in the darkness, her body still joined to *Etienne's*, her bottom resting snug in the cradle of his thighs. Even in sleep, he kept her close, a wondrous hand cupping her breast, a solid thigh bracketing hers to keep her where he needed her to be when he awoke.

And oh, how he needed her! What had begun in anger and bitterness due to loss of power over his destiny had quickly turned urgent and *greedy* for contact, for respite from the shadows that had haunted him. She'd sensed that, over their hours of loving, he'd relinquished the horrors that stained his soul.

How she knew this, wasn't exactly clear. But somehow, she could see into his soulful eyes and reach into the heart of the man. In just hours, she felt connected to him, part of him. But did he feel the same way for her?

And what would become of this blossoming connection when they reached Euphrazha? Already, Carillon would have sent the encrypted message to the Queen, informing her that her son was found and on his way. He might be swept away from her in the homecoming. When he was no longer near, would she still feel he was part of her?

Mariska bit her lip and blinked away tears. Foolish girl! Her importance in the larger picture was as the deliverer of their salvation—not as bride or consort. When the time came, she would simply fade away and return to her post—fulfill whatever destiny remained for her to complete in this life.

That she had served as his *vessel* for a short time was a privilege and a joy she would hug close to herself for the rest of her life. As a fightership commander, she'd never had any expectation of falling in love. This short, glorious time with her king was a gift for which she would be forever grateful.

Etienne stirred beside her, murmuring softly in his sleep, and his arms tightened around her as though he couldn't let her go.

Mariska closed her eyes and let the tears leak onto her pillow.

His mouth brushed her shoulder. "*Cher*, what's wrong?" he said, his voice a low, sleep-filled rumble.

She sniffed and forced a little laugh. "Nothing. But I need to rise."

"I already have," he said, proving his point with a sexy surge that pushed him deeper inside her.

Although her body was a little sore from their previous play, Mariska returned the movement with a little inner-muscular squeeze. "You are very dedicated to fulfilling your mandate. Your nursery will be quite full in the next year."

"My nursery will need room for only one occupant."

Mariska stilled, part of her hoping she'd translated his meaning correctly, but the other part equally dismayed. "Sire—"

"*Etienne*," he said, his voice holding a hint of warning.

"All right, *Etienne*, it is your duty to impregnate as many of your wives as you can," she said, but didn't really mean it. The thought of him *regenerating* with any other woman sucked her breath from her lungs.

"I will have only one wife—and not because I'm breeding the next generation of a ruling class."

Oh no! This was worse, so much worse than she'd suspected. "But it is your duty to—"

"But not my choice. My mother chose to send me to Earth—well, she should have done her homework. America isn't ruled by a monarchy. We elect our leaders."

"Oh, this isn't good. It's all my fault. You're just resentful of how you were taken."

Etienne disengaged from her and rolled her to her back, then quickly settled his body over hers. "Lights on!"

He hadn't just figured out the identi-locks! Did he also know how to pilot her ship? Mariska wondered, irritation overriding her need to get him to listen to sense. She glared up at him, not the least surprised to greet his scowl—he was one stubborn man.

"*Cher*, I'll say this once. I nearly died fighting for what I believe in, and I lost friends to ensure a country ruled by a dictator—*not* a leader chosen by his people—wouldn't remain in power. If I become your king, I'm betraying everything I believe in."

How could she make him understand? "But what about the Sister planets? What about what we believe? Without strong rulers, our civilization is vulnerable to the Gracktiles—and I can tell you now, they won't offer us elections to decide who remains in charge."

"Not my problem, sweetheart. You'll all have to figure it out yourselves. Or better yet, open up the discussion to the people."

She snorted. "You don't understand our history. Our ruling class liberated us from oppression by their might, and they continued to breed the strongest warriors. Without your seed to strengthen the warrior caste—"

"It's not always about who has the biggest muscle, is it? If that were the case, wouldn't I still be on my own planet?"

That shut her up. That and the kiss he pressed to her lips. Her days as a fightership commander were numbered. She didn't have the attention span of an *argnat* when he continued to stir her libidinous pot!

Mariska wrapped her arms around his strong back and opened her legs to allow him entrance.

Just as his cock nudged her weeping portal, a siren blared its warning.

"What the—" Etienne began.

Mariska shoved him away and rolled off the bed. "Carillon, report!" she shouted to the intercom in the ceiling as she hurriedly pulled on her clothes.

"Riska, the queen's sent an escort. Get the king ready for transport."

# Chapter Four

Etienne paced the length of the solar, unaware of the opulence of his surroundings, wishing the coming minutes were already over. How long did it take to escort one slim girl from the military base?

"Son, you weary me. Come sit beside me. Your little fighter will be here any moment now."

He turned to the queen, whom he still had difficulty thinking of as his mother, despite the fact they shared a strong resemblance. At their first meeting, he'd recognized the truth he'd tried to deny in his heart. The woman he'd called his mother all his life, Estelle Lambert—wasn't. The queen's tall, robust figure, swarthy complexion, and stern features were a mirror of his own. Today, dressed in a long, dark green gown with a high, embroidered collar and starched cuffs, she looked every inch a monarch.

"It shouldn't take this long," he grumbled. "She doesn't want to come."

"Then you should command her," she said with a brisk nod.

He shot her a baleful glance. This was one of many things they'd argued about over the past weeks. "Well, I handled it my own way. Don't interfere."

She sniffed. "Your wishes should be acceded to without question. However odd they may be," she said, nodding again.

"Mother, everyone has free will."

"You are the king, whether you call yourself one or not. The people insisted on retaining this custom—and on looking to you for guidance."

"I'm no king. Hell, I can't command myself. What do I know about diplomacy or governing? I was a grunt in the Army—a non-com, at that."

She shook her head. "You confuse me with your manner of speech. But you are wrong—look at what you have accomplished. A treaty with the Gracktiles! Never would I have thought it possible to sit at a table and negotiate with those creatures."

"The trick, *Mom*," he said just to annoy her, "was figuring out why they wanted these worlds in the first place. They need the minerals we mine, we need their markets. If you'd ever bothered to ask—" He broke off when he saw her lips press together to suppress a smile.

"Already, you sound like a king, my dear."

The sound of booted feet marching in the outer hall brought his gaze to the tall, wooden doors. "Well, watch this king grovel," he muttered.

The door opened and a contingent of the castle guard entered. At their center strode Mariska, her slim straight figure held rigid, her eyes blazing. She was in a magnificent rage. *Good!* Let her stew in her juices for a minute or two more after the merry chase she'd led him. His gaze drank her in, thirsty for the sight. It had been too long since he'd last seen her aboard her small spaceship.

"You!" she cried out, halting five paces away from him, when a guard lowered his laser-lance to halt her progress.

Etienne waved the man back and folded his arms over his chest, staring at her, absorbing the fact that at last she was here.

Mariska cast a scathing glance at the guard, and then turned to Etienne. Her face screwed into a scowl very like a bulldog he'd once owned. "By what right did you have me arrested?"

He ignored his mother's muffled laughter and kept his gaze on the woman who'd caused him sleepless nights for weeks. "You deserted your post—again." Etienne nodded to the man, standing at the rear of the guards. "Commander Zahra reports that you filed an illegal flight plan and fled with your ship—my property now, by the way—weeks ago. What do you have to say for yourself?"

Her expression smoldered, a flush of outrage tingeing her dusky cheeks red. "I had a mission."

"Not one condoned by me."

One dark, elegant brow lifted. "How quickly you assumed your mantle of authority," she almost sneered. "After all that fine talk about not wanting to be a king— 'Let the people elect their leaders'," she mimicked.

"They did." He narrowed his eyes. "They elected me. If you'd been here, you would have known that."

He could tell his statement took a little of the wind out of her sails. She took a deep breath, no doubt to harness the anger still roiling in her eyes. "Well, congratulations then," she said, her words grudging at best. "I'm happy for you—and your wives."

That one betrayal of anger told him what he'd wanted to know. She was jealous! He could feel the tension of the last minutes roll off his shoulders. Etienne turned from her to take a moment to get control of the smile threatening to curve his lips.

His glance caught Commander Zahra's—who seemed to have a similar difficulty.

The man hid a grin with a cough.

Etienne scowled at him, then turned back to Mariska. "As to wives, your disappearance delayed my wedding."

Her jaw tensed. "I'd rather hoped it was all out of the way by now," she muttered.

"How could it, when I had a fightership go missing in the midst of delicate negotiations with the Gracktiles?"

"Negotiations?" Her eyes rounded. "What did you negotiate with those lizards?"

"Peace and a trade agreement."

Her mouth gaped. "I don't believe it."

"Don't believe what? That they were willing to parlay? Or that I could do it?"

She remained still for several moments, then her eyes grew moist. "I never had any doubt you were meant for greatness, Sire," she said, her voice soft.

Etienne swallowed, and the room and people around him seemed to fade away as he stared into her tearful eyes. "I wanted a peaceful world to raise my children, Mariska. No more wars for me. No more bloodletting on my watch."

She let out a shaky breath. "Well, now you have it."

He fought to keep his face a stern mask. "But what am I supposed to do about you?"

Her chin lifted, but she didn't offer a suggestion.

"You've committed an act of treason. May I ask why?"

"I had a special cargo to retrieve," she said through stiff lips.

"Was it worth your life?"

She swallowed, but her gaze didn't waver. "I wanted to give you a wedding gift."

Etienne rocked back on his heels. "Clear the room," he said, never taking his gaze from hers. When the last of the guards and his mother had departed, he spoke. "Explain yourself," he said, his voice gruff.

Mariska cleared her throat. "After you left my ship, I got to thinking about how difficult it must be for you in a strange place with so many people around you, but none familiar to you." Her eyes held a sadness that made his heart ache. "I asked your family to come here for a visit, or to stay if they like it here."

"My family? *Maman*, Arnaud?" He had to force the words past a throat suddenly thick with emotion.

She nodded and gave him a little smile. "And Uncle Jacques. He's forgiven me, by the way."

"As long as he wasn't expecting another probing," he muttered.

Her lips twitched. "No, he was quite willing to come this time."

"Mariska—" Etienne closed the distance between them. "I was worried about you. I never expected that you wouldn't be here when I arrived. And when they told me you left…"

Her eyes filled, and she shook her head. "You needed to find your own way." She glanced around the spacious chamber. "And it seems like you're acclimating well."

"No, I'm not. I've hated every minute."

She looked at him, a question in her eyes.

"I needed you."

Her lips parted, and she drew in a deep breath. "I missed you," she whispered, "but I couldn't bear to see you with the other women."

Etienne bit back a curse. "Do you see other women in this room?"

She shrugged. "I assumed they were in their quarters."

"That *harem* has been dismantled, and every woman released to her family or married to another of her choice."

She stood so still, he wondered if she'd understood what he'd just said.

This time he did swear and knelt awkwardly on his good leg, pressing his forehead against her thigh in a symbol he'd come to recognize as one of respect and obeisance to the ruler.

He gazed up into her startled eyes and took her hand in his. "In my culture, when a man wants a woman to be his wife, he kneels at her feet in supplication to ask her for the privilege."

Tears filled her eyes and rolled down her cheeks. She hastily scraped them away with the back of her hand. "I won't share you," she said, then sniffed.

"Goes the same way for me, *cher*." He pressed a kiss against her palm, then rose to stand in front of her. "Will you?"

She opened her arms to encompass the room, looking a little lost in the large space. "Your mother—"

"Has already filled the dining hall with people who are waiting for us to say our vows."

She glanced down at her brown uniform, and he grinned. Even on Euphrazha, brides worried about their dress. "If I tell you what the sight of you in that uniform does to me, will you come now—just as you are?"

"How about if I find out for myself," she said, sliding him a glance from beneath her eyelashes.

"By all means," he murmured, dying for her touch.

She chewed the corner of her lip, then reached and cupped his sex with her hand.

He couldn't help the sudden tightening her touch produced.

"He seems happy to see me. Why aren't you wearing your uniform?"

He snorted. "No way—I'd look like one of those guys in a ballet with his package out there for anyone to see." Then everyone would know about his almost constant state of arousal whenever she was near. He inhaled her scent and felt his body tighten further.

"I like your trousers—and I don't want anyone else looking at your...package. I wondered who started the new fashion." She withdrew her hand, giving him a little squeeze as she did.

Etienne caught her chin with his fingers, and tilted back her face. "You still haven't answered me," he said, his mouth a breath from hers.

"You don't have to ask," she murmured. "I'm yours to command."

"I wish everyone would stop saying that." His brows furrowed in a frown. "I want you willing."

"I've always been willing, Sire." This time the dimple peeked out from her cheek.

Etienne gritted his teeth. "You know that's not what I meant."

"Why should I lay my heart open when you haven't told me why you want me for your wife? Is it because you think I may have conceived? Well, I haven't."

"If *we* never conceive, it won't be from lack of trying. What the hell do you think I was saying when I knelt at your feet?"

"That you *want* me for your wife—it's what you said."

"Fuck me!" He blew out a breath, irritated and anxious.

She leaned so close her breasts scraped his chest. "Can we reconnoiter first?"

"Mariska?" His voice rose in warning.

She kissed him. "Why do you want me, Sire?" She kissed him again.

He groaned. "*Etienne*, dammit!"

"But we're not naked." There was no mistaking the light of mischief in her eyes.

He gripped the neck of her uniform and slid the material down to expose her breasts. "Now!"

"All right. *Etienne*."

"No. Now. Here, beneath me." He could barely force the words from his mouth. He had to be inside her—now!

"Are all our conversations going to end the same way?" She sounded irritated, but her hands tugged her belt open, and it dropped to the floor.

"We'll never talk—that way I won't ever be tempted to strangle you." He shrugged out of his jacket and pulled the shirt beneath it over his head. By the time his sight was clear of clothing, he noted she was already naked and grinning.

He opened his trousers and shoved them past his hips. Then he grabbed her by the waist and lifted her in his arms. Mariska wrapped her long legs around him and centered her sex over his cock.

Dipping his hips despite the sharp pull of muscle in his damaged leg, he entered her with one rough thrust. Then his hands settled on her hips and he held her immobile. "Tell me, Mariska. Tell me, or there will be no fucking."

"That's not fair. You can't stop now." She pressed on his shoulders trying to rise, but his hands were firm.

Held high against his body, her face even with his, she scowled so fiercely he almost laughed. "I said no fucking—not until you tell me."

"Yes, I'll marry you," she said, gritting her teeth. "Now will you give me the fucking?" She wriggled in his arms, trying to start the sliding motion he knew she craved.

"It's not good enough, Mariska. I want the words, too."

"Which words?" she moaned, her body quivering, her breaths coming in shallow gasps.

"Tell me you love me."

"You first," she said, her expression pained.

His smile broke through. "You're a very stubborn woman."

"I have to be. I want everything, Etienne."

"How about we go at the same time?"

She nodded quickly.

"All right, get ready." He jostled her a little to move his hands lower to cup her ass.

She dragged in a ragged breath and clenched her pussy hard around his cock. "I'm ready."

"Now!" he said, lifting her, then driving her down hard along his shaft. He gritted his teeth, fighting the urge to pump hard and fast inside her.

"I love you," she gasped.

"I love you."

"I said it first!"

"I'll say it more," he said rocking his hips, driving his cock inside her, again and again. "I love you, Mariska," he groaned, and squeezed her ass so hard he knew he left bruises.

She wrapped her arms around his shoulders and leaned back a little, angling her hips to take him deeper. "I love you," she keened, her voice rising higher. "Deeper, oh pleeeaase."

He ground his hips into her, rubbing close to scrape the base of his cock against her clit. "*Cher*, hold me tight. I can't wait!"

She cried out and her channel rippled along his shaft, pulsing as he exploded, cum erupting deep inside her body.

As his cock emptied, Etienne pulled her close, hugging her tight, not wanting to set her down. Not yet.

"I tol' him pussy make him happy."

Cursing, Etienne jerked his head back and stared toward the open door. Arnaud and Jacques stood there, grinning in the entrance.

"Your new *maman* tol' us to tell you to hurry it up," Jacques said, with an embarrassed shrug of his shoulders. "We'll tell her you did just that." He gripped Arnaud's arm and pulled him from the doorway, shutting it behind them.

"Your family is going to make life interesting here, Etienne," Mariska said, a smile curving her lips. "I really like your brother."

"Do you suppose they'll keep quiet about what they just saw?"

She shook her head. "Not a chance."

"Well, seeing as how we're already late..."

Her dimple deepened. "Are you thinking to add to my vocabulary?"

"Ever heard the phrase 'going down'?" he asked, quirking a wicked eyebrow.

Mariska's eyes glittered with happiness. "I'm assuming it has a meaning other than directional?" At his nod, she whispered, "Tell me."

"Better yet, I'll show you, *cher*."

# About the Author

Delilah Devlin dated a Samoan, a Venezuelan, a Turk, a Cuban, and was engaged to a Greek before marrying her Irishman. She's lived in Saudi Arabia, Germany, and Ireland, but calls Texas home for now. Ever a risk taker, she lived in the Saudi Peninsula during the Gulf War, thwarted an attempted abduction by white slave traders, and survived her children's juvenile delinquency.

Creating alter egos for herself in the pages of her books enables her to live new adventures. Since discovering the sinful pleasure of erotica, she writes to satisfy her need for variety—it keeps her from running away with the Indian working in the cubicle beside her!

In addition to writing erotica, she enjoys creating romantic comedies and suspense novels.

Delilah welcomes mail from readers. You can write to her c/o Ellora's Cave Publishing at 1056 Home Ave., Akron OH 44310.

# Also by Delilah Devlin

Ellora's Cavemen: Tales from the Temple III *anthology*
Fated Mates anthology
Lion In the Shadows
My Immortal Knight: All Hallows Heartbreaker
My Immortal Knight: Love Bites
My Immortal Knight: All Knight Long
My Immortal Knight: Relentless
My Immortal Knight: Uncovering Navarro
Garden of Desire
Nibbles 'n' Bits anthology
Prisoner Of Desire
Slave Of Desire
The Pleasure Bot

# TIGHT PLACES

Arianna Hart

# Chapter One
## *New York City*

Savannah Malone hated rain. Especially cold rain. Most especially at night after working a ten-hour shift in spike heels and a pencil-straight skirt that cut into her waist more and more as the day wore on. All she wanted to do was get home, get into her cozy pajamas, and have a glass of wine.

Was that too much to ask for? Apparently it was, because she'd missed her bus by a mere two minutes and had to wait in the rain with nothing but her purse for protection for another half hour before the next bus came.

Her stomach growled with hunger as she sloshed through yet another ankle-deep puddle on the way to her high-rise. A bolt of lightning flashed, illuminating the city around her. Savannah walked faster.

Digging her keys out of her pocketbook with half-frozen hands, she managed to open the door to the building and squish her way into the lobby without anyone witnessing her sodden state. She prided herself on always looking together, and right now she was anything but. If she had to look like she'd been dumped in a lake, at least no one was there to see her.

Thank God. Something went right for the first time all freaking day. Absently checking her reflection in the shiny elevator doors, Savannah almost groaned out loud. Her normally impeccable French twist was askew, with tendrils of wet hair clinging to her face. Streaks of mascara ran down her cheeks, making her look like a clown, and her white blouse was practically see-through.

Great. She was soaking wet, freezing, *and* looked like death warmed over. What a day. At least it was almost over. If the elevator would just get here. It was taking its own sweet time coming down to the lobby.

Five more minutes. She'd be in her flannel jammies in five more minutes. And maybe tonight she'd have a second glass of wine as a special treat.

The bell signaling the arrival of the elevator sounded abnormally loud in the empty lobby.

"Well, it's about time," she muttered as the doors slid open on a thankfully empty car.

She punched the button for the twenty-second floor with a bit more force than absolutely necessary.

"Hold the elevator!"

Savannah stuck her arm out to stop the doors from shutting, and tried to jam her finger on the "door open" button at the same time. Her purse fell from her shaking hands, spilling the contents all over the floor.

"Got it, thanks." A rich, male voice sent shivers down her spine.

Oh my God! It was the hottie from the penthouse!

In the elevator with her.

And she looked like she'd been hit by a truck.

"You're welcome. These things take forever to come back to the lobby." *Stop babbling.* Savannah took a deep breath and bent down to pick up her scattered belongings on the floor.

"Here, let me help you with that, since it's my fault you dropped your purse."

"No, really. It's fine."

Large hands with a light sprinkling of hair brushed hers as she picked up her lipstick. A bolt of pure lust shot from her hand straight to her pussy, lighting fires in her bloodstream along the way. She looked into his face and was captured by the bluest eyes she'd ever seen.

"Th-thank you." Savannah knew she was staring but couldn't seem to help herself. High cheekbones highlighted a masculine face with a touch of stubble on it. A strong jaw was softened by full lips and a dimple in his chin.

She was a sucker for dimples.

"That looks like everything." He winked at her and smiled.

As he stood to his full height, Savannah got a quicksilver view of muscled abs and rock hard thighs.

"Yes, that's everything." Although how she'd know when she wasn't even looking was anyone's guess. She'd been lusting after him from afar ever since she moved into the building six months ago. The close-up view was even better than the glimpses she'd seen of him from across the lobby.

*Come on idiot! Here's your chance! Don't waste it.*

"Savannah Malone, I live in 2217." She stuck her hand out to shake his

"Carrick MacNamara, I have the penthouse," he said, his hand engulfing her much smaller one. Another blast of heat slammed into her.

"Really?" As if she didn't know. "You must have a great view of the river from up there."

Before he could answer her, the lights went out and the elevator was plunged into darkness. Savannah stumbled against Carrick as the car came to a screeching halt. The part of her that wasn't cringing in embarrassment at knocking Carrick against the wall sighed in female appreciation at his steely chest.

"Are you okay?" His deep voice whispered across her ear, sending chills down her spine and making her pussy lips swell and moisten. "We must have lost power from the storm. The emergency generator should kick on soon."

Savannah hoped it took its time coming back on. She could stay pressed against his chest in the dark for the next lifetime.

* * * * *

The generator better kick on soon, or he was in serious trouble. Carrick couldn't believe his rotten luck. Of all the nights to get stuck on an elevator with the redheaded bombshell, it had to be on a full moon. Any other night he could control himself, but tonight, just the sight of her lacy, white bra showing through her shirt was enough to bring on the change in him.

The feel of those heavy breasts pressed against his chest wasn't helping his control much either.

A grinding jolt rocked her against him even harder, and Carrick gritted his teeth against the temptation to rub his growing cock against her soft mound. The emergency lights flickered on as the elevator started moving up again.

He looked down into her surprised, emerald eyes.

"There, see? No problem."

Reluctantly, he set her aside and tried not to stare at the hardened points of her nipples. It had been tough enough not to ogle her rear end when she bent over to pick up the contents of her spilled purse. Maybe the safest place to look was at the ceiling.

His nostrils flared as he caught the scent of her pussy juices mixed with rain and a hint of jasmine. The trip to the penthouse never seemed so long before.

"This seems to be taking a lot longer than normal, doesn't it?" Her voice was thick and slightly raspy, sending more blood to his dick.

"Probably on half power, or something." He didn't mean to sound so clipped, but it was getting harder and harder to hold back his instinct to explore just how turned on she was.

She might be able to hide her arousal from a normal guy, but not from him.

And it was driving him mad!

"Man, this is the perfect ending to a miserable day. I just want to get home and undress— change—and this thing is slower than taking the stairs."

Carrick's brain instantly flashed a picture of her stepping out of a bubble bath into a filmy robe, her face flushed with heat. His imagination tortured him with images of rosy nipples and creamy thighs. It took all his considerable strength to hold back a groan.

Lights flickered, dimmed, and finally died completely as the elevator shuddered to a stop once again.

"Not again!" Savannah cried in obvious dismay.

Carrick swore under his breath. "Let's not panic, I'm sure there's an emergency button around here somewhere. We'll hit that and someone will be able to get us out." He could probably get out through the trap door above him and climb the cables to the next floor, but that wasn't something he could do and keep his cover. Millionaire CEOs didn't rip open metal doors and claw their way to freedom with inhuman strength.

"I'll get it. I have a pen light in here somewhere." She fumbled around in her purse. "Here we go."

A tiny beam of light flashed in the dark interior, and Carrick got a brief look at worried green eyes before she turned the light on the control panel. Her hands must be shaking, because the beam wavered and danced.

"Nothing's happening. Isn't this supposed to have some sort of alarm bell? I know the time that kid on the floor below me hit it, the thing rang loud enough to wake the dead."

Shit.

"I thought the alarm was supposed to have a separate power supply, but maybe it's tied into the generator. I'm afraid I don't know too much about elevator mechanics."

"Well, you know a lot more than I do. If I didn't live twenty-plus floors up, I'd never take the darn things."

His sensitive hearing picked up the sound of her teeth chattering.

"Are you cold?"

"I'm fine. Just a little wet. I didn't realize it was supposed to rain today and I missed my bus so I got soaked. I'll take a nice, hot shower as soon as I get out of this sardine can, and be good to go."

The thought of her see-through blouse burned in his brain. His pulse hammered through his body and his loins grew heavy with need. The pull of the full moon pounded his self-control, and she was temptingly near. And aroused as well.

The pheromones his body emitted during the full moon must be working on her already. Christ, he had to get out of this elevator before he attacked her.

"Let me try," he said, pushing by her to the panel.

"Help yourself, but I don't think your finger pushing the button is going to make much more of an impression than mine did."

He didn't care if she thought him arrogant. He needed to get out of here!

* * * * *

Savannah breathed in the lemony scent of his cologne as Carrick brushed by her. She wasn't sure if she should be amused or annoyed that he thought she couldn't push an emergency button correctly. But maybe he was a touch claustrophobic too. Lord knew she didn't enjoy being trapped in this small space.

Her body shivered again, a combination of his nearness and her wet clothes. Her jaw ached from trying to keep her teeth from chattering. Thank God it was dark and he couldn't see what a mess she was. Wet stringy hair, running makeup, and sopping clothes clinging to her. What did she ever do to deserve this?

"I guess you're right. Looks like we're stuck here until the power comes back on or they fix the generator."

"G-g-great," she stuttered through chattering teeth.

"Good Lord! You're freezing!" He clasped her hands and began to rub them briskly.

"I-I'm fine." She shivered violently.

"No you're not."

Savannah thought she heard him swear under his breath, but wasn't sure. Her toes were so cold they were beginning to cramp in her high heels, and the pain distracted her from the man in the elevator with her. What a freaking night!

"Take this."

She heard a rustling of cloth and felt the weight if his jacket in her hands.

"If you take off your wet clothes and put this on instead, you should warm up in a snap." His voice sounded strained.

What did he have to be tense about? She was the one freezing to death, being told to take her clothes off in front of a total stranger. If she was going to get naked with him, she wanted it to be between clean sheets and with a box of condoms nearby.

"No really, I'll be fine." She handed him the jacket as more shivers shook her frame.

"Ms. Malone, I promise you, I'm not suggesting you take off your clothes for any prurient reason. It's basic survival. You'll be a lot more comfortable if you're dry."

"No kidding."

"I promise, I won't look." Laughter tinged his voice.

Savannah snorted. He could look all he wanted. It was so dark he wouldn't be able to see anything anyway. She was being ridiculous. Her muscles ached from the shivering, and her teeth couldn't take much more chattering without breaking her jaw. What he said made sense.

"I'll trust you to be a gentleman and not mention this to anyone," she said, unbuttoning her blouse.

"Scout's honor."

It felt strange and kind of exciting to take off her clothes in front of a gorgeous man as he watched. Even if he couldn't see anything, he *knew* she was stripping. Desire swept through her, sending tingles between her legs.

The wet blouse dropped from her shaking shoulders with a plop. The pencil thin skirt was next, and she peeled off her slip with it. The heels and panty hose went until she was wearing nothing but her lacy bra and thong.

"I-I'll t-take the jacket n-now."

"Sure." His voice was almost a growl.

His hands brushed hers as he gave her the jacket. More tingles shot through her body. Her pussy swelled and a trickle of fluid moistened her legs. She was standing next to the hottest guy in the building, wearing nothing but a bra and panties, was it any wonder she was turned on?

The jacket was still warm from his body and carried the same lemony smell, and something else too. A hint of musk that had nothing to do with manufactured scents, and everything to do with the man. Heat enveloped her as his essence surrounded her and seeped into her brain.

"Better?"

"Ummm, much. Thank you." She snuggled deeper into the jacket.

"Glad to help."

# Chapter Two

His night vision easily pierced the darkness of the elevator. He could see her pale body clearly as she took off each article of clothing and let it drop to the floor. With each garment she lost, the animal inside him grew. Her full, ripe body was inches from him, and his hands itched to touch her.

The smell of her arousal filled his mind and spurred the lust within him. His scent mingled with her hint of jasmine, blending and forming a new essence that teased the senses. She had no idea that by offering her protection and marking her with his scent, he claimed her as his. Any other Were in the city would recognize his mark. Werecats might not mate for life like werewolves, but no other cat would mess with his mate while he laid claim to her. And she didn't even realize it.

But his body did. The pull of the moon, the scent of her nearly naked, aroused body so close to his shredded his control like a tissue.

"Are you cold? I could share the jacket with you."

Carrick didn't feel the cold, even in the deepest of winter. His Were blood kept him warm all year long. But before he could protest, she'd opened up the jacket and snuggled against him.

The feel of her breasts pressed against his chest was too much for him to ignore. Need drove him to the edge of reason, and he jumped off without looking. A groan escaped him as he tipped her face up for a kiss.

Her lips were as rich and luscious as he'd thought. More so, even. She tasted of mint and heat, and he slipped his tongue in her mouth to explore further.

Savannah's hands traced his chest through his shirt, and he shuddered with pleasure. The shirt was a nuisance, he wanted nothing between his skin and hers. With a growl, he ripped the expensive silk shirt open until her hands could touch his flesh.

"Oh my!" she gasped against his lips. Her nails dug into his pecs, then brushed against his nipples. "You have a great body," she murmured before licking her way down his chest.

"Not nearly as impressive as yours." Carrick unsnapped her bra and let her breasts spill free into his hands. The creamy mounds were a heavy weight, and felt soft as silk. She had curves to spare and he wanted to explore every inch of them.

The feel of Carrick's hot hands on her breasts sent a fresh flood of need through Savannah. Cream drenched her thighs through the thong, and she rubbed up against the steely-hard erection he was sporting.

God! She'd never been this turned on in her life! His lips were a drug, obliterating any will to resist, and his hands, oh his hands were magical. The rough pads of his fingers pinched and teased her nipples while his palms caressed the lower slopes of her breasts. Savannah had the wild urge to push him against the wall and climb on top of him until he fucked her brains out.

Her blood was on fire and she was more than happy to get burned. His hand drifted lower to tease her through her underwear, and she wanted to scream in frustration. She didn't want anything between her skin and his. With trembling fingers, she undid his belt buckle and unbuttoned his fly. The rasp of the zipper was overly loud in the quiet elevator.

His penis jutted out, large and impressive. Savannah wished she could see it, but the pitch black of the elevator was unrelenting. Instead, she explored his cock with her fingers, marveling at the length and thickness. A shiver of fear and excitement chased down her spine.

She bent her knees to go down on him, but he pulled her upright.

"Allow me."

His hairy chest brushed against her stomach and thighs before she felt his hot breath over her soaking wet pussy lips. The air caught in her throat as his fingers slowly traced her clit through her underwear.

"Do you have any attachment to your panties?" Carrick asked, his deep voice thrumming through her body, adding to the ache growing between her legs.

"Right about now I hate them." She wanted him to touch her, damn it!

"Good."

She felt a slight tug, and then the snap of the thong tearing. Hot, wet lust rolled over her body like a tidal wave. Her pussy grew so swollen, every shift of her legs sent arrows of heat straight to her core.

Carrick's fingers parted her curls and traced her slick labia. "So hot, so wet," he murmured before sliding his finger inside her waiting sheath.

The rasp of his finger along her nerve endings made her knees buckle. He knew just the right tempo to use to push her to the edge but not take her over.

"Hurry!" she whimpered, as the heat grew inside her.

"I've barely started," he whispered against her clit before sucking the engorged nubbin into his mouth.

A scream built in her throat and she couldn't hold it back. Her hips bucked against him as her body supernovaed. Flashes of light danced behind her eyelids as waves of pleasure washed over her again and again. Still he didn't stop. Carrick lapped up her juices like a cat with a bowl of cream.

She tasted as delicious as he'd thought. Savannah's taste filled his mouth and rolled over his tongue like fine wine. Her cries of pleasure were music to his ears and a spur to his already charging desires. Carrick wanted to draw out her pleasure over and over again, but his control was slipping by the second.

If he could slam into the hot sheath of her body and find release quickly, he might, just might be able to survive without changing. Maybe.

It didn't matter. He *had* to have her. With one last lap of her clit he nipped and licked his way up her stomach and over her breasts until he could stand against her.

"I don't suppose you have any protection in that pocketbook of yours?" he asked her, sanity reasserting itself momentarily. As a Were he wouldn't transmit diseases, but she didn't know that.

"As a matter of fact..." She fumbled for her purse, dropping it twice before she found what she was looking for. "I've got three condoms right here. They were a joke from a friend of mine. Bless her heart."

Carrick couldn't have cared less why she had them, he was just glad she did. The rip of the foil package was followed by her hands on his cock.

"I hope it's big enough."

"They stretch." He had to clench his teeth to keep from growling at her to hurry. Her hands teased his length mercilessly as she eased the condom over him

"Good thing I do too." She cupped his balls gently.

This time, nothing could keep the growl back. It rumbled up from his chest as he hauled her against him. He leaned against the wall and ran his hands down to her sweet ass. Lifting her up, he probed her entrance with his cock as she wrapped her long legs around his waist. Her hands gripped his shoulders and her nipples teased his chest.

With a groan he sunk himself deep in her wet sheath, hilting himself in her warmth.

"Holy shit!" she cried.

He could feel her walls spasming around his cock. "You are so fucking hot!"

Her reply was a whimper of pleasure as her legs tightened around his waist and she rocked against him. His night vision clearly showed her upthrust breasts and the long column of her neck. The rapture on her face was complete.

His was only starting.

"Hold on tight," he ordered, grabbing her ass in both hands and slamming her down on his cock. His fingers squeezed the globes of her butt hard enough to leave bruises, but he couldn't stop. It was all he could do to keep his claws from digging in and claiming her *his* way. Another werepanther would understand.

Savannah wasn't a werepanther though. The thought sobered him slightly, forcing the beast back down.

"Oh God! I'm coming again!"

That wasn't going to help him maintain his control.

In desperation, Carrick clamped his mouth over hers in a feral kiss and drove his hips harder.

Her muscles squeezed him, milking the climax from deep within him. The force of it took his breath away. He held back a shout of his own as he spurted his semen with the force of a fire hose.

The beast subsided, appeased for now.

\* \* \* \* \*

Every muscle in her body was relaxed. Relaxed? Hell, every muscle in her body had the consistency of wet pasta. Somehow they had ended up on the floor of the elevator but Savannah had no idea when that had happened. She was propped against the wall, and Carrick knelt next to her.

His heavy breathing blended with hers in the still air. The brush of his hot breath over her heaving chest sent new tingles through her over-stimulated body. Had she ever come so hard in her life?

Nope.

Hell, even her vibrator didn't push her over the edge that hard or that fast. He was a frigging sexual dynamo in a three-piece suit.

And she was the manager of a restaurant.

An upscale restaurant, sure, but she wasn't exactly his social equal. People in his tax bracket rarely looked at the hired help. His shoes were probably worth more than her monthly salary. After they got out of the elevator, she'd be lucky if he even remembered her name. But she'd remember his, that was for damn sure.

If this was the only chance she'd have to be with him, then she'd make every minute count. And by God, when they got out of this tin can, she'd have enough memories to keep her company for the rest of her damn life.

Savannah's eyes were getting used to the dark. A little bit anyway. At least things looked gray now instead of black. She could tell he was kneeling next to her, and could almost make out his shape. Easing away from the wall, she took him by surprise and pushed him onto his back.

"Hey!" he barked as his head thumped against the floor.

"I'm not one for awkward morning-after conversations, are you?" She crawled between his legs and stroked his penis until it flared back to life. He'd gotten rid of the condom somewhere along the way. Boy, the cleaning crew would have all sorts of questions after this.

"It isn't morning yet." He inhaled quickly as she licked his rounded tip.

"I'm planning ahead." She sucked him deeply into her mouth, cupping his balls with one hand.

He tasted salty from his own fluids. The taste was the only clue she had that he'd already come once. His cock was as rock-hard as if he'd never spent himself. Hunger built in her core. Her pussy swelled even more, and she rubbed her slick lips against his hairy leg.

Relaxing her throat, she drew him in deeper and deeper. She wanted to taste all of him, suck his entire length into her mouth.

"Mother of God!" he shouted as pre-cum dribbled out of his tip.

Savannah sucked harder, trying to give him as much pleasure as she could in return for the pleasure he gave her. Releasing his sac, she pressed down on the nerves running from his scrotum to his anus.

Carrick uttered a guttural shout, and she could hear his hands scratching against the rug.

Sharp claws sprang out against his will. Savannah's mouth shredded his control. Her fingers teased and tormented him until the beast within broke loose. Fangs pushed through his jaw, but the pain of the change wasn't enough to snap the hold pleasure had on him. A ridge of hair sprouted along his back, and Carrick fought to keep from changing completely.

His balls throbbed painfully, preparing to release their contents, and he clutched the cheap carpet with his nails. When Savannah's fingers teased his anus playfully, any hope he had of holding off his climax went straight to hell. Tremors shook his body as hot cum shot from his cock. Savannah's mouth worked around him, pulling more and more out of him as he bucked against her.

The shout of relief that tore from his throat sounded too much like the snarl of a panther for his comfort.

"What the hell was that?" Savannah jumped back and looked around.

With her weak night vision she couldn't see his changes. He hoped.

Shit. He should never have let her touch him again.

"Maybe someone's working on the elevator. It sounded kind of like gears moving." *Yeah, right.*

"It sounded like a cat stuck in a blender! Do you think some poor cat is stuck inside the elevator shaft?"

"No." A cat stuck in a blender! He was relieved she didn't realize it came from him, but honestly! No one had ever accused his growl of sounding anything less than feral.

Savannah must have sensed his annoyance because she moved away from him. He could clearly see her fumbling for something to cover herself with, but perversely he didn't tell her his shirt was inches from her outstretched fingers. For one thing, it would blow his cover if she knew he could see perfectly in the dark, for another, he liked watching her breasts sway as she crawled around.

She was built like a brick shithouse. Large breasts with rosy tips, a flat stomach and curvy hips that felt too damn good against his. Her legs were long and lean, and a few drops of fluid dripped down her inner thighs as she crawled closer to him.

Maybe night vision wasn't all it was cracked up to be.

He tried to ease the changes back down, but once loose it was almost impossible to recage the beast. The full moon worked against him as well. He was a fool to let his desire for her overrule his good sense.

What an idiot. With anyone else, one round of hot sex would have taken the edge off and he'd have been able to hold off until they were rescued. He was lying to himself if he thought once would be enough with Savannah.

For months now he'd stalked her, waiting for just this opportunity to get her alone and charm her. Charm her?

Ha! He hadn't expected to get stuck on an elevator with her. His pheromones pushed her to the edge, and his hands had done the rest.

"I don't know what got into me," she said from the other side of the elevator. She sat, her back against the wall and her knees drawn up to her chest. His shirt covered her luscious breasts and his jacket draped over her knees.

Damn.

"I do." He smiled wryly as a blush stained her cheeks, but didn't comment on it. "When people are trapped in unusual circumstances they do things out of the norm. Your psyche is just reacting to the situation. It feels trapped so it's responding by doing all the things you want to do before you die."

"Oh really? Guess you don't have any self esteem issues."

"I'm not being arrogant, just giving you the facts. If it was any guy in here, you'd probably respond in a similar fashion." Not really, but if it made her feel better the lie could be forgiven. His pheromones worked against any inhibitions she might have harbored. The full moon made them particularly strong, and he'd wanted her since the minute she'd moved into the building. The combination of his inner desires and his Were instinct for procreation was too much for her to resist.

Whether she realized it or not.

"I don't think I'd have stripped down to my undies if it was Bob the doorman in here with me."

Carrick laughed despite himself. "I'm glad I rate higher than an eighty-year-old man."

She was shivering again. Did he dare warm her up? Even now, after two explosive climaxes, the lust grew in him. The higher the need built, the more difficult it would be to control the change. He was better off keeping his distance.

"How long do you think we've been in here?" Savannah asked.

Much too long. "I don't know. About an hour or so, I guess."

"Lord. That's a new record. I've never even kissed someone on the first date, and I've done way more than that with you in under an hour. Honest, I'm really not a loose woman normally."

She looked so embarrassed. Carrick's heart ached for her.

"I know that. And believe it or not, I don't usually have sex in elevators on a first date either. Let's chalk it up to the situation and agree not to cast aspersions on one another. Okay?"

A small smile crossed her face and her shoulders lost some of their tenseness. "Okay. It's just... I don't know. I don't want you to get the wrong idea about me."

"I won't. I can see you're a respectable young lady. You just hide the heart of a tiger behind tightly buttoned blouses. Don't worry, your secret is safe with me." A surge of possessiveness shot through him at the idea of her hiding that highly sexual side of herself from everyone but him. His muscles began to shift as the chain on his inner beast slipped some more.

Damn!

He had no business feeling possessive about this woman. And those thoughts would get him into deeper trouble.

"Well, I'm not the genteel southern woman my mama always wanted, but I'm not a tramp either," she laughed.

"I thought I detected a bit of a southern drawl in your words. With a name like Savannah, you could only be from Georgia."

"Yup, that's me. Grits to the core. Girl Raised In The South. I had a coming out party, went to cotillion dances and can drink red punch without getting any on my dress or my white gloves."

"Impressive. So what's a gently bred Dixie girl like yourself doing in the big bad city?" He eased closer to her, unable or unwilling to stop himself. Besides, she could use some of his body heat.

*Sure.*

"Oh, the usual. I wanted to get out from under my mother's thumb, so I went to college in New York. Graduated and decided to stay on. Now, if I could only get a job up here."

"You must have some job. You can't live in this building without one."

Her laugh caressed him like unseen hands. It was rich and sweet like honey. His cock jumped to attention.

"I sublet one of the tiniest apartments in the building from a friend of my father's. It's his way of keeping tabs on me. I probably pay half of what everyone else in the building pays. But yeah, I have a job. If you can call it that. I manage the Oak Grove."

"The Grove? That's pretty prestigious. I've had my name on the waiting list for months to get reservations for a dinner party. Hell, even the President of the United States has to wait to get a reservation there."

Savannah snorted. "Yeah, it's snooty alright. But when push comes to shove, it's no different than working at the diner back home. Same problems, different atmosphere."

"I'm sure Chef Armond would love to know you're comparing his dynasty to a greasy spoon," Carrick laughed.

"Are you kidding? I'll let you in on a little secret. I got the job there because I used to work with Armond at my little greasy spoon in no-man's-land Georgia. Only we called him Arnold."

"Bullshit! Armond is famous worldwide. He trained in France! The Queen of England raves over his food."

"Yeah, I know. Between you and me, Armond worked his way through culinary school slinging hash. He's a genius, don't get me wrong, he knows his way around a kitchen, but that French accent is as phony as my leather purse. Where did that end up anyway?" she asked absently.

"About a foot to your left," Carrick responded without thinking.

"How the hell did you know that?" Savannah grabbed her purse and turned in his direction.

"I have great night vision. I eat a lot of carrots." Shit! He'd relaxed so much he forgot to pretend he was as blind as she was.

"You'd have to be a damn rabbit to see that clearly. I can make out your shape, but can't see any details." She pulled the shirt closer around her.

"I can only see a little better than that. I, ah, bumped the purse when I was getting up."

"Oh." She relaxed a bit.

"So Armond is really Arnold from backwater Georgia."

Savannah looked at him a bit nervously. "Please don't say anything. He got me the job and he's a good guy. He only puts on airs because that's what people expect from him. And he really is a good chef. He's earned all the success he's gotten."

"Don't worry, what happens in the elevator stays in the elevator." God he hoped so.

"I guess that works to your advantage too."

"Oh?" Shit! Had she figured out his secret?

"Yeah. I doubt you'd want it getting out to your crowd that you had sex in an elevator with the manager from The Grove." She looked down and fiddled with the button on his jacket.

He took her hand in his and pulled her closer to him. "That's not something I'm ashamed of. In fact, I'd been looking for an opportunity to ask you out on a date."

"Get out of town! I've been here six months and I've never been within five feet of you." She bit her lower lip as if to bite back the words.

"I know, but I've watched you plenty. Although now that I know you work at The Grove, I have an added incentive to get to know you better." Like he needed any after she tore his control to shreds. "Maybe if I wine and dine you enough, you can move my name up on the waiting list." He brought her hand to his lips and drew her finger into his mouth.

"That could be arranged," she said with a breathy sigh. He could smell the desire coursing through her at his touch and it triggered his already rampant lust.

She leaned towards him, her eyes hot with desire, and the bottom fell out from beneath them.

# Chapter Three

Savannah's stomach lurched as desire slammed through her and the elevator fell. The combination of Carrick's mouth around her finger and the free fall made her lightheaded.

The car stopped with a jolt and she tumbled into him.

"What was that?" Her finger hurt where it scraped against one of his sharp teeth. Cripes, what did he have in his mouth anyway?

"They must be working on the cables. We'll probably be out of here in no time." His hand caressed her hip and drifted over the cheeks of her ass.

"Oh. Um, that's good." Wasn't it? She couldn't think with his fingers teasing the cleft of her behind.

Her nipples stood at attention, begging for his touch, and all her thoughts of proper behavior flew out the proverbial window. If this was her last chance to be with Carrick, she was going to take advantage of it. Hell, he was the one who said everything they did would stay between the two of them. Why shouldn't she give in to the urges she was feeling?

He didn't seem to be bothered by any such self-recriminations. Savannah pulled the shirt off her shoulders. A shiver ran through her as her naked breasts brushed against his hairy chest. The solid muscle of it took her breath away. He must find time to work out in between business meetings.

"You have the sweetest ass." His hands molded her cheeks, and one of his fingers darted in to tease the opening.

Savannah's blood boiled in her veins at his touch. Tingles spread from her pussy through her entire body. She rubbed her swollen nether lips against his steely thigh. The hair on his legs teased her nubbin and sent shock waves straight to her core. More fluid dripped from her as Carrick squeezed tighter.

"I could spend hours touching you all over. You're like a smorgasbord of all my favorite treats, and I don't know where to start," he growled in her ear.

"Don't let me stop you." Having him touch her for hours sounded pretty damn good to her.

In a stunningly quick move, he laid her flat out in front of him on her stomach. "There, now I can touch every inch of you and not get distracted by your clever fingers."

"You're not exactly clumsy yourself." How had he moved so fast? One second she was rubbing against his thigh, practically ready to come with little help from him. The next second, she was sprawled on her stomach and he was kneeling next to her.

He lifted her foot and massaged the arch.

"Oh my," she groaned. That felt so good after wearing heels all day.

"Did you know the foot is an erogenous zone?" He placed a kiss on her arch and continued to stroke it.

"Ah, no, but I'm starting to figure that out." Every touch of his hands shot straight to her aching pussy. Her clit throbbed with need for him, but he still confined his attentions to her foot. He was about as far away from where she wanted him as he could get, but what he was doing felt so good she couldn't complain.

Strong fingers pressed against the muscles in her calves, kneading away aches and pains from her long day. Carrick didn't seem to be in any rush to get to her dripping pussy. Savannah spread her legs wider, hoping he'd get the hint and use those fingers on something a bit higher up.

He either didn't catch on or was deliberately ignoring her, because his hands stayed around the backs of her knees. When his hot breath brushed across that sensitive area, she almost jumped out of her skin.

"Easy there, honey." His voice was low and throaty, almost a growl.

Ha! There was nothing easy about lying still while he licked and kissed his way up and down her legs. She felt him move between her spread thighs, but he only knelt there, he didn't move any closer.

God! She could feel the tip of his cock brushing against her thigh as he moved. This was torture! She wanted that cock slamming inside her, not teasing her with its nearness.

Carrick's hands moved higher up on her thighs until his fingers grazed the lower slopes of her ass. Slowly enough to make her scream, they slid back down again. Over and over he followed the tantalizing path, coming closer and closer to her pussy, but never touching it.

Savannah whimpered in frustration. He kept her on the razor edge of exploding, but never let her go over it.

"I can smell your cum," he growled, his lips against her butt.

Hot breath blew over her wet nether lips, and his voice vibrated through her pussy. Could you overdose on lust? Her heart pounded with need.

"There's plenty for you to smell." Her voice was faint, but she didn't care. She was lucky she could even speak.

His lips and tongue set her on fire as he kissed and licked his way around her butt. Every nerve in her body was on overload, and still he pushed her higher. As he drew closer to her pussy, she lifted her hips in supplication. Dear God, if he didn't touch her soon she would just die!

"Patience."

*Patience my ass!*

He chuckled and the vibrations made her shiver. Had she said that out loud?

One finger circled the opening of her swollen lips, wetting itself in her juices.

"You're so wet for me." He pushed his finger in slowly. "So hot."

Hot? She was a freaking inferno! A damn volcano just waiting to explode. His finger slid slowly in and out of her channel, scraping nerve endings as it went. His free hand pressed against her abdomen above her pubic bone and every pulse of his finger pushed her closer and closer to the edge.

Her breath came in tiny gasps, and sweat ran down her face as she strained to go over the edge before he stopped. Savannah almost cried when he drew his finger completely out of her pussy.

"No!" she wailed.

"Shh. I won't leave you hanging."

She wanted to cry in frustration. She was so damn close. He dipped his finger into her juices again, and then used it to lubricate her anus. Her muscles clenched automatically.

"Trust me, I won't do anything you don't want me to do. Relax." His finger stroked a trail of flames between her pussy and her rear, making her soften against him. She melted more than she relaxed.

Carrick pushed his finger back inside her pussy and added another digit, stretching her even more. Savannah pushed herself against his hand. It felt like flying, it was so good it made her dizzy.

"Trust me," he whispered, pulling her to her knees without removing his hand. She whimpered with need as he moved behind her.

His hand pushed faster in and out of her, and his other thumb pressed against her anus ever so gently.

Savannah jumped at the incredible pleasure of it. Her breasts swung below her, grazing the rough carpet and adding another caress to her overwhelmed senses.

"Come for me," he growled against her back, biting down hard enough to hurt.

Before she could yelp in pain the surge of her climax swamped her with its ferocity. Waves and waves of pleasure rippled out from her throbbing pussy, melting her bones to water on their way. Her hips bucked against his hand, wanting the tsunami to go on forever.

Before she could recover from the devastating climax, Carrick clasped her hips in his hands and slammed his cock inside her pussy, hilting himself completely. Another wave slammed into her battered senses, drowning her with its force.

"Again!" he snarled, slamming deeply inside her and bending down to capture her breasts in his hands. "I want to feel you come around me, your muscles milking me." His teeth sank into her shoulder and the pain mingled with the pleasure until she couldn't tell which was which.

The feel of his hairy thighs pressing against her ass and his chest rubbing along her back gave her a protected feeling, even as it kept her nerves buzzing. She felt surrounded and cherished, and hot as hell.

"Come for me, Savannah. You're mine." He bit her neck this time as he squeezed her nipples lightly.

With every stroke of his cock inside her, she flew higher and higher. When his hand slapped her ass, it was too much. Even if she had wanted to stop it, she couldn't have. An eruption of desire destroyed everything in its path and shot her mind into oblivion.

Barely conscious, her body shook with aftershocks as Carrick pounded harder and quicker into her pussy. His nails dug into her hips, but she hardly noticed. She was beyond caring what he did to her now. She knew she'd never be the same. Nothing and no one could ever compare to that experience.

"Yes!" he shouted from behind her.

Or at least she thought that's what he said. It came out as a savage snarl.

"Carrick?" There was no way she'd believe it was the elevator this time. That cat-like snarl had come from his throat. How, she had no idea, but it had.

He pulled out of her without speaking. The wet, slurping sound of his penis leaving her body sounded obscene in the silence.

"Carrick? What's going on?"

"Can't—stop—it."

"Can't stop what? Talk to me! Tell me what's happening." She reached for him in the darkness, but couldn't find him. "Where are you?" Her hand landed on something soft.

His jacket?

The lights flickered on and as she blinked away tears of pain from the bright light, she stared directly into the blue eyes of a panther.

\* \* \* \* \*

"Nice kitty." Savannah saw the something soft she'd had her hand on was the big cat's tail and snatched it away. She backed slowly to the corner of the descending elevator and reached for something to cover herself with.

Where the hell was Carrick? Risking a glance around the car she searched for him. He was gone.

"Carrick?" she called in a panic, hoping he'd spring out of thin air.

The panther let out a muted purr.

"Carrick?" she asked again, staring at the cat.

It cocked its head to the side and looked back at her. When its eyes drifted to her exposed pussy, it licked its chops.

"Holy shit! It is you." She grabbed his shirt and yanked it on.

Her head spun and she couldn't put a coherent thought together. She was in an elevator with a panther, who was the CEO of a multi-million dollar company.

And had just fucked her senseless.

"Is that really you?"

He purred again.

"I'm losing my mind. It's finally happened. Old crazy Aunt Lucy's genes went to me and I've gone insane." She clutched her purse to her chest and slid down the wall. The panther/Carrick took a step towards her, but she flinched so he stopped.

The ding of the elevator stopping sounded obnoxiously loud.

\* \* \* \* \*

Carrick lost sight of Savannah as a the doors opened and a crowd of people pushed inside. They were in such a hurry to get in they didn't spot him until they were in the car with him.

When the front-runners stopped dead the folks behind them kept pushing, knocking them to the ground. Cries rang out as people got trampled in the rush. Carrick snarled and jumped over the fallen victims into the crush of people waiting in the lobby.

People streamed into the building, rushing to get out of storm. He took advantage of their distracted state and raced for the front door. With a final snarl he dodged the doorman and shot out into the night. There was nothing he could do until the moon set and he could change back. Fear for Savannah raced through his mind as he ran down the wet streets.

Did she really believe what she saw? Or would she chalk it up to the insanity of the moment? Did she hate him now?

She'd looked so afraid when the lights came back on. Hell, he'd probably be afraid too if the person he'd been screwing turned into a wild animal afterwards.

But God, it'd been good. Even if word got out that Carrick MacNamara, high-powered CEO, was a Were, it was still worth it. He'd never felt like that before. That instant sense of connectedness. Like two pieces of a puzzle joining perfectly.

Fate had a fucking poor sense of humor. He'd been stalking Savannah for months and when he finally got his hands on her he scared the hell out of her. And he'd have to do it again before the day was over.

# Chapter Four

She got her hot shower and her glass of wine. Somehow they didn't make her feel much better. Savannah prowled the confines of her living room, her socks swishing silently on the rug.

What the hell had she done?

Were any of the night's events real? A reflection in the glass of the entertainment center caught her attention. She moved closer to get a better look. Just peeking out from the edge of her t-shirt was a perfect half-circle of teeth marks.

With two startlingly clear fang punctures.

*Guess it was real.* Savannah poured herself another glass of wine.

Sipping her drink she continued to pace, trying to sort out her thoughts.

Okay, let's put this in logical order. First, she knew she'd been alone with Carrick in the elevator. There had definitely not been a panther in the elevator with them before the power went out. Therefore, if Carrick was gone and a panther was in his place, it had to mean he was a were-creature. Panic threatened to overwhelm her, but she forced herself to stay on the path of logic. Curling up into the fetal position and jibbering in fear wouldn't help straighten out the situation.

Okay, Carrick was a Were. And she'd had sex with him. Mind numbing, shoot her to the stars, completely ruin her for any other man sex. And during that multi-orgasmic experience he'd marked her.

More than once.

Did that mean she was going to be a Were too? She took a peek out her sliding glass door. It was a full moon. It would take an entire month of wondering and worrying before she'd know for sure if she'd sprout fangs and grow her own fur coat. Great.

And she'd thought having to wait a few extra days for her period was nerve-racking.

Good God. When she fucked up, she did it big-time. No, she couldn't just have sex in an elevator with some run-of-the-mill hunk with whom she could laugh about it later. When Savannah Malone screwed up she did it full force. She had sex, multiple times, with the CEO of a Fortune 500 company, who just happened to be a freaking Were.

Where was that bottle of wine?

Flopping onto the couch, she resisted the temptation of getting rip-roaring drunk. It wouldn't solve anything and the wine hangover would be miserable.

Like the morning after wasn't going to be bad enough.

She'd have to face all those people who'd charged into the elevator—with her thong and panties lying out in the open—every time she left the apartment. There she'd been, wearing Carrick's shirt and nothing else, with a damn panther in the elevator.

Maybe she could just hide under her covers until her lease was up, then move in the dark of night.

Sighing heavily, she heaved herself out of the comfort of the couch and padded to the kitchen for a bottled water.

As she passed the foyer, the pile of clothes she'd dropped on her way in grabbed her eye.

Her wet blouse and skirt made a puddle on the tile, soaking Carrick's jacket and pants. His shirt was in the bathroom where she'd dropped it on her way into the shower.

Curiosity drove her to pick up the jacket again. Savannah breathed deeply of his scent and a spark of unwanted desire shot through her. He might be a great big cat, but as a man he sure as hell knew his way around a woman's body. Her breasts tingled in remembrance, but she pushed the feelings aside.

Reaching into the pocket, she found his wallet and a set of apartment keys. He'd be needing those eventually, wouldn't he? Which meant she'd have to see him again after all. A brief flicker of hope flared.

Wait a second, sister! Did she want to see him again? I mean, what if he turned her into a Were? Was that a good thing? She couldn't exactly call out of work three days a month because of the full moon.

Somehow, she didn't think the customers at The Grove would appreciate a panther in their midst either. Was there a way to control the transformation? How would she know if she was changed for sure? And what was all that talk about him wanting to date her for months?

She had a lot of questions for Mr. MacNamara.

Now she just needed to wait until he showed up.

\* \* \* \* \*

Savannah woke up with bright sun shining in her eyes and a foul taste in her mouth. She should never have had that extra glass of wine. Her head throbbed and muscles that had been dormant for longer than she wanted to remember felt sore and stretched.

For one blissful moment she remembered nothing of where those aches came from. Then reality came crashing down around her. Somehow, without her realizing it, she'd grabbed Carrick's shirt and brought it to bed with her.

His scent clung to the expensive fabric and mingled with her own. The combined fragrance made her heart trip in her chest and tingles spread downward to her pussy. How could she be mad at him and yet still want him?

With a groan and a curse she got out of bed and stumbled to the kitchen to make coffee. There was no way she could ponder such philosophical thoughts without caffeine. As the heady brew dripped and gurgled into the pot, Savannah brushed her teeth. The area around the bite on her shoulder was only a little sensitive to touch.

The orgasm she'd gotten when he'd bit her was more than worth any minor pain she felt. Her knees buckled as lust tore through her. So much for being mad at him. If he walked through her front door right now it would be all she could do to keep from jumping his bones.

As if her thoughts conjured it, a soft knock sounded. She crossed to the foyer slowly, and tried to gather her wits before she answered the door. Without even looking through the peephole, she knew it had to be Carrick. After all, she had his house keys and wallet.

With shaking knees, and an even shakier breath, she opened the door. Carrick leaned casually against the frame looking too damn good for having turned into a panther the night before.

He wore a snug white t-shirt and faded jeans. On his feet were beat-up loafers with no socks. His face was slightly stubbly, and he looked good enough to eat.

"It isn't very smart to open your door without asking who it is, you know." His deep voice vibrated along every nerve ending in her body.

"We're in a locked building. And besides, I knew it was you." She stepped back so he could come in.

"Then I'm doubly surprised you opened the door. About last night—"

"Would you like some coffee? I just made a fresh pot." A flood of fear made her cut him off. She hurried to the kitchen to grab some mugs. If he was going to tell her he was sorry, she could wait until after some coffee fortification.

"Sure. That would be great." Carrick watched Savannah move around the small apartment like a mouse in front of a cat.

She was only partially wrong.

Had he scared her that badly? She hadn't seemed so nervous when she first opened the door. It wasn't until he started talking that she ran off.

His nostrils flared at the smell of her. Some of his scent remained on her, even though she looked freshly showered. Possessiveness bloomed hot and heavy inside his chest. There had to be some way to salvage this. Some way to make her give him another chance.

Carrick racked his brain for a way to explain everything, but there was no good way to spin it.

*How about the truth?* a small voice in the back of his head taunted. Hell, she'd seen the truth up close and personal last night, what'd he have to lose now?

She handed him the steaming cup of coffee and their fingers brushed. Her emerald green eyes met his, and her pupils dilated with quick desire.

Maybe it wasn't just his pheromones that had worked on her last night?

"Do you take anything in your coffee?" Her voice was husky and her fingers trembled.

"No, thanks." He watched her avidly as she added milk and sugar to her cup and sat down at the tiny kitchen table.

"So. I guess you want your clothes and stuff." She made a move to get up and get them.

"Eventually. Sit back down. They can wait."

"Yeah, I can see that. Where'd you get the clean clothes? Last I saw you, the only thing you had on was fur." Her eyes challenged him.

"I have—friends who store some changes of clothes for me in case I get caught unprepared. I stopped there first."

"Ah. I see. I guess you couldn't very well walk around the city butt naked."

"I try to avoid it when I can." He took a sip of coffee and braced himself to open Pandora's box. "I imagine you have some questions for me."

Savannah snorted. "That's an understatement."

"Fire away. I'll answer them as truthfully as possible."

"That would be a nice switch." She stood and dumped the dregs of her coffee in the sink. "First, am I going to become a Were too? I don't know how all of this works, but I'm pretty sure you get changed from being bitten by a Were. And you bit me."

More than once. His dick sprang up at the memory. He clutched the coffee mug in his hands and fought for control. She deserved to know if she was going to switch. "No, I didn't break the skin deeply enough to exchange the enzyme that would cause you to become a Were. You won't have to worry about that."

"Well, that's one thing anyway."

She didn't seem overly relieved about his news. What else was she worried about? "What else is on your mind?"

Her hands fluttered along the thin chain she wore and back down to fiddle with her rings. She wouldn't look at him either. Finally she looked a foot to his right before speaking. "Would you have—you know—had sex with me if you weren't so close to changing?"

The leash on his control slipped another notch. "I might not have acted on my desires so quickly if I hadn't been fighting the change too, but I've wanted you for a long time. My need for you had nothing to do with the change, that only sabotaged my control." He stared at her until she met his gaze. He didn't want any misunderstandings. "If I had been stuck in that elevator with another woman, I wouldn't have lost all control over my lust or my form. In fact, that's the first time I've ever blown my cover during sex with a human."

"Oh." Her shoulders relaxed a bit and he could smell her juices beginning to flow. She wasn't immune to him, pheromones or no.

"Yes, oh. As you can imagine, it would be professional suicide for word of my nocturnal tendencies to get out."

"I'd never say anything! Honest!" She looked offended.

"I know that. I'm just trying to emphasize that I have never lost control before. Too much rides on my discretion. Only you have been able to break that control." He stood and crossed to her, invading her personal space. "And just being this close to you is doing it again."

"Really?" She released a breathy sigh. "I didn't think you'd want to see me again after we got out of the elevator."

Carrick brought his hand up to brush her cheek before sliding his fingers through her scarlet tresses. "Honey, you couldn't keep me away. All I could think about while I waited to turn back was that you'd refuse to see me. That I'd scared you too much. Or worse, that you thought I didn't care about you as a person."

"We didn't exactly have time to delve into deep, personal discussions." She licked her lips and it was all he could do not to lean down and taste her.

"No, but I know in my gut what I feel had nothing to do with the phases of the moon and everything to do with you. I want to spend more time with you, have those deep discussions. Hell, take you out to dinner and a movie, for God's sake."

His thumb traced the line of her cheekbone as she looked up at him.

"Dinner sounds nice. But do we have start at the dating phase? I mean, can't we skip the wooing and go right to the doing?"

She reached her arms around his neck and pulled his head down to hers. Soft lips teased and tugged at his slack ones until he snapped out of his shock and responded with enthusiasm. Carrick probed her lips with his tongue until she opened her mouth and let him in. The taste of her was like honey to his starved senses.

Had it only been hours since he last touched her? It felt like days. Weeks. He couldn't get enough of her. Her breasts swung freely under the thin shirt she wore, and he slipped his hands under it to cup the creamy mounds.

Savannah moaned low in her throat and rubbed her pelvis against his throbbing cock.

Carrick tore his mouth away from hers and captured her face in his hands. As much as he wanted to lose himself in the carnal pleasures she offered, he needed to make sure he was reading her right. "You're sure you're okay with this? It's not often I can't hold back the change, but you do something to me, lady."

"Good, cause you destroy any control I ever had over my body too."

"I don't mean that. I mean are you comfortable with the fact that I'm part cat and that I have to keep it secret."

She met his stare with one of her own. "As long as you don't try to change me, I'm perfectly fine with it. I don't know if I'm still caught up in all the emotions of last night, but all I know is that my biggest worry was that you'd say it was a one-time thing and I'd never see you again. I should probably care that you're a Were, but honestly, if that's what was at work last night, then I'm all for it."

"You might change your mind when you're thinking clearly again." The words stuck in his throat, but he had to offer her a way out. He didn't want her going into this with her brain clouded by passion.

"So might you."

"Bullshit! I know what I'm feeling," he denied hotly.

"So do I. You're not the only one who's wanted a chance meeting in the elevator."

Carrick stopped fighting the pull of desire and crushed her to his chest. "Thank God for power failures and tight places."

"You said it. But now I have another tight place for you to explore—in the full light of day."

Savannah undid his jeans, spilling his cock into her hand. Carrick growled as it jumped in impatience. He would not fuck her on the floor of her kitchen. Where the hell was the control he was so famous for?

"Bed. Where's your bed?"

"Down the hall, on the right." Her eyes were closed and her hand pumped his length.

Carrick scooped her up and ran down the hall before his need to be inside her overcame his need to lay her out on a bed and make love to her slowly.

The sun shone through her bedroom window and set her hair aflame as he laid her down gently on the rumpled sheets. Her hands reached to pull his pants down even as he pulled her pajama pants off. Bright red curls gleamed between her pale thighs, and his mouth watered with the need to explore her pussy.

"Hurry, hurry!" she whimpered, pulling off her shirt and reaching for his.

"What's the rush?"

"I want to see you naked. Last night I only felt you, and good as that was, I want to see all of you now."

Her words sent a fresh surge of lust to his groin. Carrick kicked off his jeans and sprawled on the bed next to her. "Look all you want—as long as you keep touching me."

"I don't think that'll be a problem."

Savannah ran her hands through the hair on his chest and teased his nipples with her nails. He sucked in his breath as her fingers drifted lower—and lower—until she grasped his cock again.

"You have a great body. I love all these muscles." Her tongue traced a ridge of his abdomen. "But I really love this. You have a beautiful cock." She smiled at him mischievously before drawing it into her hot, wet mouth.

"Uh, thanks." No one had ever said his dick was beautiful before. He didn't care what she said about it, as long as she didn't stop what she was doing. "You're killing me," he groaned. His balls were almost bursting with the need to come, but he held it off.

Carrick reached for her, pulling her head away from his dick and drawing her body up his. "I want to come inside your pussy, not your mouth."

"That can be arranged." She rubbed her breasts against his chest and poised her entrance over his tip.

"Aren't you accommodating," he said, thrusting himself up inside her dripping channel.

She threw her head back, and the sun danced lightly over her creamy breasts. "It's that southern hospitality."

"Must be." Carrick couldn't say much more because all the blood had left his brain. She rode him hard, pumping her hips up and down and gripping him with her inner muscles. Her breasts bounced in front of him, teasing him with their nearness. He grabbed her hips to try to get her to slow down the pace so it wouldn't be over with so quickly, but it was too late.

"Don't stop now!" she cried. Her nails dug into his pecs and she pushed harder against him, grinding her clit against his pelvis. "So close."

Carrick reached between them and stroked her nubbin as she pounded above him. Her face glowed with rapture as the orgasm overcame her. Seconds later, her squeezing muscles milked his own climax out of him. His stream shot out into her body and his hips bucked against hers, trying to get every last ounce of pleasure.

Savannah collapsed on top of him, her body still quivering. He stroked her smooth back softly, luxuriating in the feel of her on top of him and clean sheets under him. Who would have thought getting stuck in an elevator would lead to finding his mate? There was something to be said for the comfort of tight places.

# About the Author

Arianna Hart lives on the East Coast with her husband and three daughters. When not teaching, writing, or chasing after her children and the dog, Ari likes to practice her karate, go for long walks, and read by the pool. She thinks heaven is having a good book, warm sun, and a drink in her hand. Until she can sit down long enough to enjoy all three, she'll settle for the occasional hour of peace and quiet.

Arianna welcomes mail from readers. You can write to her c/o Ellora's Cave Publishing at 1056 Home Ave., Akron OH 44310.

# Also by Arianna Hart

By Honor Bound *anthology*
Lucy's Lover
Rebel Lust
Silver Fire

# *Pleasure Port 27*

Kate Douglas

# Chapter One

Evan shifted the window blinds to one side, tilting the metal strip just enough to allow the eye of the telescope entrance. He took a long time adjusting the focus, getting it just right, making it perfect.

She was there. She was always there at night, her heavy drapes open as if in invitation, lighting just so, the mirrors positioned as if she had him in mind. Sometimes he wondered if she'd subconsciously invited him, if she knew he watched.

If she performed, just for him.

Leaning closer to the eyepiece, he pushed his unruly hair out of his eyes. He adjusted the towel covering his bare hips and legs.

He watched.

And waited.


Mira checked her make-up, applied a bit more blush to her high, well-defined cheekbones, ran her hands along the form-fitting gown that barely covered her hips, and stared at the closed door to the apartment.

Her first of the night would be here any minute. She sighed, wondering what he might want from her, wondering what it would feel like to actually care about the man she fucked.

She'd been doing this so damned long. She glanced back toward the mirror, saw nothing but perfection—a slim woman who appeared to be in her mid to late twenties, long of leg with fair, almost translucent skin and thick blond hair falling straight and heavy to just below her waist. She ran a finger across her eyebrow, smoothing its contours, and once more studied the door.

No one. She looked at the slim watch on her left wrist, noted the time at just before nine. If he wasn't here in five more minutes, she might begin to worry, but so far he wasn't really late.

She was used to travelers showing up early for their appointments. Each was allotted the standard three-hour visit and they rarely took a chance arriving late. Mira's interstellar reputation meant she always kept her nights booked.

Lately, though, she'd felt anxious, uneasy. At first she thought someone was watching her...maybe quality control from the head office? All it took was a single complaint and she knew she could end up deconstructed just as easily as she'd been constructed.

Did her customers sense a change in her? Was the perfect body she'd been endowed with no longer attractive? Was she growing less desirable, looking used up...old?

*Never.* She knew better, though she'd held this post longer than most. Constructs eventually aged here on Earth, but on her home world her productive life span with her perfectly endowed body would still far surpass that of the normals.

A slight tapping drew her out of her musings. Smiling, she shook off the vague sense of unease, sauntered across the room and opened the door to her first visitor of the night.

Evan adjusted the focus on his telescope and sighed as the tall blonde opened the door. The men who came to her were all huge, ruggedly handsome, not the type he'd figure on needing a prostitute. This one was no different.

He was shrugging out of his odd coveralls before the woman had even closed the door. Evan's breath caught in his throat as he watched the now familiar ritual — the blonde's long fingers slowly sliding across the man's broad chest, the look of anticipation on the face of yet another male sharing the favors of the most perfect woman Evan had ever seen in his life.

She tugged the man's suit down over his lean hips, following the trail with her mouth. Within moments, she knelt before him, their bodies a perfect tableau in the lens of Evan's powerful telescope. The man's un-circumcised penis twitched and bobbed in front of her mouth, almost knocking against his flat belly, but she waited, licking her lips and smiling up at the visitor.

Evan felt the tight curl in his belly and shifted himself in his chair. He stroked the smooth frame of the telescope as if it were his cock, heating the cold metal beneath his large hand.

When she finally took the man's penis in her mouth, Evan sighed. Good Lord, she was gorgeous, her throat convulsing as she swallowed the guy's cock deep, her cheeks hollowing with each suck and pull, her eyes closed in obvious pleasure.

The man tangled his hands in the mass of long blonde hair spilling over her shoulders. He kneaded it in rhythm with the woman's mouth. Her hands swept over his lean flanks, the one nearest Evan slipping around the firm curve of the guy's muscular ass, the other sliding down between his legs.

Her hair blocked much of Evan's view, but from past experience he knew exactly what came next. His body clenched in almost unbearable anticipation.

Suddenly the man's body stiffened, his hips thrust forward as he buried his cock in her mouth. Her throat worked convulsively until his entire cock disappeared between her lips, the rippling, swallowing motions easily visible in the telescope's powerful eye.

Her left hand moved against the man's buttock and Evan imagined the thrust and jab of that long, perfectly manicured finger slipping in and out of his tight ass. Her other hand held the man's testicles as he climaxed.

Evan tried to imagine how that would feel. Was it a smooth, squeezing rhythm? Did she hold him softly or crush the tender sac to the point of pain? Were her fingers tickling that sensitive spot of flesh behind the man's balls, or wrapped fist-like around them?

Suddenly, his mouth wide and gasping for air, the man slumped forward, resting his hands on the woman's shoulders. She slowly pulled her head back until his flaccid cock popped from between her full, red lips.

Evan watched as she licked the last few drops of semen from the tip, his heart aching, his thoughts a painful combination of guilt and regret.

He sighed as the image faded into a bright blur.

Once more he'd managed to fog up the lens.

\* \* \* \* \*

Mira licked the man's cock clean, barely aware of the taste. They all tasted pretty much the same anyway, though she recalled a time in her long career when she'd noticed each man's unique flavor and had rejoiced in it.

Now this was merely a job, one she'd been genetically engineered to fulfill, one she should enjoy for many years to come. Where had the joy gone? What was happening to her?

She glanced up and saw pale starlight though the open window. She tried to guess which one was home. Once a man had pointed to a star far to the north and said it was closest to their world. She couldn't imagine choosing to travel so far, leaving everything familiar to go off and explore new worlds.

Of course, she'd traveled to this one, though she'd had no choice and didn't recall the journey. Newly created, she'd been placed here on Pleasure Port 27 for the sole purpose of easing the strain of star chasers, those extraordinary space pilots who traveled the known—and often unknown—universe, slipping between dimensions as easily as they traversed worlds, always searching for new goods to trade, new civilizations to conquer.

Three different men a night, almost every night. The routine rarely varied. The men were all clean, attractive and free of disease. Of course, if any of them arrived at Pleasure Port 27 with any kind of bacteria, illness or injury, she had the ability to cure, repair and heal.

Just another duty for a pleasure port construct.

A strong hand grasped hers, and the man helped Mira to her feet. He stepped out of the skinsuit she'd left tangled around his ankles and led her to the large bed.

Slowly he lifted her gown over her head, as if he savored each inch of skin he uncovered. She reveled in his sigh of appreciation, the soft smile hovering about his full lips. Smiling seductively, she thrust her breasts forward in a well-practiced invitation.

Neither one of them had spoken, but there was no need for words. He knew why she existed just as well as Mira did. Without instruction, she lay back on the silken sheets, spread her legs wide and tilted her hips, mimicking the age-old rhythm of procreation while she slipped one finger between the wet and ready folds of her sex.

She'd never understand why some men more than others seemed to enjoy watching her fuck herself. Not all of them, but this one obviously loved it. He'd already taken his partially erect cock in one meaty fist, sliding his fingers back and forth over the smooth skin in a slow and steady motion that matched her speed.

He grinned at her and Mira smiled back. Nice. This one appreciated her skills. Some men just wanted a couple of hard, fast fucks, maybe a quick blow job. A few wanted anal sex, and there was always the occasional weird one who showed up and just wanted to talk.

It was a pleasure to have a man who relished good sex, especially with a woman whose body was literally designed for the carnal arts.

His cock was huge now, already bigger than when she'd taken him in her mouth, the foreskin fully retracted around his sizable girth. She buried two fingers deep in her pussy and closed her eyes for a moment of pure pleasure, then slipped her fingers out and raised them to her mouth.

The man grabbed her hand and sucked both her fingers between his lips, encircling them with his tongue as if he savored each drop of her juices. Mira raised her hips in open invitation and glanced at the clock. They still had almost two and a half hours. She wondered if he might be good enough to make her come. They had plenty of time, but it was such a rare gift. She'd almost forgotten what real sexual satisfaction felt like.

Breathing hard, Evan adjusted the focus and quickly wiped the steamy lens with a tissue. He loved the way she had her room arranged, so that the foot of the bed tilted perfectly toward his window.

The large man had stood beside her, his hand squeezing his cock, his other hand fondling his own balls, but the woman had shown Evan everything. Lying back on a mound of pillows with her knees slightly bent and legs spread wide, she'd fucked herself slowly with her fingers.

Damn, she had the most gorgeous pussy he'd ever seen. It was cleanly shaved, and the folds of flesh glistened a deep rose, the lips thick and wet with her fluids. He wondered what she'd taste like and tried to imagine putting his mouth on her, sticking his tongue as far inside as he could while he slipped at least one finger up the tight channel of her ass.

He'd seen her take men that way, men with bigger cocks than his, but he wasn't sure how much she enjoyed it. She always acted like she loved every act, every man with equal emotion.

He wondered if she could ever love him?

The question faded from his mind as he watched the man climb between her raised legs, hiding the view of her beautiful sex from Evan's line of sight. Now all he could see was the man's tightly muscled ass, his heavy testicles swinging between his legs as he thrust his cock into the woman.

Evan took another deep breath and pulled the telescope out from between the metal blinds. They rattled and banged against the window when the lens caught one edge, but he twisted it loose and set the telescope aside. He brushed his hand across his lap, smoothing the towel over his flat belly and even flatter groin, then leaned back against the headrest on his chair.

Watching another man screw the woman he'd begun to think of as his own wasn't entertaining at all. He wanted to see her face, not some nameless jerk's ass, wanted to watch her hot, quivering sex, not another man's body tightening with an orgasm she'd so unselfishly given him.

Evan thought about that a moment. In all the time he'd watched her, he'd never once seen her come.

She had to know he watched.

Maybe she waited for him.


Mira caught a reflected motion in the big mirror beside her bed. Without breaking rhythm, she tried to focus on the image and suddenly realized she was watching someone watch her!

Lifting her hips to each thrust, she kept her partner entranced with her practiced body while she traced the reflected image to the apartment directly across the street from hers. A flash of light from a passing car glinted off a round lens, then disappeared as the window blinds settled back to a smooth, dark surface.

Whoever, whatever had been spying on her, no longer watched. She turned her attention back to the man thrusting deep inside her body, and remembered to tighten her muscles in perfect counterpoint to his strokes.

Her directive from the company was explicit and to the point. Discovery was not an option. Whoever studied her, for whatever reason, must not be allowed to live.

A quick burst of adrenaline flashed through her body and tightened her with a sensation she'd not felt for years. Her breasts suddenly tingled with new sensitivity, her large nipples peaked into tight points. Riding the man's huge cock, Mira's body surged close to his groin and she rubbed her sensitive clit hard against the root of his cock.

The climax caught her by surprise, lifting her hips closer, tighter as he drove hard and deep inside her spasming folds. Panting, gasping, her hands clutching at his broad shoulders, she cried out just as he joined her, surging deep with a long, low growl of his own.

Her partner collapsed over her shivering body, then rolled his heavy frame to one side. He grinned at her. Playfully, he flicked one of her nipples with his fingertip, fully aware he'd just done something not many men could manage—he'd brought a pleasure partner to climax.

Mira stroked his shoulder as she struggled to catch her own breath, then slowly tilted her head to one side. She saw their sweat-soaked bodies reflected in the floor-to-ceiling mirror.

And in the small reflection of the window across the street, once more she saw the round, smooth glare of a lens. Her nipples tightened even more. Her breath caught, released, caught again. It took an act of will to look away from the lens.

Mira's body trembled, but she wasn't sure if it was anger or excitement affecting her most. She tried to figure out her own response, the fact she'd climaxed with the full knowledge someone watched.

Her partner stroked his hand along her thigh, then buried his fingers deep inside her soaking pussy. Her muscles clenched, holding onto him. She put her silent watcher out of her mind and turned her full attention back to the man who owned her favors for this next two hours.

She had two more scheduled for the remainder of the night. The thought of performing for her unseen audience was oddly unsettling…and tremendously arousing.

She could close the curtains.

She could even turn out the lights.

Or, she could let him watch while she studied her own reaction, then make him pay for it in the morning.

Since he had just this one night left to live, Mira decided to make it a good one.

# Chapter Two

She'd intended to march across the busy street and give her voyeur hell before she killed him. Unfortunately, her third caller this night had shown a penchant for really rough sex. Mira knew it would take her a full day's sleep to recover, if she ever got out of the shower.

The hot water blasted her breasts and belly, easing some but not all the aches from her bruises.

Her watcher would have to wait to die...at least until she healed.

Oddly enough, she'd climaxed with her second man after fairly boring, vanilla sex, something that never happened. Of course, she'd made it a point to keep an eye turned to the window across the road where the round eye had watched her.

It was gone by the time her third man arrived. She'd actually wished he'd been watching then, if only to see if her voyeur was the reason for her earlier climaxes.

*My voyeur.*

She grinned in spite of her badly split lip. She was growing possessive of her watcher.

There'd been no orgasm with number three. Merely a torn and bleeding ass where he'd forced entrance, a couple of cracked ribs from her aborted retaliation against the brute and a case number after she'd reported him to the company's head office.

Pleasure partners were well built, well trained and very expensive. It was not a good idea to damage one.

She flipped off the water and grabbed a towel, then wandered back into her bedroom. The apartment across the street was in shadow. She looked into the reflection of the mirror, unwilling to actually stare in her search for the telescope's eye. She couldn't tell if he watched or not, but suddenly, in spite of the pain, Mira felt the first tingling rush of sexual excitement.

He definitely had to die, but not necessarily right away. Smiling, she slowly, reluctantly, pulled the drapes shut and crawled into her bed.

Shocked, Evan pulled the telescope back from the window. Her body was bruised, her lip swollen and split. Somebody'd hurt her last night. Badly.

It had to have been her third john because he'd watched the second guy until the man left, even though all the two of them did was screw a couple of times. If he had her, Evan knew he wouldn't waste their time on the missionary position, not with a gorgeous woman like her.

He'd want her every way possible, all night long. He'd want to know he was the only man she'd need. As if that was ever going to happen!

She took three men a night, each for three hours. He'd studied her long enough to know her schedule by heart. He wished he could watch her all night long, but even a voyeur needed sleep.

*Voyeur.* That's all he was. A watcher, not a doer. A pathetic shell of a man, if he could even call himself a man. Sighing, suffused with guilt, Evan realized his gaze had once again settled on the loaded pistol sitting beside his bed. He found himself staring at it more often lately, finding an almost sexual allure to the smooth metal of the barrel, the fine-grained wood of the handle.

The gun was heavy, the grip a perfect fit. He closed his eyes, imagining his fingers wrapped around the cool wood, waiting while it warmed to the temperature of his hand. He thought of the muscles he'd use to raise the muzzle to his temple, the way his finger would twitch against the trigger just before he fired, the cool ring of steel against his skin, the sharp retort he probably wouldn't even hear.

Sighing, he closed his eyes and bowed his head, aware that the nightly view of the woman across the street was all that kept him alive.

Now she was hurting. He thought about going over to check on her, to make sure she was all right.

*And how do you explain knowing about her bruises?*

If she didn't appear tonight, he'd take that risk. Even slipped the telescope into its case and prepared for work. He knew he'd think about her all day.

Mira was jolted awake by a knock on the door. She'd overslept! Her first man of the night was here already and she hadn't even brushed her teeth or combed her hair.

*Unforgivable.* She leapt out of bed, took a quick look in the mirror and saw that her bruises were gone and the split lip nicely healed. No wonder she'd slept so hard. Healing took a lot out of her. Even her ribs felt fine, and she was certain at least two of them had been cracked.

Another tap on the door, harder this time.

"Coming." She belted a robe around her waist, bent over and fluffed out her waist-length hair then flung it, properly tousled, back over her shoulder. When she finally glanced through the peephole, she sighed with relief.

This was one of her regulars, a fairly nice guy with a most amazing tongue. Though he'd never brought her to orgasm, she'd always enjoyed his attentions. She opened the door and stepped aside. He nodded and immediately began to unfasten his skinsuit.

Smiling, Mira opened the curtains wide. Now she knew exactly where to look, she spotted the eye of the telescope immediately.

Her pussy clenched and she almost laughed out loud. She'd never once dreamed she was an exhibitionist, but something about the unmoving eye, watching her in secret, made her hot. She shimmied out of her robe in full view of the window, palmed her breasts with a smooth, practiced sweep of her hands, and turned to her visitor.

Swaying her hips as she walked, Mira strutted for her watcher. She moved close to the man, more aware of the eye of the telescope than the male staring at her out of wide, surprised eyes as she stalked him like a hungry tiger.

Her watcher had this one last night to live. She might as well give him a good one.

She'd be sorry when he was gone. Knowing he watched excited her. Made every move more thrilling, every touch more sensitive. She knelt in front of her surprised man and wrapped her hands around his lean hips, drawing him to her mouth.

She'd never gone down on this one before. He'd never asked, she hadn't offered. She noticed, with that small part of her mind not concentrating on the glass eye watching her, that he wasn't shying away.

His cock was long and thick, the sac hanging below, full and lightly furred. She lifted his balls in her palm and heard the soft moan that escaped his lips.

A sense of power infused her. One man watched her and found pleasure, another accepted her touch and found even more pleasure. She shifted her stance just a bit, enough so that she and her client created a perfect silhouette. Still cupping his testicles with one hand, she used the other to guide his swollen cock between her lips.

The moment she wrapped her mouth around him, his hips thrust forward, almost choking her.

"I...I'm sorry." The words were choked, strangled sounding. "You surprised me."

She slipped her mouth away from his engorged cock. "Would you like me to stop?"

"Oh...no. No! Don't stop. Please, don't stop."

His hands fisted in her hair and she drew him once more between her lips, suckling hard and deep, swallowing as she pulled him into her mouth, down her throat.

The moment she had him, all of him, enclosed within her mouth, she opened her eyes and looked up. His head was thrown back, his lips stretched wide in a pained grimace. He breathed in short, sharp gasps. Mira smiled around the throbbing penis filling her mouth and throat, then began to slide him in and out, sucking hard, harder until her cheeks drew in and her tongue tightened along the base.

She heard him whimper, felt his legs tremble, knew he wouldn't last much longer. Suddenly, his body jerked and his hips thrust forward. She bit down hard, trapping his cock between her teeth, within her lips, holding him with her tongue.

He bellowed, a cry of pain and pleasure, his hips thrusting, fingers digging into her shoulders. She took his release, swallowing, holding his testicles in her palm, scratching at his buttocks with her free hand.

He cried out again, thrust deep into her throat, his body twitching and trembling in smaller and smaller spasms. Finally, with a small, broken whimper, he leaned over her, pressed down on her shoulders, and slowly withdrew his cock from her mouth.

She looked up at him, saw that he was okay, then smiled at the open window. She raised her hand, wiped the smear of semen off her cheek, and returned her attention to her shell-shocked customer.

This guy was going to get the most amazing three hours he'd ever spent at a pleasure port. Her watcher wouldn't be disappointed.

It was the least she could do before she killed him.

\* \* \* \* \*

Evan wiped the sweat from his brow with a clean handkerchief, and pressed his eye to the glass once more. She was working the second guy of the night. He couldn't believe she was working at all, as badly beaten as she'd appeared last night. She must be on some kind of powerful painkillers to go at it the way she was tonight.

The first man had left after three hours of absolutely mind-boggling sex. This one looked ready to drop, but she kept bringing him back for more. They'd done it at least six times in two hours.

The woman was amazing. She was also watching him watch her. He wasn't sure when he'd finally realized she was aware of him, but once he figured it out, there was no doubt.

Evan felt a great sense of relief, unexpected but welcome. He was afraid he'd truly become the voyeur, had developed some perverted need to watch without being seen. Knowing she was aware of him, knowing she practically performed for him, made him feel almost a part of each intimate act.

When she stroked the john's ass, he imagined her hands on him. When her full lips encircled an engorged cock, Evan practically whimpered with the sensation.

Lost in her world of sex and sensuality, Evan almost missed the second man preparing to leave. The woman always disappeared from his view for a few minutes. He assumed she took the time to bathe or at least refresh herself between customers, because each man was met by an absolutely gorgeous, fresh-looking woman.

Normally, he would have gone to bed by now, but there was something extraordinary about this night. He focused the telescope just in time to see her walk back into his line of vision. She stopped, turned, pulled her robe aside to expose one full breast, then slowly, seductively, making the most of her beautiful green eyes, she winked.

Winked!

Evan almost dropped the telescope. He knew it wobbled because he heard the shutters rattle, but he had his eye back against the lens in time to catch the woman walking to the door with an exaggerated sway of her hips. Just before she reached for the knob, she turned and blew Evan a kiss.

He burst into uncontrollable laughter. Tears leaked from beneath his lashes until he gasped for breath. Dear God, he hadn't laughed like this in years…seven years, to be exact.

*Oh shit.*

*No.* He didn't want to think about that now, not now when her hand was turning the doorknob and her last guy of the night was probably standing just outside. Not now when he knew she was aware of him, obviously didn't mind the fact he watched.

He glanced at the clock by the bed. 3:00 a.m. Damn, if she stayed on schedule, she'd be busy until at least six. He'd never make it into the office at this rate.

*So, I'll call in sick.* It wasn't as though he didn't have an excuse. Turning the eyepiece a fraction of an inch, he tightened the focus just as the woman led a large, muscular man across the room. She turned him perfectly so that Evan had an excellent view of her face, then knelt and drew her customer's cock into her mouth.

Once more, she serviced the man as if she hadn't had sex in months, as if she were starved for the taste of his ejaculate. Once more, she performed flawlessly, keeping her eyes on Evan even as she suckled her man to orgasm.

At some point, when she was on her knees with the man's cock in her mouth for the second time, or maybe it was later, when she knelt on all fours and the man took her from behind, when she fixed her gaze on the eye of Evan's telescope, her full breasts swinging with each lunge and thrust, Evan realized he was crying.

Tears ran slowly down his cheeks, blinding him to more of her beauty. He was still sobbing quietly when she finally sent her last man home and closed the shades.

Hours later, he awoke in the semi-twilight of his room. Sun filtered dimly through the blinds, his head ached and the first thing he saw was the handgun on the table by his bed. He stared at it, wondering what had awakened him, aware on some level that all was not right.

Suddenly the door burst open. It hit the opposing wall with a loud *crash*, then bounced back against the outstretched hand of the blonde in the doorway. She stood there like an avenging angel, her body encased in a skimpy silver suit of some odd type with form-fitting black leather boots that reached almost to her thighs.

A weapon of some sort was strapped to one hip and her hair was no longer hanging long and straight, but was instead bound behind her in a tight knot at the base of her neck.

Evan leaned back in his chair to see her eyes. Damn, they were as green as new grass, and while the look on her face was pure anger and aggression, he thought he saw something more, something almost like regret in her eyes.

"Enjoying yourself? Like the show?" She sauntered into his room, closing the door carefully behind her. He was partially hidden in shadows, so he reached for the switch beside him and turned on the lamp.

Brilliant light splashed across the room. She blinked. Her expression altered in a heartbeat. "Ah…so this is why you watch?" She waved her hand, encompassing the window, the telescope…and Evan in his wheelchair.

"I guess I should apologize. I thought, after last night, that maybe you enjoyed being watched. You certainly played to my telescope."

He wished he could read her better. Her accent was unusual. That alone confused him. Cops knew accents. It was part of the job, but her accent was totally unfamiliar.

He watched warily as she moved closer to him and sat on the edge of his unmade bed. He glanced around the room, trying to see his messy studio apartment as she might.

The view left him disgusted with himself. "If I'd known you were coming, I might have cleaned the place up."

His attempt at humor fell flat. She waved her hand, dismissing him, the mess, whatever. "Why are you crippled?"

Well, the broad didn't pull any punches.

"I was a cop. Shot in the gut—shell blew through my lower spine on the way out. It was a bank heist. The crooks had AK-47s. My little handgun was no match for theirs."

"They can't fix you?"

He laughed, but barely recognized the sound for what it was. "I'm lucky to be alive, they say. There's not much left of my spine. I'm sitting upright because of some strategically placed metal rods, though I'll be the first one to debate how lucky I am."

"You can no longer fuck?"

"You got it, sweetheart." He gestured toward the telescope. "That's the closest I get. Your little business is the only sex I'll ever have."

"Business? What do you mean, business?"

It was Evan's turn to look confused. "All the men. You're a prostitute, right?"

She laughed. "Ah, now I see...I think. Prostitute...that is a woman who sells her body, no? I am a pleasure partner, a construct. My people placed me here at Pleasure Port 27 to service lonely travelers from our world. I make no money for what I do. I was created to fuck, genetically engineered, to be exact. That's all I'm good for."

She said it in as straightforward a manner as if she were telling him she was a secretary for the phone company.

"Okay...run that by me one more time. You're telling me you're not human? Not from Earth?"

"Human is what you are? No, I was created on my world and delivered to Pleasure Port 27 about eight of your years ago. Our people do not call themselves *human*. We are..."

If he'd wondered before if she were telling the truth, the odd sounding syllables issuing out of that gorgeous mouth would have convinced him she was from anywhere but here.

"My God...I find it hard to believe. You've been here, living among us for eight years, your men come and go on our world and no one even knows you're here? How come you're telling me?"

She smiled, those beautiful full lips that could wrap themselves around the biggest of cocks, and slowly nodded her head. "I can tell you the truth because no one will find out. I've come here to kill you."

As soon as the words left her mouth, Mira knew she couldn't kill him, at least not right away. His poor broken body called to her...that and the fact he was physically the most beautiful man she'd ever seen.

It was difficult to judge his height in his wheelchair, but she knew he was taller than most humans. His hair was long, reaching almost to his shoulders. It glistened black as night beneath the harsh light of the bedside lamp. He had dark brown eyes and his skin was a deep olive, though she imagined it would darken if he spent more time outside.

His shoulders were massive, the muscles on his arms rock hard, evidence of his upper body strength to make up for the wasted legs below. There was so much pain in his face, so little hope. It was criminal no one had healed him. That alone kept her from killing him.

She could heal his injuries. One night, that's all she'd need. Just one night.

"There's a gun there, on the table." He pointed toward a primitive looking weapon. His voice was flat, totally without inflection. "I'd planned to use it on myself, but if you want the pleasure, go for it."

He stared at her with so many expressions crossing his face. Pride, anger, desperation...and need. So much need — whether for death, or maybe a meaningful life.

She sighed, knowing full well her decision would end her own career, possibly even her existence. "Later. I have other things to do now."

She stood up and inspected his room, opened his closet and peered inside, checked the bathroom. "I want you to rest. Sleep today, eat well when you awaken. I will return by nightfall."

He frowned. "What about the men? You're busy every night."

"So, I will take a night off. I'm allowed two nights each Earth week. I never take them because there's nothing else for me to do. I enjoy what I was created for."

"Except when someone beats the crap out of you." Now he merely looked angry.

She laughed. "Ah, I wondered if you saw me. That man was a bastard. He will not be allowed access to any other pleasure ports because of his behavior. I have reported him." She turned and grabbed the doorknob in her hand. "Sleep. That is a command, not a suggestion. I will see you tonight."

She stepped through the doorway and paused on the landing just outside, computing the number of days she had free. Eight years without a day off should be good for a bit of a break. Smiling, she headed for the elevator. She'd still have to kill him, but there was no reason she couldn't enjoy him first.

One good thing would come of her beating. The company couldn't deny her request for a vacation.

Evan lay in bed, his mind spinning, his upper body tense. From the middle of his chest down he felt nothing, though it wasn't all that hard for his mind to fill in the blanks.

Sleep, she said. Right. Like any man could sleep after a conversation like they'd just had. An alien! He'd been watching a damned fucking alien...a whole shitload of fucking aliens, to be precise. He owed it to his commander to let the man know what the hell was going on in that apartment across the road, but for the life of him he couldn't bring himself to make the call.

*She's coming back tonight.* That didn't make any sense at all. First she said she was going to kill him, then she was saying he needed sleep and she'd be back. He thought of all the sexual acts he'd watched her perform, thought of the looks on those men's faces as she'd given hours of pleasure.

*She's coming back tonight.* The phrase stuck in his head, like some sort of mantra. Over and over again, the words blended, one into the other, until a light tap on the door told Evan he'd slept and she was here.

He didn't know what he expected, but the blonde standing in his doorway wearing men's flannel pajama bottoms and a faded tank top with a small backpack thrown over one shoulder certainly wasn't high on his list. Dressed so casually, she looked about 18, as innocent as a schoolgirl on a sleepover.

"You haven't eaten a thing, have you?"

Before he could do more than shake his head, she walked into the room and headed straight for his small kitchenette. Within minutes she prepared a sandwich and heated a bowl of soup in his microwave, bustling about the kitchen with an easy familiarity like any middle-class housewife.

His heart actually hurt, watching her like this, wondering what might have been.

*She's not human.*

*So what?*

"What's your name?"

He fully expected another set of her odd syllables, but she turned around and smiled when she answered him.

"Mira. Apropos, don't you think, since it means *look* in one of your languages."

He still couldn't believe she was standing here in his studio, conversing with him. His voice cracked a bit when he spoke. "*Mirar*, to look. It's Spanish, the language the Mexican people speak. Part of my own heritage, actually. I'm Evan Torres. My father was Mexican. It's nice to meet you, Mira."

Suddenly he realized he was smiling when he added, "Even if you do plan to kill me."

She laughed and it carried like the sweet sound of a bubbling creek. "Well, not right away. I'm going to feed you, first. Then, with any luck, I will make you walk again. And fuck. I really want to fuck."

She grabbed the plate with the turkey sandwich, used a hot pad to lift the soup bowl in her other hand and placed them on the table, as if nothing at all had changed.

Nothing. As if the words she'd just spoken hadn't totally upended his world, as if she hadn't just proclaimed something so life-altering, so unbelievably amazing that Evan felt as if he'd fallen down the proverbial rabbit hole.

His mind should have keyed on the word *fuck*. It didn't. All he could think as he wheeled himself slowly to the small kitchen table was one simple word she'd spoken as if it were of no great importance at all.

*Walk.* She said she could help him walk. Bemused, more than a little rattled, he picked up his sandwich and began to eat.

He really was a gorgeous man. He seemed very nice, very friendly, once she saw him as an individual, not as a stranger behind a powerful telescope, watching her. Now she'd met him, talked with him, Mira realized he had every reason in the world to be angry, to feel depressed, to watch.

She sat on the kitchen counter, idly kicking her heels against the cabinet while she watched him eat. Everything about Evan fascinated her. As a construct, she lacked the history of a woman born and raised in a normal family, but she'd had enough memories implanted to be able to appreciate the sight of a good-looking man enjoying his food.

Memories were important. The company required all constructs be able to carry on a decent conversation, to fit in to whatever civilization their pleasure port was located on. She'd added to her repertoire and now knew enough to pass as human in any situation, though she'd rarely had the opportunity to practice.

This was the first time she'd actually prepared a meal for someone, though, simple as it was. She'd enjoyed it, surprisingly so. For a few moments, while Evan finished his soup, she let herself imagine a future other than working in a pleasure port. A future such as any human woman on this world might expect.

*Bad idea.* She'd always been perfectly content with her life. There was no point in wishing for something she couldn't have.

Evan carefully wiped his mouth on the napkin. He glanced at her, then seemed to come to some conclusion.

"I need some privacy for a few minutes." His skin suddenly darkened to a brick red.

"Ah." Now she understood. His injuries had taken more than his ability to walk. His basic human needs for elimination were affected as well. How demoralizing that must be, for a man who was once a powerful policeman, capable of protecting others.

Even more reason to help him. Killing Evan could definitely wait.

"I'll be outside. Call me when you are ready. We have a long night ahead of us."

# Chapter Three

Evan blinked, startled by the bright rays of morning sunshine breaking through his window blinds. For a moment, he felt as if he'd had a strange, unsettling nightmare. His mind was filled with vague images of himself crying out in pain, of a woman holding his shaking body, of someone sleeping beside him.

He turned his head and almost fell out of bed.

*Mira!*

Dark circles of exhaustion smudged the fair skin beneath her closed eyes. Her long blonde hair twisted around his waist and one arm was thrown across his chest.

Her leg covered his thighs...*and he felt it!*

Unwilling to wake her, Evan ran his left palm along his side, reaching the spot near his hip where all sensation usually ended.

His skin felt cool beneath his heavily callused palm.

*His palm felt rough and dry, passing over his hip and thigh.*

*Dear God...but how?*

Mira shifted beside him, her thigh brushed against his cock.

As if it were surprised at the touch, his long-dead penis slowly swelled to life. Almost afraid to move, Evan savored each sensation, the tension in his balls, the tight, stretching feel of his cock rising to full erection.

Within seconds, it stood at attention, leaning just a bit to the right, touching Mira's smooth thigh. He remembered, now, how she'd insisted he lie on the bed without inserting the catheter he'd needed for the past seven years. Without the diaper he wore at night.

He'd stretched out on his bed, naked and unfettered for the first time in seven long years, fully expecting to wake up in time to change the fucking sheets.

The bed was dry.

His cock was hard as a rock.

His heart pounded in his chest as he slowly wiggled all ten toes. He felt his breath rasping in and out of his lungs as, uncaring now whether or not he woke the woman sleeping beside him, he moved her aside, slowly pushed himself up on his elbows and even more carefully pivoted on the bed to place his feet on the floor.

"Ah...you're awake."

He snapped his head around to stare at her. Mira had raised herself up on one elbow and was shoving the mass of tousled hair out of her eyes. She still looked half asleep.

"How do you feel? Do you have any pain? It was a more difficult healing than I'd imagined."

It took him two false starts before he could get the words out, and then his voice cracked so badly he hardly recognized himself. "No shit, Sherlock. How?"

"Stand up. Let's make sure I did it right before I start bragging about my skills." She slipped around beside him and crawled out of bed, still wearing the faded flannels and tank top, then leaned over and put an arm around his back to support him.

With Mira's help and a good push with his left arm, Evan slowly rose to his feet. Standing beside him, Mira suddenly appeared smaller, more feminine. Her shoulder was under his arm, supporting him, helping him to straighten.

Slowly, she stepped away until Evan stood alone. His legs trembled, as much with emotion as the strain on long unused muscles. He tried to take a step and stumbled.

Mira caught him. "Take it slowly. Ease back down. There. Sit. For seven years your muscles have not received any messages to work. They will need to build back slowly. I can repair damage, but I can't make you stronger. That you will need to do on your own."

"How?" Evan slowly sat back down on the edge of the bed. "What did you do? The doctors said there was no hope of recovery, the damage was too great. How?"

Mira shrugged her shoulders in a most human manner. "I told you I was not born. I was genetically engineered by the company on my world that supplies pleasure ports with sexual companions. I am a construct. We ease the journey of interstellar travelers. They are often injured and need healing, so we are given the ability to heal, both ourselves and our visitors. I healed you. It would have been easier if I'd not had to remove the steel rods in your spine, but if I'd left them, you would not have had the mobility you need."

Evan ran his hand along his back. "How'd you get 'em out?"

She bowed her head and looked terribly guilty.

"I vaporized them." She grabbed his hands in both of hers. "I'm sorry. I know it was horribly painful for you, because I had to use extreme heat, but I've tried to block your memories of the pain. I healed the burns once I removed the last remnants, but I do apologize."

Vague memories of excruciating pain, searing heat, his own ragged screams, then Mira's soft hands touching, cooling his body. Evan shook his head. "A small price to pay. I don't know what to say, how to thank you."

She laughed. Lord, how he loved that sound. "Ah, you will thank me. First you will grow strong, then we will fuck. That will be my thanks. That is what I was created for. I would like it, just once in my life, to be with a man of my choice. For this I choose you."

She brushed her smooth palm across his lower belly until she reached the root of his newly awakened cock. Slowly, she stroked him with her long, slim fingers. "You are not yet ready for pleasuring me, but there's no reason I can't pleasure you."

Evan was so caught up in the vision of those beautiful fingers sliding up and down his cock, he almost missed Mira's comment. Suddenly she was down on her knees in front of him, spreading his thighs apart so she could fit herself between them.

When she licked him from the tender spot between the base of his penis and his testicles to the smooth crown at the top, he almost lost it. She knew what she was doing, though, and her fingers pressed down on the thick base as she slowly drew him into her mouth, controlling his sudden urge to ejaculate.

He balanced himself on his wide-spread palms as she slowly suckled his long-dormant cock. It was a struggle not to tip his head back, close his eyes and go along for the ride. Instead, he forced himself to watch, to savor each touch, each lick, both visibly and tactilely.

Scared to death he might wake up and discover he'd merely fallen asleep in his wheelchair, Evan wanted enough images for a lifetime of dreams. She was gorgeous, she was every man's wet dream, she was kneeling before him right now with his cock disappearing completely down her supple throat.

Her fingers cupped his hot sac, squeezing lightly until he practically whimpered with the pleasure. He couldn't take any more, not after seven long years, not after...

Her other hand slid beneath his thigh. Before he had time to consider her next move, she'd slipped it neatly into his tight ass, breaching the muscle, pumping slowly in and out with the same rhythm as her mouth and tongue, deeper with each small thrust, deeper until she found whatever she was looking for, and Evan knew all was lost.

He arched off the bed, driving his cock deeper into her mouth, clenching his buttocks down on her hand, crying out as she sucked him hard, squeezed his balls, filled his ass and managed to strike sparks off every nerve he'd ever missed.

From arcing burst of power to boneless in a heartbeat, Evan slumped backwards on the bed, gasping for air, fighting the conflicting urges to either laugh or cry.

Instead, he lay back and grinned, knowing he looked absolutely foolish as Mira suckled his now-flaccid cock, licked him clean with her very talented tongue, then crawled up beside him to lie across the bed, her head on his shoulder.

"That's never happened before."

Her whispered comment caught him by surprise. Slowly raising his eyelids, he stared at her. She looked out of focus and blurry, so close. "What's never happened?"

"I came without touching myself. I came without anyone or anything even close to my clit." She pulled herself up on one elbow. "You just gave a construct a climax merely by shooting into her mouth. Now that has to be a first. We're notoriously difficult to bring to climax."

Evan laughed. Once started, he couldn't stop until the tears were rolling down his cheeks and his breath was once more caught in tight, ragged gasps.

"Just wait..." He grabbed another lung full of air. "Just wait until I get to touch stuff. Then you'll find out what a real climax is."

Mira reached out and brushed a damp lock of hair away from his forehead, then leaned over and kissed him hard on the mouth. The look on her face was sad, pensive. "You have just one week to show me. Grow strong fast, okay?"

*One week. She must have really meant it when she said I had to die.*

Evan nodded. One week as a man was worth whatever years he might have had in that damned chair. He planned to enjoy every moment.

"Take your clothes off, Mira. Now. We don't have time to waste."

She tilted her head and smiled at him. "But you're not strong enough. You need to gain strength."

He sat up and began tugging her worn tank top over her head. She raised her hands, laughing at his obvious impatience.

"We'll call this a training workout. No pain, no gain." He tossed her shirt across the room and tumbled her lightly, playfully, to her back. "Lose the pants. Now."

Laughing, Mira lost the pants.

\* \* \* \* \*

Mira held her face up to the stinging spray of the shower and tried to remember ever feeling such complete satiation. As a pleasure construct, she'd had sex with three different men a night, every night for almost eight years. Give or take a few missed appointments, that was well over eight thousand different men and at least four times that many sex acts.

The last five nights with Evan had been unbelievable. Beyond imagination. She'd never been with a man who put her pleasure first, who insisted she join him in each miraculous climax, who never hesitated to try something new, to give her the lead or to take control and lead her down paths she'd never imagined.

There was a lot to be said for human innovation.

She turned off the water and grabbed the towel hanging beside the door. Evan should be back in a few minutes. He'd called his office and taken the week off, but he'd finally had to make a trip to the store for groceries, fully disguised so no one would question his sudden ability to walk. He hadn't even needed a reminder to take care. In fact, with his hat pulled down over his eyes, his long hair tied back and a big coat disguising his body, even Mira would have had trouble identifying him.

She wrapped the towel around her body and wandered out into the main room. With Evan gone, she'd managed to straighten things up, change the sheets on the bed and clean up the dishes. Now, it seemed so empty without him here.

Something caught her attention. She turned, realized she was staring at her backpack, and sighed. She'd fully expected someone from the company to try and contact her. After eight years without a break, they probably wondered how she was faring.

She unzipped the small pouch in the front and drew out her orb. The small crystal globe, about the size of a tennis ball, cleared immediately, as soon as she touched it.

Mira's immediate supervisor, an identical appearing construct now long retired from her own pleasure port, smiled at Mira through the glass.

"Ah, Mira. It is good to see you. You're okay? I was beginning to worry. You have healed from your injuries?"

The language of her home planet sounded foreign to her after so many days speaking English with Evan. Mira considered her words a moment, translating before she spoke.

"Yes, Sona. Thank you for asking."

"Where are you? I don't recognize the room behind you."

Evan's room. It had become more of a home to her these last five days than the rooms she'd lived in for almost eight years.

"Sona, you have been my only friend since I first awoke in the generating tanks. Please tell me this—is there any way at all I can leave service?"

Sona dipped her head. "Of course. You may return for deconstruction."

Death.

"No other option?"

"Mira, tell me why you ask? As a pleasure construct, you should be happy at your post for at least twenty more earth years, if not longer. What happened?"

"I've fallen in love, Sona. He's human. He knows about us."

"Constructs don't love, Mira. How could this happen? You know what you have to do."

"I know. I don't want to, but I understand my duty. Please, I still have a couple days left. Let me have them with Evan."

"As you wish." Sona's features began to fade, then suddenly filled the orb once more. "Don't do anything rash. Talk to me first. You are my friend...if constructs can have friends, why can't they love? Goodbye, Mira."

She slipped the orb back into her pack just as the door opened. Mira watched Evan walk across the room and felt each step as a beat of her heart. He brought with him the scents of fresh rain and wind-blown leaves, of warm coffee and hot, male body.

All things she'd grown to love on this world.

Mira stood up, dropped the towel to the floor and threw her arms around Evan.

"Help! Don't make me spill this. I brought you coffee." Laughing, he hugged her tightly with his one free arm and leaned over to set the bags on the kitchen table.

Mira rubbed her damp, naked body against his like a cat in heat. "This was your first walk to the store. You must be exhausted."

She smiled up at him, practically falling into the deep coffee brown of his eyes. "Should I put you to bed for a rest?"

He kissed the tip of her nose. "No, but you can take me to bed. There are still a few things I haven't done with you. Don't want to miss anything before my week is up."

"Please…" She wrapped her arms around his neck and buried her face in the warm space at the base of his throat. "Don't talk about endings. I want this week to be about beginnings. Evan, I hate what I have to do. I love you."

"As I love you." He slipped her arms from around his neck, turned away and slowly removed his coat. Then he sat on the edge of the bed to take off his shoes. Mira saw one large tear land on the back of his hand.

"Evan, you know what I am." She practically cried the words, falling to her knees in front of him. "If I don't do it, they'll send someone else to finish you. I never should have…"

"No!" He reached for her, pulled her into his lap and kissed her, his lips punishing, his breath hot and sweet against her face. "A week in heaven is an irreplaceable gift to a man facing a lifetime in hell." He tugged at her earlobe with his teeth, kissed a fiery trail under her chin, down her throat.

She arched into him, crying out when he latched onto the taut nipple on her left breast, biting down and suckling hard as he tucked her body beneath his.

His wool shirt abraded her chest, the belt buckle and snaps on his jeans cut into her soft belly and she felt the hard ridge of his erection beneath the zippered teeth of his pants.

Their hands met, struggled together, and finally managed to undo his belt buckle and shove his pants to his knees. His cock surged hard against her pubic bone as he continued his desperate assault on her breasts. He tugged at first one, then the other, squeezing and kneading her buttocks with his hands, rubbing his cock up and down, in time with his biting, suckling and squeezing.

Already his thighs were gaining muscle and strength and he pushed harder against her. She grabbed his swollen cock in her hand and aimed it at her moist, wanting center. Her pussy clenched against the rounded crown, spilling fluids over his hot skin, easing his entry into her sex so that his first hard thrust buried him all the way to his balls.

She felt them against her ass, the hot sac filled with his seed. She grabbed his buttocks, rocking with him as he thrust almost angrily into her. Harder, faster, his rough shirt rubbing her sensitive nipples, his lips now hot against her throat, laving kisses over her lips, her neck, her eyes.

He'd never been this way, so out of control she felt as if a wild animal took her here in this small apartment. His emotion, his passion, spilled out with each manic thrust and she knew he loved her, desperately wanted all of her, if not forever, for as long as they might have together.

Two more days. Only two more days, when two hundred years would never be enough.

She felt the hot coil of her climax unwinding from belly to clit, a deep, pulsing wash of power that tightened the genetically engineered muscles in her vagina until she held him deep inside, like a key within a constricting lock, held him as he roared out his own climax, stiffened in her arms, then collapsed slowly against her trembling body.

"What the fuck was that?" Evan raised himself up on his arms in an attempt to ease his weight off Mira, but his upper-body strength had totally deserted him. Still gasping for breath, he rolled to one side.

"What?"

"That thing, whatever you did with you pussy. Shit, woman." He started laughing, gulped a great draught of air, and tried, unsuccessfully, to wipe the smile off his face. "That's a new one. It felt like my cock was caught up in one of those little Chinese toys, the woven tube where if you stick your fingers in you can't pull them out."

"Oh..." She blinked, as if she might cry and Evan saw her throat contract when she swallowed. "I didn't mean to hurt you. It's something we're engineered to..."

He held a finger across her lips, then kissed her lightly on the tip of her nose. "I'm not complaining. My God, Mira...that was *absofuckinlutely* amazing. How come you've never done it before?"

She smiled, almost shyly. "I wasn't sure if you'd like it, so I've been controlling it. I sort of lost control this time."

*Idiot woman.* "You go right ahead and lose control anytime you like."

# Chapter Four

Dying hadn't bothered Evan the first time Mira told him how short a future he had. Hell, he'd had nothing to live for.

Now, though...he turned and looked at the woman sleeping beside him and thought of all the tomorrows they'd not have, all the things he wished he could do for her, show her. They'd spent their week making love, barely venturing out at all.

Not only because he'd been scared to death someone would recognize him and wonder what the fuck he was doing walking, but because he wasn't willing to share even a second of Mira's time.

Sometime tonight it would all be over. He looked down at his legs, tangled in the soft blue sheets, and thought of going on with his life as a whole man.

*What's the point, without Mira?*

Evan leaned over and took her breast in his mouth, suckling her nipple into a taut peak even as she slept. He rolled the other one between his thumb and forefinger, then slowly kissed his way down her belly. Her smooth pussy fascinated him.

He knew her body was designed not to grow hair except on her head and eyebrows...and her eyelashes. She had absolutely gorgeous eyelashes. He looked up, surprised to see her watching him through half-lidded eyes.

He smiled and returned to her smooth pussy. She spread her legs wide, giving him complete access. He shifted on the bed until he was kneeling between her legs and grasped her taut buttocks in his palms.

She grabbed her own nipples, continuing the foreplay he'd started. He watched her a moment, more turned on than he could believe to see her tugging and rolling her nipples between her fingers. When he was sure she was doing a good job, he turned his attention once more to her pussy.

Her clit was an absolutely perfect pink pearl, engorged and peeking out between the lush folds of her labia. A small trickle of moisture glistened on her nether lips. Carefully, he traced it with the tip of his tongue.

She cried out and arched her back, but he controlled her with his hands. Her legs rested on his forearms as he raised her higher, nuzzling at the soft skin between her legs, slowly licking the damp crease between her buttocks from her ass to her clit.

He brushed lightly over the moist opening to her vagina the first three or four times, then stabbed deeply into her with his tongue. She cried out, a whimper more than a scream, so he did it again.

By the time he moved on to her clit, Mira's legs were trembling and sweat matted the hair around her forehead. Her hands still tugged at her breasts, her eyes were closed, her lips parted.

"Please, Evan. I need to come. Please?"

"Soon." He licked her pearl lightly.

"Now? Oh..."

He licked her again, then circled the sensitive flesh with the tip of his tongue.

Her hips twisted and turned as she tried to force him to take her, but he continued his teasing, taking her to the edge, then backing off. A quick lick, then suckling the lips into his mouth, nipping lightly at her engorged flesh, spearing her with his tongue.

Her moans were a constant plea now, her body bathed in sweat, her lips parted as she finally gave up on her breasts and clutched at the blankets beneath her. Evan felt as if his own cock might explode merely from watching her hanging in the throes of orgasm, so close yet so far away.

He blew a cool puff of air between her legs, leaned closer and swept his tongue her full length before settling his lips around her clit. Drawing it gently into his mouth, he sucked and licked at the tiny organ, barely touching yet applying just enough pressure to drive her wild.

She clamped her knees against the sides of his head, arched her back and practically vibrated with the power of her climax. Evan sucked harder, knowing just how sensitive she was, then eased off and softly laved her quivering flesh with the flat of his tongue.

Sobbing, shivering, she slowly came down from her orgasm, her hands futilely clutching at the blankets, her lips parted wide to let the whimpers escape and the air in.

Evan nuzzled her belly, kissed her gently where her belly button would have been had she been human, and snuggled his face against her breast. "I love you. Even when I am gone, I will always love you. Whether it be in heaven or hell, you cannot escape my love."

Her arms lifted slowly from the twisted sheets and she smoothed his long hair back from his eyes. There were no more words to say. He felt her chest heaving with barely controlled sobs and knew his words were truth.

He would never, not even after death, forget this woman.


Mira let the tears fall as she swept her hand through his silky black hair. They still had a few more hours, but he slept now after a glorious night of lovemaking, and the time was right. She didn't think she could handle a goodbye from the man she loved more than life itself.

She hoped Sona knew what she was talking about. At least it meant Evan would live. He'd have no memory of his alien lover and he'd have to deal with the unanswerable questions about his sudden mobility, but if Sona's suggestions worked, it meant Mira didn't have to kill him.

She wondered if he would remember anything about her. She knew she'd never forget him, though deconstruction would take care of that whether she wanted to forget or not. She'd broken every law the company had. She'd healed a human, told him about the pleasure ports, the fact she was from another planet. Even pointed out the sector in the northern sky one night when they'd stood together on the rooftop and stared at the stars.

So many things Evan had said he'd love to show her. Mountains, oceans, rivers, forests…she'd been delivered to the apartment across the street directly from the generation tanks and had rarely left, other than to replenish supplies. Constructs were not allowed to mingle. There were to be no friendships and as little human interaction as possible. No exploring meant no risk of discovery. Mira'd followed the rules to the letter...until she'd ventured across the road to Evan.

And what was the first thing she'd told him? That she was here to kill him. Now she kissed the top of his head, inhaling the sweet male scent she'd grown to love.

Then she placed both hands at his temples, one on either side, closed her eyes and let the power flow.

One by one, she found and removed all his memories of the two of them. She took away the many nights he'd watched her through the telescope, stole each kiss and warm caress. Took away the pounding rush of each climax, the taste of bodies trembling with sexual need, the soft, quiet moments when they'd made foolish plans and talked of a future that wouldn't be.

She took them all. Then, praying that Sona was right, she left one tiny thought. Only one.

And prayed it would be enough.

* * * * *

Later that night, brokenhearted, her soul in tatters, Mira waited for her regular client to arrive. She was still sitting on the edge of the bed, alone, when the first rays of the morning sun peeked over the building across the street.

Evan's building.

There'd been no glint of telescope, no sign of Evan at all. Neither had there been a traveler looking for a night of pleasure. Relieved, confused, Mira waited.

Money appeared on schedule, enough to pay her rent and buy what few groceries she needed. Money, but no contact from the home world. The crystal orb remained silent.

No contact from Evan, either. Obviously, Mira had been successful and all incriminating memories were gone. Now she waited for the deconstruction team to take her away. She dreamed of Evan and what they'd lost, and wept.

However, when she thought of Evan going on with his life, his body whole and healthy, Mira discovered she still knew how to smile.

Days passed. Weeks. Mira waited. A construct existed at the whim of her superiors. Their wishes remained a mystery.

Then, one morning, the crystal orb shimmered and began to glow.

Mira gazed into the orb, unable to fully comprehend what Sona was saying. The other construct's words tumbled out in a breathless rush.

"I don't believe it, either. You're free of your contract. You have to return the orb and find another place to live. You'll age at a normal Earthling's rate. In case you're interested, you're twenty-nine Earth years right now. Twenty-nine and free, Mira!"

Mira's breath caught in her throat, her heart pounded, loud, out of sync. "Sona, I don't understand."

"There will be no deconstruction, Mira. You're free."

"Free? But how...why?"

"You fell in love, Mira. You're flawed. The company can't use you. They can't salvage your brain if it's no good.

It's cheaper to set you free than bring you home for deconstruction."

Mira practically dropped the orb. "But his memories of me are gone. I wiped them all."

"Which is the only reason you're not an anonymous murder victim on Earth. The company would have seen to it immediately. They have your orb records of the mind-wipe, proof you followed orders. There's a packet in your top dresser drawer with all the paperwork you'll need to set up your new life."

"Sona, I can't thank you enough...I..."

"Yes, you can. You can be happy. You can find Evan and hope your implanted memory took hold. It's been three months, long enough for him to get his life in order, long enough for the media to leave him alone after his miraculous cure. Go to him. Be happy. Be alive, Mira. You've given me more hope than you can imagine."

"Goodbye, Sona. Thank you. I'll miss you."

"As I will miss you. Put the orb across the room. I need to retrieve it, and there's always risk of a malfunction. Good luck, my friend."

Mira set the orb on the dresser and stepped away. The room spun, shimmered, returned to normal.

The orb was gone. She grabbed the dresser drawer and ripped it open, spilling the contents on the floor. With trembling fingers, she leaned over and picked up a small packet filled with a birth certificate, medical and school records and a thick wad of American dollars.

She opened the birth certificate and peered at the name typed neatly on the first line—Mira Amore—and burst into tears.

\* \* \* \* \*

Evan helped the truck driver load his old wheelchair into the back of the van along with the other donated items. Someone, somewhere should be able to use his stuff.

He didn't need it anymore.

He still woke some mornings, wondering if it was all a dream, if he were still paralyzed. He truly lived a miracle, one without explanation. With the insurance settlement he'd received after the shooting, he didn't need to work. He'd stayed on at the department to keep from going insane when he couldn't walk.

Now, he had things to do, places to go.

Still, it was nice knowing they wanted him back on the force.

*Sorry, but no thanks.*

He slung his pack over his shoulder and headed for the train station. He'd thought if he ever got his legs back, his life would be complete, but for some reason he felt as if a huge part of him were missing.

Hopefully, a little travel would cure whatever ailed him.

"Evan?"

He looked up, blinked. Caught his breath as if he'd been sucker punched in the gut. "Mira? Mira from Penn State University?"

The backpack fell from his fingers and landed on his left foot with a loud *thud*.

"Yes, it's me! I can't believe…"

"I haven't seen you since college." He grabbed her hands, secretly pleased when her fingers tightened around his. Good Lord, she was gorgeous. Prettier even than he remembered.

"Evan, I've…I've thought about you so much. How are you?"

"I…" He stopped and looked around. The coffee shop across the street looked almost empty. "Do you have time for a cup of coffee?"

She smiled up at him, her green eyes curiously glistening with unshed tears. "I'll always have time for you, Evan. I've never stopped thinking about you."

Evan shivered as he leaned down and grabbed his pack. Now that she mentioned it, he realized he'd never forgotten her, either.

He tugged her close and wrapped his arm around her waist as they started across the street. She slipped into his embrace as if they'd never been apart.

Squeezing Mira against his side, Evan realized the feeling of something missing had completely disappeared.

# About the Author

For over thirty years Kate Douglas has been lucky enough to call writing her profession. She has won three EPPIES, two for Best Contemporary Romance and a third for Best Romantic Suspense. Kate also creates cover art and is the winner of EPIC's Quasar Award for outstanding bookcover graphics.

She is multi-published in contemporary and paranormal romance, both print and electronic formats, as well as her popular futuristic Romantica ™ series, StarQuest. She and her husband of over thirty years live in the northern California wine country where they find more than enough subject material for their shared passion for photography, though their grandchildren are most often in front of the lens.

Kate welcomes mail from readers. You can write to her c/o Ellora's Cave Publishing at 1056 Home Ave., Akron OH 44310.

# Also by Kate Douglas

Just A Little Magic
Luck Of The Irish
More Than A Hunch
Ellora's Cavemen: Tales from the Temple I *anthology*
StarQuest 1: Lionheart
StarQuest 2: Night Of The Cat
StarQuest 3: Pride Of Imar
StarQuest 4: Synergy
StarQuest 5: Bold Journey

# LICENSE TO THRILL

Sahara Kelly

*Acknowledgement*

*For my Partner – again.*
*With thanks for the ear, the input, the laughter and the*
*wisdom.*
*Not to mention the shoulder to cry on, the musical*
*education –*
*and the midgets.*

# Chapter One

*Pooiinnngggg.*

"Oh *shit*." Jane Bradford clenched her teeth as the button at the waistband of her skirt shot across the silent office. "I never should've had that frickin' cheesecake for dessert."

She groaned.

There wasn't one goddamned safety pin in the entire office, either.

She mangled a paper clip into a sort of pointy sculpture, pierced the waistband of her skirt and prayed it would hold. She also promised herself she'd give up cheesecake for the rest of her life, but knew *that* was a flat-out lie.

It was unusually quiet in her office, since just about everybody had the flu.

Why *she* hadn't gotten the bug, she had no idea. But for once, she was rather thankful for her robust constitution, even though it came with a rather robust figure. Women with lush curves like hers didn't get sick much. They did things like eat regular meals, stayed away from germ-breeding environments like health clubs, and of course, never kissed anybody with bacteria that might be infectious.

Never kissed anybody at all, infectious or not.

Jane shrugged, grappled with a load of files that needed to be entered into the database and promptly tore her last pair of stockings on her desk drawer.

"Fucking hell. Mother*fucking*...piece of *shit*...crappy damn *pissy* drawer..."

Taking full advantage of her solitude, Jane recited a litany of every foulmouthed curse she could think of. And added a couple in Italian for good measure.

"Ms. Bradford."

A stern voice at the door interrupted her caustic litany, making her jump and drop the top batch of the files in her arms. More oaths trembled on her lips, but died when she saw who was standing there.

The head of the Agency. Steven Turner.

"Er...good evening, sir." Jane nodded at him. Fuck it. He must have heard every damn swear word. There goes my year-end bonus.

She blushed.

He ignored it. "You're the only person here?"

"Yes sir." She shrugged. "The flu's taken out everybody else at the moment. Was there something you needed?"

He frowned. "There's *nobody* else here?"

Sheesh. Boss he may be, but apparently not too bright. "That's correct, sir. I'm it."

Mr. Turner sighed. "Well, you'll have to do, I suppose."

Jane blinked. "Do what?"

He turned away. "Follow me."

"Huh?"

He gritted his teeth. "It was a simple instruction. You are to follow me. To the communications center. Now move your ass."

He stalked off, not even waiting to see if she obeyed.

Suppressing yet another curse, Jane shoved the remaining files onto a desk and left her office, grabbing at the waistband of her skirt as she went..

What the *fuck* was all this about?

\* \* \* \* \*

Some distance away, another member of the Agency was cursing. Only this time, he was softly and fluidly uttering words beneath his breath that were close to a thousand years old.

His contact had stood him up. There were several unfriendly looking individuals leaning up against the bar of the seedy strip club, eyeing him. Their expressions were not unlike the look a dog gives to that last piece of pizza – hungry, with plenty of teeth.

Edvarde Przybyl wasn't too concerned. He could handle them if he had to. But he wasn't about to blow his cover to a bunch of liquored-up, brain-dead morons.

He casually lifted a hand to his ear and, as he brushed his long hair out of the way, he surreptitiously tapped the small receiver that lurked behind his lobe. It was part of the earring he wore – in his *left* ear, not that the patrons would know the difference.

The stripper, however, had noticed. She knew the difference.

He raised an eyebrow as she gyrated over to him, the sequins on her thong reflecting the neon lights that blinked up a nearby pillar. Her large breasts swayed precariously and for a second Eddie braced himself to catch her if she tipped over.

Her waist was slender and her hips lean. It was a pity her plastic surgeon hadn't kept the rest of her in proportion. Eddie sighed. He did like a little something to grab hold of in the ass department, since fucking a bony woman wasn't his idea of fun.

Even if she was about to thrust her pussy into his crotch and do some kind of hip wiggle guaranteed to produce a hard-on in ninety percent of the male population.

"Uh…not tonight, okay?" Eddie produced a bill, folded it, held it out between two fingers, and smiled politely as she lowered her mouth on it and whipped it away.

"Thanks, baby. Maybe next time?" She brushed her solid breasts over his arm.

"Maybe."

"I won't forget, you know." She teased herself against his shirt, nipples hardening as she moved in time to the music.

"That's nice." Where the hell was his Control?

He needed to leave, to get the hell out of this dive, but couldn't—not until Control had confirmed his contact as missing. There were other channels of communication between contacts and the Agency, but only one between the Agency and the agents in the field.

Control. That voice on the commlink that filled an agent in on the up-to-the-second details of each mission. The voice that had decided to take a hike right at the very moment he needed it most.

Inwardly, Eddie seethed. Outwardly, he continued to smile at the stripper. Given the lack of customers, she'd obviously decided he was her best bet, in spite of his protests and the fact his smile was about to crack his cheeks.

"My name's Lulu." Her breasts wobbled in confirmation.

"Ah."

"And I'll just bet you've got a mighty big cock down there."

"Hmm."

"I love cock. Love sucking cock. Licking it, running my tongue up and down, right round that sensitive bit at the veeeery tip…" She giggled. "Especially on quiet nights like this. My pussy loves big cock too."

* * * * *

*"My pussy loves big cock too."*

"Good God. What's that?" Jane's jaw dropped as Turner pushed her into the chair in front of an electronic console.

"That's your agent's conversation. His Control…er…was taken ill." Turner looked embarrassed. "Rather suddenly."

Jane winced. "Threw up, did he? There's a lot of that going around."

*"I'm sure it's a lovely pussy, but really, not tonight. Thanks anyway."* The male voice oozed through the speakers like warm honey.

"Oh for heaven's sake, turn that to headset, will you?" Turner looked helplessly at the console.

Jane efficiently settled the earpiece unit over her head and clicked a switch. Now that voice would ooze for her alone.

"Where is he?" She toggled various switches eliminating background interference.

Turner sighed with relief. "He's in a strip club, at a supposed meet, but his contact just called in to change the location. Can you tell him that?"

"Of course." Jane hit the "send" button. "This is Control. Repeat. This is Control."

*"Well, it's about time...for me to leave, baby."*

Hmm. Quick thinking on his part. Probably leaving one sad and horny woman behind him, though, if he looked anything like his voice sounded.

Turner passed her a slip of paper. "Here's the new information. Get it to him as soon as he's clear. You're in contact with Agent EP-9 – his Control for the moment, Ms. Bradford." He moved to the door. "Get that stuff to him, and stay live while he makes the meet. That's all."

"Uh...what do I do? I can use the machine, but I have no clue about Control responsibilities."

An odd grin curved Turner's mouth. "That's one thing you don't have to worry about with Agent EP-9. He'll take care of himself. He always does. Your job is just to monitor him. Give him whatever information he needs."

"Ah." *I can do that. I think.*

Turner's cell phone chimed and he answered it, cutting off the conversation abruptly. "I have to go. I'll be back in a while. Keep up the good work, Ms. Bradford."

*Right.*

Jane was alone in a strange cubicle, in front of a multi-gazillion dollar piece of equipment, connected electronically to the most seductive male voice she'd heard in years.

*"All clear, Control. Come in please."*

*Damn. That was one hell of an offer. I wonder what he looks like?*

She squelched down her hormones, gathered up her work ethics, and settled in to do her job. "Control here."

*"Where the fuck is Kurt?"*

Jane frowned. "Kurt, who I assume was your previous Control, is probably sucking down some sort of flu medication. And then barfing it back up again. In case you missed it, buddy, there's an epidemic going around here."

A gusty sigh blew into her ears, making the hairs on the back of her neck stand on end. What the hell was it with this voice? *"Yeah. I'd heard. So I get a newbie. Swell."*

"Look Agent EP – er – nine, I've had a shitty day too. Let's just get this over with, shall we?"

Silence reigned. Then a small chuckle sounded. *"Okay, darlin'. You got a new contact point for me? Since this one's a bust. In more ways than one."*

Jane overlooked the endearment. This agent was probably as much of a self-absorbed horny asshole as some of the others she'd seen. Sex and secret agents seemed to go hand-in-pussy these days. She wrinkled her nose and read off the address over the mike.

*"Oh lovely. A whorehouse."*

Jane chewed her lip. Obviously Agent EP-9 knew the area better than she did, since this fact was news to her. "Ah."

*"About fifteen blocks or so south from here, I think. Hang on…"*

There was an odd whistling sound, like the one reporters do their best to avoid on windy days. She tapped the gain control.

*"Okay. I see it."*

Jane blinked. "I thought you said it was fifteen blocks. How'd you get there so fast?"

*"Shortcut."*

She opened her mouth to question that succinct non-explanation, but was stopped by his next transmission. *"Shit."*

"What?"

*"I've got company. Three of them, leaving the entrance right now. Not happy."*

"Three who? Not happy about what?" Jane sat helplessly, staring at blinking lights with unseeing eyes. This was like walking into the last reel of a mystery movie, or reading the last chapter of a juicy murder novel. She'd missed all the explanatory action and had no idea who the fuck he was talking about.

*"Ssshh."*

Jane shushed.

For about five seconds. "Look, I'm supposed to be your Control. I'm here to help you."

*"Then shut the fuck up for a minute or two, will ya?"*

Jane snapped her mouth closed. *Asshole. Thinks he's God's gift to national security.*

The silence was broken by the sounds of doors opening and closing and muttered conversations. There was a giggle, a shout, more giggles — what the hell went on in those places anyway?

Jane did her best to stay professional about the whole thing. So Agent EP-9 was in a whorehouse. *Big deal.* It would've satisfied a rather naughty curiosity if he'd described it for her, of course, but she was a professional first. Okay, and a nosy woman too, but that was a distant second. Right at this particular moment, anyway.

*"Control, I'm approaching his room."*

"Roger that." *Call* me *a newbie, will ya?*

He chuckled again softly, and Jane had the oddest feeling it was for her alone. She shook it off and focused, closing her eyes and envisioning a door opening onto...what?

*"Oh — merde."*

Okay. There was nothing in the rulebook about not responding to French curses. "What?"

"I said *shit.*"

Jane sighed. "I speak French. I understood the word. I wanted to know why you'd said it in the first place."

*"It's not good."*

"Huh?"

*"My contact's dead."*

# Chapter Two

Eddie stared at what was left of Sully "The Sneak" Adams. It seemed he'd departed this life unwillingly, since his hands were bloody and bruised, his body twisted, and his knees were clenched tight into the fetal position as if to protect himself in his final moments.

Eddie frisked the body carefully, but there was nothing in his pockets.

"Control, notify the locals. DB at this location. Definitely homicide."

"*Roger that.* Dead body at your location."

She was efficiency personified when she remembered to be, and a delight when she didn't. In spite of the carnage inside the room, Eddie grinned. He wanted to meet this one. But first things first.

"*Authorities notified. Also Mr. Turner. He suggests you return to base and regroup.*"

"I'll just bet he does." Eddie shrugged. "Tell him I'll be there ASAP."

Looked like he was going to get to meet his new Control sooner rather than later. A prospect that lightened Eddie's thoughts considerably. While a portion of his mind worked over the new dynamics of the case, another part considered his options concerning *her*.

Fuck, he didn't even know her name yet.

A few minutes later, he was walking in the door of the Agency and running his hands through his hair. Flying always made one annoying bit stick out from the back, and he wanted to look his best.

There she was.

Eddie stopped for a moment or two in the doorway, staring at her. Intent upon her console, she leaned over it, sandy brown hair tucked neatly into one of those scrunchy elastic things. Her blouse was taut over her back, showing the outlines of a lace-trimmed bra. Full hips were planted firmly in her chair, their swell making Eddie's mouth water. He did so *love* a rounded ass.

He cleared his throat and she glanced over her shoulder. "Hi."

She turned back to whatever it was she was doing. Calling *him*, by the sound of things. "Agent EP-9. This is Control. What is your location? I repeat...what is your location?"

"Right behind you."

She spun around, giving him a perfect view of the full breasts that pushed out the fabric of her blouse. *Niiiice.*

"Look buddy, the trash is over there, okay? I'm kinda busy here."

"Uh...I'm Eddie Przybyl."

"Good for you. Like I said," she nodded her head to the corner of the cubicle. "Trash is over there. Now take a hike, will ya? I don't have time to chat."

"Ah good. You're both here." Turner walked around the corner and pushed Eddie into the small room in front of him.

Jane gaped. "Huh?"

Eddie smirked.

"I forgot. You've only met over *that*." Turner pointed at the console. "Eddie, this is Jane Bradford, your temporary Control. Jane, this is Agent EP-9. Edward Przybyl."

"*Not* the janitor." Eddie couldn't help adding the taunt. He was mostly amused, in spite of a little hurt she'd confuse him with the maintenance staff.

She leaped from her chair, color spreading over her cheeks in a hot blush. "Jeez, I'm so sorry. I thought...I mean you look like...uh..." She stuttered to a halt. Then gasped as a slight rustling sound followed her words and her skirt dropped from her body to puddle on the floor around her feet.

Eddie couldn't help it.

He looked.

* * * * *

Jane wanted to die. Right then and there. But of course she didn't. She just gasped out her horror and glanced up from her fallen skirt into Eddie's eyes.

*Big* mistake.

Glints of fire flickered behind his gaze as he stared at her panties. Damn, he was staring *through* her panties. She could feel her pussy begin to moisten and swell under that look. Something in her gut made her want to part her thighs so he could get a better look. Maybe even touch her.

*Shit, it's hot in here.*

Her nipples beaded up inside her bra, rubbing against the lace and making her breath catch in her throat. Feather light touches were sliding up her thighs, invisible fronds of sensation sending flickers of electricity to her clit.

*This is fucking unreal. Why didn't I wear a slip today? What the hell is this guy doing to me?*

The harsh sound of Turner clearing his throat distracted Eddie and his gaze moved away from her crotch. She sagged and then hurriedly retrieved her skirt.

"Stop it, Eddie."

"Sorry." Eddie grinned at his boss. "Some things I can't control."

"I don't understand all this." Jane looked at both men, confused, embarrassed and a bit wet in some private places that she didn't want to think about.

Turner awkwardly pulled at his collar. "Agent Przybyl is one of our best agents. Very talented."

Eddie raised an eyebrow.

"In many unusual ways." Turner finished with his explanation.

Jane still didn't understand, but before she could pursue the subject, it got changed in a hurry.

"So your contact got himself killed before he could pass the information along. That's bad. The good news is that we know who he was with before his scheduled meet with you." Turner flicked his cell phone, reading off a message. "Apparently he went to see a Blanche Overjoy." He glanced at Eddie. "The name mean anything to you?"

Eddie nodded. "Yep. Ex-hooker. Now she trains girls for escort positions. Sully could've left the disk with her."

Jane looked skeptical. "Escort positions?"

Eddie stared back at her, and instinctively her hands went to the waistband of her skirt. She was almost afraid that it would drop off of its own accord if he looked too hard.

"I've got an idea." His gaze turned back to Turner.

*Me too. No. Bad girl.* Jane slithered awkwardly back into her chair, ashamed of the direction her thoughts were taking. Which was pretty much into the nearest dark closet with Agent Prizzy-whatever.

"I'll need her for cover. Forget about a Control on this. I'll take care of it."

Turner blinked. "Uh…"

"Good." Eddie snapped his fingers and Jane jumped. "You. Jane. Come with me."

Jane stood once more, hanging on to her skirt for dear life. "Come where?"

"I told you where. With me. What're you waiting for?"

*An explanation? A "Would you mind helping me out, Jane?" Or perhaps "Jane, I'd like to fuck you silly after this mission?" She was getting rather fed up of being told to follow men around this evening.*

Eddie reached over and grabbed her wrist. "Move it, baby. Time's wasting."

The words of outrage at being called "baby" died in her throat as the heat of his grasp shimmered up her arm and into her breasts. How the *fuck* did he do that?

Sure, he was cute. And sure, he was just the right height. And those eyes…well, the less said about those, the better for Jane's peace of mind.

Of course, being tugged along behind him and getting to see his butt in his tight pants did nothing at all for the few shreds of peace left in her mind. He was one delectably yummy hottie.

And he was dragging her into a closet. *Oh goody. Great minds do think alike.*

* * * * *

The "closet", however, turned out to be a small locker room, one wall of which was covered with a variety of clothes neatly hung within dry-cleaning bags.

"Here. Strip and put this on."

Jane blinked. "What?"

Eddie sighed. "Look, you can't go out undercover dressed like a...a..."

"A what?" Jane bristled.

"An efficient office manager with torn stockings and a busted waistband."

"Oh." Jane chewed that one over and looked at the dress he was holding out. It was red, short and glittery. "So I'm supposed to put this on and look like...oh gosh, let me guess. A hooker?"

"Right first time. Good catch. You'll do just fine." He undid his shirt and tore it from his body without a second thought.

Jane couldn't manage a second thought, since her first one threatened to choke her. *Oh yum.* She stared at the chest in front of her, trying not to drool or lick him, both of which urges were duking it out in her head.

"Jane...c'mon. Time's wasting." Eddie snapped his fingers at her again, and she jumped.

"Don't do that finger thing, okay?" She took the plastic cover off the dress. "Damn. This won't fit *me*."

"Yes it will." His eyes raked her. "You're a fourteen, I'd guess. 38C or D."

She glared at him. "Stop right there."

"Well, put the damn thing on or I'll tell you your weight and age, not to mention when you shaved last and when your next period's due."

Jane screeched. "What are you, some kind of pervert? You been nosing around in my personnel file?"

Eddie sighed. "Put. The. Dress. *On*." His hands dropped to his waist and he unsnapped his pants.

Jane blushed and turned her back on him, struggling out of her skirt and blouse and hanging the dress in front of her.

"You won't need this, either." Hot fingers brushed her skin and her bra fell away.

She squawked, grabbing for the garment as it dropped.

"Ssshh." A warm body pressed up against her back. "You need to relax. Close your eyes while I fill you in on the mission."

*Fill me with something else, you lovely hunk of man, you.* Jane sighed against the thought.

Then tensed as arms surrounded her and cupped her full breasts. "What the *fuck*…"

"Close your eyes, Jane. I need to tell you about the mission. Open your mind. Hear my thoughts."

Jane snorted, aware of her nipples budding hard just above his fingers. "Right. You grab my boobs and we do some kind of science-fiction mind meld thing."

"You got it. I knew you were smart the minute I saw you."

"On TV they touch the *head*, buddy."

"My name is Edvarde. And this – " His hands firmed around her breasts, covering them completely, " – is a *much* better way, don't you think?"

*Actually, yes.*

Experimentally, Jane closed her eyes. She was getting paid by the hour, right? Might as well enjoy it.

And suddenly, the room filled with light. Eddie – no, *Edvarde* – was there. Facts, figures, times and places flooded her mind. The mission, spelled out simply and clearly. Retrieve critical information, either on disk or a CD of some sort, from the man who had been killed earlier that evening.

This was super weird. Like a mental connection that allowed the flow of data between two minds, slicker than silk.

Jane moaned, aware of the burning heat of hands on her breasts. Now the images were changing. It wasn't Agency mission information any more. It was her. And him.

And they were...oh my *God*.

Jane stared up at him as he held himself above her. His eyes glowed, a red flame shining through brown irises. She felt his cock, hard and heated, nudging at her pussy lips.

Her gut contracted, ready...wanting...needing his penetration into the trembling depths of her cunt. She was so hungry for this, soaking wet with her own juices and desperate to get him where she needed him to be.

"Jane." He sighed her name. "Let me in."

"*Edvarde…*" Christ. Was that *her* purring out words like some sex siren? Oh yeah, baby. It was her. In her vision, she parted her thighs and reached for him.

He was there. As real as could be. Sliding past her pussy lips into her slick cunt, stopping only when their bodies touched. Filling her to bursting, marking his passage into her with electric sparks of sensation.

"*Oh sheeeiiittt…*" The breath left her lungs as he pushed even deeper, pressing against her clit with his groin and the neck of her womb with his cock. They fit. Yin and yang blending in a timeless, seamless coupling of male and female.

His gaze held hers with an almost physical intensity. She couldn't look away, couldn't close her eyes, could barely blink. She'd never imagined a man could find his way into her very soul, or bury his cock so deeply within her body that she had no clue where he ended and she began.

Then he moved. Rapidly, ferociously, he took her, giving so much more than he could possibly receive. Her clit pulsed in rhythm with his thrusts, and her hands grabbed his biceps as her mouth fell open on a silent scream.

She shattered, body exploding around his as every cell, every nucleus that was Jane Bradford detonated into an earth-shaking eruption of orgasmic pleasure.

"Jane, stop daydreaming. We've got a mission."

The words acted like a shower of cold water, and Jane staggered a little, amazed to find herself dressed in the hooker outfit, still in the wardrobe closet and with no man between her legs, pumping himself into her. Only a pair of very wet panties.

She blinked.

*I really* have to lay off the coffee.

# Chapter Three

"Good lord, it *does* fit."

Eddie watched in amusement as Jane made a futile attempt to pull the red glittery neckline up a little over her lovely breasts. "Told you so."

She snapped him a glare. "I really hate when people say that."

"Sorry."

She sighed. "My fault." She shook her head. "I don't know what's come over me. Probably this damn flu or something."

"Whatever. Let's roll, shall we?"

"Um…" She paused. "Look, can the security of the civilized world wait while I use the ladies' room?"

Eddie hid a grin. "Sure. Just don't take all day."

She frowned at him and disappeared through a door with a nicely tasteful little cutout on it. A cutout of a man.

She reappeared a moment later, blushing. "Do not say a word. Not *one* word." She moved down to the next door and successfully entered the ladies' room. If silence could have seethed, it would be doing it right about now.

Eddie leaned against the wall and waited. Somehow he was going to have to give her some idea of who and what he was. She was too damn bright to accept all the glib explanations he passed off to people he mentally "invaded".

And to his surprise, he found the thought exciting. He also didn't feel that he'd *invaded* Jane. There hadn't been any resistance to his mind-intrusion, just a heated welcome that had led him into places he *never* went. And turned him inside out when he got there, too.

She'd been right there with him all the way, and that fact probably had a lot to do with why she was in the ladies' right now. He'd managed to come in his old jeans, which were now stuffed in his locker. His laundry lady would have a fit, but that was nothing new. It'd probably be a shitload easier to clean *those* stains than the blood he'd been covered with after his last assignment.

Before he'd had time to consider the implications, Jane re-emerged, looking much more in control of herself. "Right. Let's go, then."

She stalked off down the hallway, and Eddie let his eyes follow the seductive bounce of her hips. Damn, she had one *fine* ass on her. He had to hurry to catch her though, since she seemed intent upon heading out by herself.

He reached the doors at the same time she did and pushed them open, nodding over to the parking lot. "The black job over there."

She crossed to the low-slung black convertible and whistled through her teeth. "Sheesh. You agents gotta clear a damn sight more in your paycheck than the rest of us."

Her hand trailed over the sleek finish. "Just putting gas in this would blow my budget to hell and back. Not to mention the insurance…"

Eddie rolled his eyes. He did so *not* want to discuss finances with this woman. They had a mission, a challenging case, and he was trying his best to ignore the other case – the one plaguing his cock and his lust. "Get in. We need to hit Blanche's place as soon as we can."

Jane slid onto the leather seat with a sigh of pleasure. "Sure. I'm okay with that. I think I understand this whole thing." She blinked. "Which brings up a question…"

*Uh oh. Here it comes.*

He started the engine and busied himself backing out of the parking lot. He could have taken the couple of hours needed to explain the case to her verbally. He hadn't really *needed* to institute that mind link. He'd just wanted to, that's all.

Eddie wrinkled his nose and stared ahead of him. If he ignored her, maybe she wouldn't ask.

*Like hell she wouldn't.*

"I shouldn't be able to understand it. There's no way that you can put all those…those *thoughts* in my head." Jane choked a little, coughed, and carried on. "The information in my brain wasn't there an hour ago. *You* put it there. Now unless there's some secret mind control program here at the Agency I don't know about – which I strongly doubt – you got *some* explaining to do, Agent Prizzybits."

She folded her arms and stared at him.

He glanced over, trying very, very hard not to look at the deepened valley between her breasts that her pose had created.

He failed.

"And my cleavage isn't asking the question here, buddy."

Eddie sighed and pulled the car into a convenient parking lot. He turned off the engine and considered his next words. Before he could say anything, of course, Jane was all over him.

"Why have we stopped? Is this Blanche's? She runs a Chinese restaurant? That wasn't in your mental briefing –"

"*Jane.*" That voice made strong men quail.

Jane simply raised an eyebrow. "What? I'm simply asking here…"

"Shut. *Up.*"

\* \* \* \* \*

The sharp sound of Jane's mouth snapping shut echoed around the interior of the car. *Arrogant asshole.*

"You ever hear of the Anasazi?"

She frowned. "No. I hate rap."

Eddie drummed his fingernails impatiently on the steering wheel. "They're not a rock group. They're a tribe of Native Americans."

"Oh…like the Sioux or something?"

"No. Nothing like them. The Anasazi used to live in what is now Colorado. Archeologists have found their homes but no clues as to what happened to them."

Jane pursed her lips and dredged up a memory. "You know, I think I saw a TV special about that once."

"Probably." Eddie continued his story. "Anyway, I know what happened to them."

"Well now, *that's* a big whoop on the scale of things." *Where the fuck is he going with all this history crap?*

"I am Anasazi."

Jane blinked. "Okay. So you're Native American. Explains the hair coloring. You got a point we're going to get to any time soon? Because we do have a mission to complete, you know."

He hissed through his teeth. "Time is irrelevant, Jane."

She opened her mouth to respond, but stopped when Eddie made an odd motion with his hand. Suddenly the silence in the car seemed like a living thing, a cavern of stillness.

"I have stopped time for us. Temporarily." He grimaced. "Pardon the pun."

"Huh?" Jane looked around, to find the car windows blank and impenetrable.

"Jane. Look at me. Discard every notion you ever had of how life, time…the laws of physics…whatever…are supposed to work."

"Okay." She was helpless to refuse this guy anything once he fixed her with that gaze. The one that did very nice things to rather private places and involved lubricating her panties.

"Now clear your thoughts and imagine someplace you've always wanted to be. Something you've wanted to do but never have."

Jane considered his words. "Hmm. Aruba. A beach in the Caribbean. I always wanted a tropical vacation."

Eddie unbuckled his seat belt and leaned towards her, nearly touching her forehead with his. "Then let's take one."

"But —"

Her vision blurred and a loud whirring sound jarred her ears, along with the pounding of her pulse.

Suddenly, she was naked. The pounding became the soft thud of surf on a sandy beach and her vision cleared to reveal a magnificent sunset.

And Eddie, also naked, between her legs.

"Is this what you dreamed of, Jane?" His shoulders were broad, pressing into the softness of her thighs, shining gold from the shimmering rays of the sun.

"Uh…not *exactly*, but it'll do…" *Like I'm gonna say no.*

"Glad to hear it." Eddie settled more comfortably, spreading her legs further apart as he nestled against her. "It'll do just fine for me too."

Jane's breath stopped as he lowered his head and found her pussy with his mouth. Heated flesh met heated flesh, and sparks sizzled in back of her eyeballs as one hellaciously fine tongue learned the finer details of her anatomy.

Unerringly, Eddie sought out her sensitive spots, probing the tender pussy lips with delicate care, making her shiver and tremble with pleasure. He stroked her, suckled gently at her juices and then pulled back a little. "Mmm. You taste…God, I can't describe it." He raised his eyes and stared at her. "Haven't had anything this good in several hundred years."

Okay. There was something in that statement she ought to be thinking about, but it would have to wait. Like a month or two. Or at least until Eddie had finished doing whatever he was doing.

And if he kept on doing *that*, she was going to be finished before he was.

He returned to her pussy, focusing his attention on the aroused nubbin of flesh that he'd coaxed from beneath its protective hood. It pulsed in time with his caresses, tingling with excitement as his tongue circled it, flicking softly across the surface then dipping beneath to spread her moisture over any place he could reach.

Hard hands gripped her buttocks, lifting her a little, and coincidentally tugging the cheeks slightly apart. The added sensation drove Jane wild. This was not only someplace where the sun hadn't shone, it was someplace no man had gone before, and she had no idea it could be so exciting.

As a matter of fact, she had no ideas at all, since her brain was vaporizing into a cloud of shaking need and funneling itself down to where Eddie's tongue met her clit.

"Let go, Jane." He sucked harder now, and slid one hand to the entrance of her cunt. "Come for me, babe. Let me taste your heat. I want my face in you when you come. Do it, Jane."

The setting sun toasted her naked skin, but it was nothing compared to the feel of Eddie pressing into her, as two hard fingers slipped through her juices and inside her cunt. He moved them around, in tandem with an extra-strong thrust of his face into her pussy.

The dual assault was more than enough to send Jane over the edge. She opened her mouth on a scream as she shattered into a million vibrating cells, pulsating over and over and jettisoning her into some far distant galaxy.

A sharp sound brought her back to earth.

"See what I mean?" Eddie's fingers were under her nose, she was in the seat of the car, and he was doing that frickin' snapping thing again.

"What the…" She blinked at him. "Will you *stop* doing that?"

"Doing what? Making you come?"

"No. Snapping your fingers at me." Jane blushed and squirmed. "I mean, yes. Making me…whatever it was you just did."

The immensity of what had just happened finally hit her, and a chill swept down her spine. She inched away from him until she was pressed up against the car door. "Just what the fuck *are* you, Mister Prizzletwits?"

* * * * *

*What* are *you?*

Eddie closed his eyes briefly, battling against memories of words similar to those. How many times had he been asked that question? How many times had people backed away from him in fear?

It had been several centuries before he'd learned to hide his talents, and a couple more before he'd mastered control of his thoughts. Now, slipping into someone's head was as *un*natural to him as slipping into their underwear. Only when a mission called for drastic measures would he be requested to utilize his "unusual" abilities. And even then, only as a last resort.

The whole thing skipped a little too close to the "Violation of Civil Rights" line, and danced lightly over it at times. It made his bosses at the Agency squirm.

He'd had no trouble keeping to the rules. Until Jane.

Something about her had ripped away all his control and driven him into her head, to fuck her, suck her, damn near get inside her soul if he could. And now she wanted to know what he was.

Eddie knew, with *this* woman, he had no choice but to tell her.

"As I said, I'm Anasazi. A thousand years ago, give or take, my people perfected various...skills. Amongst them the ability to *mind-link*, if you will, with others. We worked on it, and found that possessing such mental capacities enhanced other talents."

"Ah." Jane nodded, still looking a bit wide-eyed, but no longer squashed flat up against the window. "So you're a descendant of these – whatevers?"

"Er...not exactly."

She snorted. "No, I should think not. Your name isn't exactly *Running with Guns Drawn*, is it?"

Eddie chuckled. "You couldn't pronounce my Anasazi name. Przybyl came close to how it sounds, and people don't seem to question anything they're not sure if they can spell." He brushed a hand across her cheek. *Fuck it. I don't seem to be able to stop touching her.*

"I *meant*, Jane, that I *am* Anasazi. One of the people who lived in Mesa Verde so long ago." He paused, trying to find the right words to explain something completely and outrageously unlikely to somebody as practical as the woman sitting next to him with one eyebrow raised in disbelief.

"My people worked hard at living. At surviving hand-in-hand with the Earth that nourished them. They worshipped the elements, the Universe, however you want to describe it."

"Okay. Tree hugging hippies centuries before love beads. I got you so far."

Eddie sighed. This wasn't going to be easy. "Yeah, I guess that'll do as an analogy. Anyway, we discovered various ways to enhance our mental abilities—which led to other things. We learned how to extend our lifespan using natural energies."

Her other eyebrow went up. "Better and longer living through organic chemistry?"

"Jane, I'm serious here. Honest. We developed abilities that allow us to control our environment like you'd flip a switch, only we do it with our minds. Over generations, our Elders learned how to prolong life as well. Eventually, well, the herbs, the rituals, a lot of stuff I don't know about since it's pretty much privileged information—whatever it was, it *worked*." He stared at her, pouring every ounce of genuine emotion into his gaze. "Here I am. Here we are. There are many of us, living quietly contented lives…"

He paused once more before throwing in the kicker. "…that never end."

Jane pursed her lips. "So you're saying you're like some kind of immortal or something?" Her eyes grew wide. "Oh shit. You mean along the lines of a vampire type thing?"

"Certainly not." Eddie lifted his chin and frowned at her. "Don't be ridiculous. There are no such things as vampires."

She raised an eyebrow. "Right. You expect me to believe that you're a thousand-year-old Anasazi-whatever, and yet you tell me there's no such thing as vampires." She folded her arms across her chest and glared at him. "Try again."

Try again? How could he try again when he was telling her the truth? "There are many mysteries to our existence, you know. Can you explain dreams? Can you tell me how déjà vu works? Do you understand the relationship between brain chemistry, body fluid fluctuations and lunar cycles?"

"No. But I bloat like hell once a month when the tide comes in."

Eddie tilted his head and studied her. "You're taking this all rather calmly."

"I haven't taken anything yet." She blushed. "Well, I mean in the literal sense."

Eddie grinned. "Jane, I swear I'm telling you the truth. Very few people know what I am or what I can do. I promised myself to use what gifts I've been given to do something useful for this world. The Agency took me on, investigated and verified me, and I've been with them ever since."

He stroked her arm, loving the silky skin as it heated his fingertips. "I have no idea why you've destroyed all my safeguards. Why I can't wait to get inside...your head." He slid nearer to her and reached out his arms. "Or why I can't wait to get inside...you."

Obeying urges he'd long thought buried, Eddie touched his lips to hers. He'd intended to keep it light, casual even, but at the first taste he was lost. He pulled her unresisting body into his arms and forced his way into her mouth, desperate to taste her for real this time.

There was a microsecond's hesitation on her part, and then her tongue met his, dueling and twining around, searching out his flavors and textures and making his cock harder than the stone of his ancient homeland. Blending, melding, parting only to meet once more, the kiss took Eddie's breath away.

And apparently Jane's too, since she tore her mouth from his, lungs heaving. "Jesus *Christ*, Eddie. I'm prepared to believe you've been doing *that* for a thousand years." She panted. "That's one *helluva* kiss you're packing."

Eddie shifted uncomfortably. "It's not the only thing."

Jane looked at the bulge distorting his pants. "That's not your gun, is it?"

Her words recalled Eddie to where they were and what they were *supposed* to be doing. "Shit. This is going to have to wait, babe." He cleared the time block from the car. "Can we...continue this discussion later?"

Jane grinned. A very nice and friendly grin for a woman who's just discovered the guy she's kissing is a thousand-year-old weirdo. "Sure. Whatever. *When*ever." She stared him right in the eye. "Promise?"

"Oh yeah." Eddie started the car again, wondering if he was actually wearing what could be termed as a shit-eating grin. He glanced in the mirror and caught a glimpse of himself.

*Yep. Shit-eating grin.*

\* \* \* \* \*

The short trip to their destination didn't give Jane a huge amount of thinking time. Certainly not enough to wrap her head around the idea that the man she'd just swapped spit with was older than she was. A *lot* older.

Like a millennium or so.

She shrugged her shoulders. So what? She'd always liked older men. And this one sure was a doozy.

Thankfully, she'd been raised with a reasonably practical outlook on life, believing that science could explain most things, although not all things. But here was something that totally defied current beliefs. If she hadn't seen it—*experienced* it—she would have laughed and figured somebody was smoking something they shouldn't.

But there was no doubt about it...Eddie was real enough. As were the mental visions he'd created in her brain. She had the wet underwear to prove it. Since meeting him such a short time ago, she'd come twice, had incredibly erotic mental experiences, and developed the worst case of lust she'd had since being introduced to chocolate at a tender age.

Eddie was, she admitted, better than chocolate. And *that*, in her book, was really saying something.

Her mind tippy-toed over the possibilities such a person presented. Like a superhero come to life and sitting next to her, giving her great brain sex. *What else can he do?*

She turned in her seat. "Um, Eddie? Can you..."

"We're here." He pulled into a darkened alleyway and killed the engine, turning the lights off in a hurry.

*Shit.* Jane choked back her questions and followed him out of the car. "Now what?" She tugged at her dress, wishing it were an inch longer and two inches higher at the neck.

Eddie stared at a large house, silent for a moment, then looked down at her. "We know that Sully was here before heading over to meet his untimely end."

Jane nodded.

"I know that whatever he was supposed to give me wasn't on him when he died and the opposition doesn't have it."

She frowned. "How do you know that?"

"I picked up a great deal of anger and frustration from the three goons who offed him. And they weren't looking for his library card."

"Ah." She wasn't about to argue that point with him. Not right now, anyway. "But you couldn't get anything more detailed out of them?"

Eddie looked a little self-conscious. "There is a...a kind of distance limitation to my gifts, you know." He shifted. "I need to be within a certain distance to get up close and personal, if you get my drift."

"Hoookay. I'll go with the flow here, since this is a mission and I'm supposed to be a professional." She glanced down at her dress. "Although a professional *what* is up for debate."

"Well, that's kinda like the thing here, Jane."

She swallowed. "Why do I have a nasty feeling I'm not gonna like what's coming next?"

Eddie grinned. "You're my whore."

"*What?*"

He held up a hand to stem the screech that Jane knew had probably shattered windows in nearby buildings. "Look, Blanche Overjoy trains escorts. And you and I know what that means. So to get in, we're going to have to ask for an appointment – a walk-in consult or something – and get her involved with you somehow. Then I can find out where the damn disk is, retrieve it, and we can both make like a tree and leave."

Jane rolled her eyes. "And if we can't get to see her?"

"Then we go to Plan B."

"Which is?"

"Dunno. Don't have one yet."

Jane sighed. "Look, you're the one with all these superhero-type talents. Can't you just poof into invisibility, go pick their brains and get the damn thing yourself?"

Eddie chuckled. "I ain't *that* good, babe."

*Oh yes you are.* The thought formed in Jane's mind without volition.

"Why thank you." Eddie smiled sunnily at her.

"Don't *do* that." Christ, the man was really inside her head.

"Okay. Sorry. There's just something about you…"

Jane felt warmth cradling her breasts, like two hands stroking her and seeking her nipples, teasing them.

She squirmed. "Eddie. Cut it out." She sighed. "At least for now, anyway."

"Sorry again." The warmth disappeared, shut off like a light, and Eddie's spine straightened. "You're right. Let's get this over with and then get on to the good stuff."

*Sounds like a plan to me.*

# Chapter Four

Eddie mustered his thoughts. He simply *had* to focus on the assignment, not Jane. And it was frickin' hard when her scent surrounded him like a cloud of desire, and he swore he could hear her skin brushing against her dress.

He rang the bell of Blanche Overjoy's house with a mixture of lust and apprehension running through his brain. *Not good.* If anything should happen to Jane...

"Good evening. May I help you?"

The polite enquiry came from a man who strongly resembled an elephant in a tuxedo. Bulging muscles strained the fabric, and the fact that his dress shirt actually buttoned around his neck was a tribute to whoever had custom-tailored the entire ensemble.

Blanche sure picked her bodyguards for their strength, not their looks.

Eddie stared into the man's eyes. "My name is Edvarde Przybyl. We were wondering if it would be possible to see Ms. Overjoy? We don't have an appointment but..." He reached into that place inside him where so much magic lay, curled in a warm rope of glittering excitement.

Money. Power, sex...reputation as a playboy...

He sent images softly and patiently across the few feet between them, creating a picture of himself as he wanted the muscle-bound dude to see him.

The man's face relaxed. "Welcome, Mr. Pryzbyl. How nice of you to drop by. Would you mind waiting for a moment, while I tell Ms. Overjoy you're here? I'm not sure of her schedule this evening, but I'd be happy to check for you."

With a hand beneath Jane's elbow, Eddie followed the bouncer into a small room, tastefully furnished with expensive antiques.

"I'll be right back. If you'd care for drinks, please help yourself." He left with what was probably supposed to be a friendly grin. It was actually more of a baring of yellowed teeth, but what the hell. Eddie's plan was working – this far.

"How did you do that?" Jane whispered softly, looking around her with a rather intense degree of interest. "Is this a – whorehouse?"

Eddie grinned, picking up her torn emotions at being curious about something like that. "No. This is Blanche's home away from home. She works here because she likes the house, and doesn't, of course, actually *own* a whorehouse. Although if you track the financial records of ownership, and dismiss a variety of dummy corporations, I'd be willing to bet she's got some powerful financial interests in a few of 'em."

His attention was snagged by someone approaching. "Jane, go with me here. Don't be shocked by anything I do or say, okay?" He sent soothing thoughts over to her in a quick flash.

He physically felt her tossing them aside, as she straightened her spine. "I'm here to help you. Don't worry about me."

He blinked. *I think I'm going to worry about you a lot. More than any other woman I've met in a looooong time.* But he kept those thoughts to himself. "All right. She's coming. Here we go."

Eddie closed the distance between them, watching her eyes widen as his hands delved into the front of her dress.

He had her breasts bared and was kissing them as Blanche Overjoy walked into the room.

*  *  *  *  *

Jane experienced one flash of blissful heat from Eddie's tongue around her nipple, then froze as a woman entered.

Jerking away from that tempting mouth, she struggled to wrench her dress back into place. "Er...Eddie?" She cursed the blush that flooded her cheeks, rising hotly through her to swamp her in embarrassment. A *real* agent would've been able to do something like this without a blink. Probably. Or maybe not.

*Ah fuck it.* Jane sighed.

"Hello. I'm Blanche Overjoy." The woman raised an eyebrow. "And I can see you need my help."

Pissed off at that obvious insult, Jane raised an eyebrow, but Eddie had the situation well in hand. She rather missed him having her breasts well in hand too, but that was neither here nor there at this particular moment.

"What a pleasure to meet you." Eddie lifted Blanche's hand to his lips and smiled.

*Sheeeittt.* Jane could literally see this damned woman melting.

*He's doing his job. Do yours.* Jane's brain kicked her hormones out of the way, told them to go do a crossword or something for a bit, and tried hard to concentrate on the assignment.

Eddie turned towards Jane. "This is Janie. I'm thinking about taking her to the West Coast." He stroked his chin, staring at her like she was some kind of object. "But the parties I'd like to attend…well, let's just say she needs a little polish?"

A quick vision of Eddie lying naked on top of her sent another blush cascading across her skin.

"Yes, I see what you mean. She does blush a lot, doesn't she?"

*Well I fucking* wouldn't *if you stopped making me.* The thought obviously reached Eddie, since his lips curled in a hint of a smile.

*Okay. He wants me to blush. Keerist, Jane. Get a grip. This isn't a game.*

"It's not unattractive, of course, but probably a little too much for my associates." Eddie turned to Blanche. "Think there's anything we can do about it?"

Blanche moved to Jane, circling her with a predatory air.

Jane, in her turn, watched Blanche. Tall and slender, the woman was probably heading for middle age, but still moved with the grace of a ballet dancer. She was simply dressed, although her clothes probably cost more than Jane made in a month.

She reeked of expensive tastes, overlaid with an inherent sexuality that Jane envied. *God, I hate skinny women.*

*So do I.*

A quick impression of Eddie's words, then nothing. But it was enough to strengthen Jane's resolve, and she stood quietly, undergoing Blanche's scrutiny without moving.

"Hmm. I think there is some potential." Blanche ran her fingers across Jane's shoulders and walked around, coming to a halt and looking her up and down. "Strip."

"Pardon?" Jane blinked

"Take your clothes off, girl."

"Uh…"

*Do it, Jane. I need her thoughts focused on you. They're muddled right now. I can't read her.*

"Okay." In response to Eddie's urgent mental appeal, Jane's hand drifted to her straps and she awkwardly slid them down to dangle around her elbows.

Something shifted behind Blanche's eyes. "Good. Continue." The woman stepped back a couple of paces and rested against a convenient table, crossing her arms in front of her.

Gritting her teeth, Jane shrugged the top of her dress down.

And blushed once more as her breasts appeared.

"Don't blush. Don't *think*. It's simply skin. A body that is in no way unique." Blanche's words were like a douche of cold water.

*There's nothing like a nice compliment to stroke a girl's ego. That wasn't one of 'em.*

Getting more irritated by the minute, Jane slid her dress over her hips and let it pool on the floor around her feet. She amazed herself by straightening her spine and giving Miss Critic a damn good look at her 38Cs.

*Take that, teeny tits. These are real. I'll bet you twenty bucks yours aren't.*

Somewhere in the back of her mind, Jane heard a muffled snort of laughter. She ignored it, her gaze fixed on Blanche Overjoy.

"Lose the panties." Blanche flicked a finger at Jane's underwear. "And get yourself a thong while you're at it. Those are...well, I don't know what they are, but they're wrong."

*Fuck you and the horse you rode in on.* Anger built inside Jane. Like she really wanted to spend endless hours in her office having her butt flossed by an expensive piece of lace and elastic.

Defiantly, she dropped her panties to the floor, and stood there buck-naked in front of Blanche.

"Hmm." Blanche reached to her and ran her fingers over Jane's breasts, down to her navel and lower, just flicking at her pussy hair. "Not bad. Could certainly afford to lose some weight, but then again, some men like their women well-padded."

Jane opened her mouth to answer, temper flaring like a blow-torch.

But Blanche forestalled her. "Touch yourself."

"What?"

"Or..." Blanche stood slowly, and then closed the distance between them, licking her lips. "Would you like *me* to?"

\* \* \* \* \*

*Holy fucking shit.* Eddie's cock was a stone pillar along his thigh, and he fought harder than he'd ever done in his life to keep his mind where it needed to be.

Inside Blanche's head, not up Jane's cunt.

He tried to ignore Jane's emotions, roiling and seething around him like a wild and ravenous beast. He couldn't afford to lose himself or his focus. Not right now.

Biting the inside of his mouth and letting the small pain distract him from her nude body, Eddie lowered his eyelids and once again plunged into Blanche's mind.

What he saw there nearly sent him over the edge.

Visions of Jane between Blanche's legs. Visions of Blanche between Jane's legs. Visions of Jane and Blanche touching, suckling, writhing on silk sheets. He swallowed. It was like running a triple-X-rated lesbian porn movie.

But someplace there had to be images of the information he needed.

Part of him registered Jane's hand as she reluctantly cupped her breast for Blanche's delectation. It was actually helpful in a masochistic sort of way, since Blanche's conscious thoughts screamed into one particular place, leaving her subconscious unguarded. Of course, his cock ached like fury.

But that was something he could deal with. Later.

And *there*…just as Jane's hand slid down to her pussy, Eddie found what he was looking for.

And promptly lost it again as Jane's fingers spread her pussy lips apart and Eddie saw what Blanche was seeing. *Oh fuck.*

He could practically feel Blanche's arousal as pink and glistening flesh swelled around Jane's hand. He could taste the desire rising in this woman's brain. Or maybe it was his own. Whatever it might be, there were two of them in that room with a bad case of the hots for Jane.

But only one of them had the right equipment to satisfy her in the way she deserved. And himself while he was at it.

Once again, Eddie breathed in and did his best to clear his head, pushing away the erotic images of a nude Jane arousing herself.

And there...*finally*...

Images of Sully and Blanche, talking, arguing, and finally exchanging something. A CD. He felt around for a location, and realized it was Blanche's office. And now he knew exactly where she'd put it.

He pulled out, probably a little too quickly, since Blanche suddenly swayed and put a hand to her head. "My goodness."

Stepping to her, he solicitously touched her arm. "Ms. Overjoy. Are you all right?"

"I think so. I was a bit dizzy for a moment there." She blinked.

Eddie motioned to Jane to dress, and hid a grin at her obvious spurt of relief. Turning back to Blanche he smiled, all comfort, warmth, money and charm. "So you think my Janie has potential?"

Blanche caved before that smile. "Definitely. Make an appointment...better yet, several appointments. She needs grooming and self-confidence, that's all. I think she'll do nicely after that."

"I'm *so* happy." Eddie radiated happiness. "You've been very kind."

Blanche nodded. "My pleasure. Franklin will see you out. He'll give you my card." She glanced back at Jane. "Until we meet again." Her eyes were hot.

"Thank you very much." Jane's response was polite, although her brain was anything but. She watched the woman leave the room with an expression that made Eddie extremely glad his erstwhile partner wasn't armed.

He held a finger to his lips, stopping Jane's words before they spilled out.

"Hush. We've little time." He looked around, narrowed his eyes at a point low on the wall and concentrated.

Within seconds, there was a fizzle, a pop behind the electrical socket, and the lights went out.

"Come on. Quickly. I know where the CD is, but *they* know where the circuit breakers are."

Eddie grabbed Jane's arm and raced her out into the dark hallway, finding his way more on instinct than anything else.

Responding to the urgency he'd put into his words, Jane followed him up the stairs without a word.

"In here." He opened the door to Blanche's office, hurried to her desk, opened the top drawer and sighed with relief as he picked up the shiny CD case lying inside.

"*Shit.*" A small light blinked beneath the rim of the desk. "We've set off an alarm."

Jane looked panicked. "We did?"

"Yeah. Must be on a different circuit." He tilted his head. "And unless the circus is in town, I'm thinking Franklin and his buddies are heading this way."

# Chapter Five

Hooookay. This wasn't as much fun as it was supposed to be.

Jane held her breath and looked helplessly at Eddie. She had no clue what to suggest, what to do or where to hide. This *sucked*.

"Control?" She wondered if anyone was listening at the Agency.

"No time."

"Can't you *freeze* time or something?" It was all she could think of.

"Too many of 'em. Too open. Won't work here. Ahh…." Eddie dragged her over to the French doors that opened onto a small veranda.

Jane shivered as they stepped out into the cool night air. She looked down. "Uh – Eddie? We're two flights up here. I don't see a drainpipe, and I'm not real good at doing that rappelling thing, even if we had a rope – which we don't."

He ignored her, just putting his arms around her waist. "Trust me. You have to trust me, Jane. Can you do that?"

She looked at him. For an instant out of time, parts of some kind of psychological puzzle clicked into place for Jane. Parts that were shaped like Eddie, thought like Eddie, felt like Eddie and loved like Eddie.

She realized that for the first time in her life, she was whole.

"Yes." It was a simple answer, but for Jane it was a truly life-altering moment. She trusted this man. Whatever he said he was, or might or might not be, she trusted him. Simple as that. Complicated as that.

*Whatever.*

"Good." He hugged her close. "Put your arms around me and close your eyes."

A nasty suspicion crept into her head. "Eddie, you're not going to *jump* with me, are you?"

"Nope. Well, not *exactly*..." He pressed his chin into her head. "Hold tight."

Eyes shut, Jane held tight. And gasped as the wind whistled around them, lashing her hair and making her dress flap against her thighs.

Then there was a solid thump and they tumbled into a heap on the sidewalk.

"Ouch." Jane rubbed one knee.

"Sorry." Eddie grabbed her and bundled her into the car before she had time to think. Then they were away on the throaty roar of a powerful engine, leaving Blanche and her muscle guys far behind.

Jane swallowed. "Um, Eddie? Did you know you've got a bit of hair sticking up in back of your head?"

He laughed and smoothed it down. "Yeah. Always happens when I fly."

"*Fly?*" This was one weird dude. Jane gulped.

Skillfully, he negotiated the streets back toward the Agency. "I was going to mention that. Sorry about the landing...I don't do as well when I've got passengers."

"*Fucking shit.*" It was all Jane could manage. Her brain blurred, trying to make the impossible merely improbable. Or somehow believable. She zoned out for a bit while her thoughts went off on a fishing trip to Alaska and her adrenaline levels retreated below their redline.

But time wasn't standing still. Soon the CD was in safe hands, the order of the civilized world restored, and they were alone in Eddie's rather luxurious office on the top floor of the Agency.

"So." He looked at her. "Jane."

She sighed. "Yeah. Me Jane. You – I don't know what."

"Me horny." He smiled at her, all eyes and lips and chest…

Jane surrendered. "Then take me, Special Agent Prizzynuts. Debrief me." She opened her arms wide. Whatever he was – or wasn't – she was totally crazy for him.

"Oh yeah. I'm gonna debrief you. For real this time, Jane." Eddie's hands stripped her efficiently. "I want my cock in you for real. I want your cunt clamping around me as you scream – for *real.*"

She found the wall against her back as she scrabbled to rip Eddie's shirt off. "Yeah. What you just said…" She bit her lip in frustration as his fly caught, then freed his cock to fall heavily into her hands. Silky and hard, it burned her palms.

Oooh. Yeah. Super dude – super cock.

Eddie's teeth closed around one nipple and bit gently as she squeezed her way up the hot length of him. "Like that?"

"Mmm." She leaned her head back. "More."

"Yes, ma'am." He pressed his weight into her, not caring about his cock, wrapped in her hand, crushed between them. He kissed her, hard and hungry, thrusting his tongue into her mouth, then investigated the skin of her neck, nipping at its base, sending shivers down her spine.

Her pussy ached and wept, moisture flooding her thighs. She opened her mouth, needing...wanting...so much. She licked into his ear and grinned as she felt him shudder all the way to his toes.

"Jane...Christ..." His hips thrust hard against hers, grinding their bodies together. "Why the hell do you make me so fucking hot for you?"

She couldn't answer, since he filled her mouth with his tongue again. "Mmm." *The feeling's mutual.*

*Thank God.* Eddie's mental words flashed into her brain, followed by images of the two of them doing impossible things to each other. It was erotically amazing, and the best mental foreplay Jane could have dreamed of.

Her clit screamed, her breasts felt about the size of watermelons, and she was hotter for him that was humanly possible.

"I'm gonna come, Eddie..." She had no idea if the words had come from her mouth or her mind. It was all one and the same with this man. If she didn't get him into her cunt within seconds, there was going to be a supernova on the surface of the Earth that would puzzle astronomers for years.

"Eddie...now, for God's sake...*now!*" She choked out a plea from her soul.

"Yeah, *now*." Eddie slid his hands under her buttocks, raised her to just the right height and thrust his cock inside her.

"Oh. My. *God*."

Jane exploded, her climax shuddering through her, ably assisted by Eddie's hips as they pounded against her. He drove her higher, the rough feel of the wall against her naked back contributing to the immense eruption threatening to blow her brains out. Then he joined her, filling her with his come, throbbing inside and sending her off all over again.

She screamed. For real.

So did Eddie.

\* \* \* \* \*

*Three Months Later*

"You sure you want to do this?"

Jane rolled her eyes. "No. Of course not. I just want to wither away, age and die while you watch." She touched his shoulder. "We've been over this so many damn times, Eddie. When are you going to believe me?"

He smiled. "Well, the last time you agreed, you had your mouth full, if I remember correctly. I couldn't quite make out what you were saying."

Jane smiled back. "Can I help it if I love your cock? I didn't hear you objecting."

Eddie's throat moved as he swallowed. "And you won't."

Jane followed his gaze as he stared at the road ahead. The phone call inviting them to meet with the Anasazi Elders had come as a welcome surprise. Whether they'd be able to honor Eddie's request to *change* Jane, to make her like him, well, that was yet to be decided.

Eddie had been the one to ask this favor of his people, explaining to them that their mental link was unique. Apparently it was, since once that bit of news had reached Elder ears, there'd been quite a bit of intense correspondence, some legal stuff to sign and a few cryptic phone calls.

Eddie had done the legwork and filed the formal request. Jane had been the one who had encouraged him every step of the way.

They both wanted it. They both wanted each other with a certainty that was absolutely and completely etched in stone.

But Eddie still couldn't resist making sure. "Giving you powers like mine, asking you to become what I am...I dunno, Jane. It's a big step."

"Look, we don't even know if it'll work yet." Jane patted his arm maternally. "This is *my* decision, Eddie. I love you. You're stuck with it. And if this whole thing works, if your Elders can make me like you, you're stuck with *me*. For a hell of a long time, too. Are *you* sure you want to do this?"

He snorted. "Like you have to ask."

"Okay then. Subject closed." She yawned. "So when do we get to Mesa Verde?"

He blinked. "We're not going to Mesa Verde."

"But — I thought we were going to see your Elders, or whatever you call 'em."

"Yeah, we are."

Jane sighed. *Patience*. He was, fundamentally, a man, when all was said and done. A pretty extraordinary one, sure, but with a lot of the basics going on there, too.

She tried again. "Eddie. Where *are* we going?"

"Weeelll..." he drawled the word out, teasingly. "How bad do you wanna know?"

There was a twinkle in his eye that Jane had no difficulty recognizing. She didn't need their mental link to tell exactly what he had on his mind.

She grinned. "Can you be bribed?"

"A blow job would be nice."

"Pull over."

The tires screeched and the car rattled and bumped onto the shoulder. Jane had his fly unzipped before he'd turned the engine off. Hers was already racing above the red line.

She loved his cock. Loved knowing how much he enjoyed it when she sucked him back as far as she could into her throat. And especially loved teasing his balls at the same time.

Yeah. The basic simple truth was, she loved *him*.

Pouring that love into her actions, Jane tugged at Eddie, getting him where she wanted him – into her mouth.

He sighed with pleasure, running his hands through her hair. "God, Jane..."

"Mmm." She teased the long vein that ran the length of his cock.

"How did I live so long without you?" he gasped.

She smiled around his heat. There was one little spot – right *there* – that rolled his eyeballs. She teased it again. "Mmm. Don't know."

As had become habit between them, Eddie dropped his mental shields and let his thoughts flow into Jane's head. His delight, his pleasure, his arousal – even an image of herself as she moved her head up and down his cock. It sure was weird watching oneself giving a guy a blow job, but she'd gotten used to it.

And yes, it turned her on. As did the images she got from him when he returned the favor. It was wild sex on so many levels, and she had to pinch herself sometimes to make sure this whole thing wasn't some kind of crazy hallucination.

But the taste of him in her mouth was real, as was the hot honeyed liquid that had started dampening her pussy. Turning *him* on turned *her* on too.

Eddie sighed, trembling as she teased the tiny slit at the tip of the swollen head. A drop of moisture oozed from it and Jane licked at it, tasting him, loving him, then swallowing as much as she could of him once more. And reaching to cradle his balls as she did so.

He was panting. "Jesus, babe…"

His thoughts lost focus, images blurred, and she knew his orgasm was nearly on him. As if his physical reactions swamped his head, even with all his super mind skills. The sex between them was *that* powerful, *that* seductive.

His thighs hardened and clenched around her, and Eddie threw his head back so sharply she heard a bone or two crack. "*Jane…*"

He came, spurts of hot seed filling her throat as she swallowed, taking every last drop of him. And loving it.

*You're wrong.*

"Huh?" Jane blinked as a weak thought entered her mind.

*It's not the sex between us. It's the love.*

Jane smiled as her heart purred contentedly. "So. Where *are* we going?"

Eddie waved his hand limply at the windshield. "West."

"Okay." She waited.

"To the Elder in Los Angeles. Grab a vacation at the same time." He stretched and moved, then slumped again. "Shit. That was sooo good. I do love you, you know."

She was not to be distracted. "And I love you too. Why Los Angeles?"

"Why not?" He blinked at her. "If you were *that* old, with *those* powers, would you want to live in a stone cave? No dishwasher? No Internet? No plumbing?"

Jane thought about that. "Uh, I guess not." She frowned. "You mean these Elders are all over the place?"

"Sure." Eddie finally found the strength to zip his fly. "There's one running a bank in New York City. Another is a writer someplace in the Midwest, I think. We're gonna go see the one in LA. He runs a movie studio."

"Jeez." Jane blinked. "I guess I was expecting something more…more…"

"Magical?" Eddie grinned.

"Yes."

"Honey, gimme a few minutes, and I'll be happy to show you some magic. Some very *special* magic all my own."

Jane looked into his eyes and believed him. She looked into her heart and that believed him too.

Her mind filled with his thoughts, him putting his mouth on her, suckling her, learning her all over again with skilled tongue and hungry lips. She closed her eyes and shivered with the pleasure of anticipation.

Whether or not she could ever share his mystical world, or his abilities, or live a thousand years alongside him didn't matter. Whether she'd become another special agent with super powers and work with him as his partner didn't matter. He was who he was.

And she loved him.

She knew she always would. And *that* was super enough for her.

*The End*

# About the Author

Sahara Kelly was transplanted from old England to New England where she now lives with her husband and teenage son. Making the transition from her historical regency novels to Romantica™ has been surprisingly easy, and now Sahara can't imagine writing anything else. She is dedicated to the premise that everybody should have fantasies.

Sahara Kelly welcomes mail from readers. You can write to her c/o Ellora's Cave Publishing at 1056 Home Ave, Akron, OH 44310-3502.

# Also by Sahara Kelly

A Kink In Her Tails
All Night Videos: For Research Purposes Only
Beating Level Nine
Detour – *with S.L. Carpenter*
The Glass Stripper
Guardians Of Time 1: Alana's Magic Lamp
Guardians of Time 2: Finding The Zero-G Spot
The Gypsy Lovers
Hansell and Gretty
The Knights Elemental
Lyndhurst and Lydia
Madam Charlie
Magnus Ravynne and Mistress Swann
Mesmerized
Mystic Visions
Partners In Passion 1: Justin and Eleanor – *with S.L. Carpenter*
Partners In Passion 2: No Limits – *with S.L. Carpenter*
Persephone's Wings
Peta And The Wolfe
Scars of the Lash
Sizzle
The Sun God's Woman
Tales of the Beau Monde 1: Lying With Louisa
Tales of the Beau Monde 2: Miss Beatrice's Bottom
Tales of the Beau Monde 3: Lying With Louisa
Tales of the Beau Monde 4: Pleasuring Miss Poppy
Wingin' It

# Why an electronic book?

We live in the Information Age—an exciting time in the history of human civilization in which technology rules supreme and continues to progress in leaps and bounds every minute of every hour of every day. For a multitude of reasons, more and more avid literary fans are opting to purchase e-books instead of paperbacks. The question to those not yet initiated to the world of electronic reading is simply: *why?*

1. *Price.* An electronic title at Ellora's Cave Publishing and Cerridwen Press runs anywhere from 40-75% less than the cover price of the <u>exact same title</u> in paperback format. Why? Cold mathematics. It is less expensive to publish an e-book than it is to publish a paperback, so the savings are passed along to the consumer.

2. *Space.* Running out of room to house your paperback books? That is one worry you will never have with electronic novels. For a low one-time cost, you can purchase a handheld computer designed specifically for e-reading purposes. Many e-readers are larger than the average handheld, giving you plenty of screen room. Better yet, hundreds of titles can be stored within your new library—a single microchip. (Please note that Ellora's Cave and Cerridwen Press does not endorse any specific brands. You can check our website at www.ellorascave.com or

www.cerridwenpress.com for customer recommendations we make available to new consumers.)

3. *Mobility.* Because your new library now consists of only a microchip, your entire cache of books can be taken with you wherever you go.

4. *Personal preferences are accounted for.* Are the words you are currently reading too small? Too large? Too...**ANNOYING**? Paperback books cannot be modified according to personal preferences, but e-books can.

5. *Instant gratification.* Is it the middle of the night and all the bookstores are closed? Are you tired of waiting days—sometimes weeks—for online and offline bookstores to ship the novels you bought? Ellora's Cave Publishing sells instantaneous downloads 24 hours a day, 7 days a week, 365 days a year. Our e-book delivery system is 100% automated, meaning your order is filled as soon as you pay for it.

Those are a few of the top reasons why electronic novels are displacing paperbacks for many an avid reader. As always, Ellora's Cave and Cerridwen Press welcomes your questions and comments. We invite you to email us at service@ellorascave.com, service@cerridwenpress.com or write to us directly at: 1056 Home Ave. Akron OH 44310-3502.

MAKE EACH DAY MORE *EXCITING* WITH OUR

# ELLORA'S CAVEMEN
## CALENDAR

✝ WWW.ELLORASCAVE.COM ✝

# THE
# ☥ ELLORA'S CAVE ☥
# LIBRARY

Stay up to date with Ellora's Cave Titles in
Print with our Quarterly Catalog.

To recieve a catalog,
send an email with your name
and mailing address to:

## CATALOG@ELLORASCAVE.COM

or send a letter or postcard
with your mailing address to:

Catalog Request
c/o Ellora's Cave Publishing, Inc.
1056 Home Avenue
Akron, Ohio 44310-3502

# COMING TO A BOOKSTORE NEAR YOU!

# ELLORA'S CAVE
# 2005
## BEST SELLING AUTHORS TOUR

erridwen, the Celtic Goddess of wisdom, was the muse who brought inspiration to storytellers and those in the creative arts. Cerridwen Press encompasses the best and most innovative stories in all genres of today's fiction. Visit our site and discover the newest titles by talented authors who still get inspired - much like the ancient storytellers did, once upon a time.

# Cerridwen Press

www.cerridwenpress.com

Discover for yourself why readers can't get enough of the multiple award-winning publisher Ellora's Cave. Whether you prefer e-books or paperbacks, be sure to visit EC on the web at www.ellorascave.com for an erotic reading experience that will leave you breathless.

www.ellorascave.com